THE
PRESERVATIONIST

JUSTIN KRAMON

PEGASUS CRIME
NEW YORK LONDON

To the memory of my mother

THE PRESERVATIONIST

Pegasus Books LLC
80 Broad Street, 5th Floor
New York, NY 10004

Copyright © 2013 Justin Kramon

First Pegasus Books cloth edition 2013

Interior design by Maria Fernandez

Library of Congress Cataloging-in-Publication Data is available.

ISBN: 978-1-60598-480-3

10 9 8 7 6 5 4 3 2 1

Printed in the United States of America
Distributed by W. W. Norton & Company, Inc.

This is where the serpent lives. This is his nest,
These fields, these hills, these tinted distances . . .
—Wallace Stevens, "The Auroras of Autumn"

Death isn't sad. What hurts is being drowned by these emotions.
—Banana Yoshimoto, *Hard Luck*

Part One

ORIENTATION

CHAPTER 1
Julia

Of all the places Julia Stilwell thought she might be on a September afternoon, less than a year after the accident, this was the last she would have imagined. College. A freshman headed out on a first date. It was too normal. She felt like she'd snuck into the wrong movie, like any minute a guy in a little hat would come running up the aisle, shine a flashlight in her eyes, and ask to see her ticket.

But here she was, ten minutes to two, fixing her hair, getting her shoes on, smiling at her reflection so she could paint blush on her cheeks, going back and forth in her mind about whether to bring a backpack or a purse. It was all the usual stuff girls do before dates, but to Julia it felt like a test, a set of pictures she had to line up in the right order. Wrong answer sends you back to go. It was a blessing her roommate, Leanette, was in class and not around to witness the chaos of these final preparations. Leanette had dates every weekend and went to all the parties, and Julia was sure this fussing would have seemed amateur to her, like a kid playing with an adult's makeup kit.

In the end, Julia decided on a messenger bag. She slung it over her shoulder, flipped the lights off, and left the room.

Outside, it was gorgeous. Cloudless and warm, the air felt like a shirt just out of the dryer. Julia lived in an off-campus dorm, and though the building was musty, with cinder-block walls and a dull gray carpet that gave off a smell like boiled milk, there was a pretty courtyard out here, a cement bench, a trellis wrapped with vines and bright flowers. She took a long breath, enjoying the weather and her anticipation, perched for a moment on the fragile edge of happiness.

Julia was headed to campus, and she decided to take the path through the woods. She could have gone through town, but didn't know whom she'd run into, and whether they'd ask what she was up to. The date with Marcus didn't have to be a secret, but for some reason she wanted to keep it to herself, like a note in her pocket.

Before the accident, it would have been different. Julia would have had to tell Danny and Shana about how Marcus had asked her out, making little jokes to play it down. They wouldn't have let her get away with the secrecy. In high school, when she wasn't practicing the trumpet, Julia had spent most of her free time with these friends. She knew everything about them, from what they'd gotten on their last history tests to what their boyfriends had whispered in their ears the first times they'd had sex.

Julia had always been a bit of an oddball, with her quirky sense of humor, the flat way she delivered jokes that caught people off guard and sometimes made them smile, sometimes give her confused looks. She was never a star in the classroom, and didn't go in for all the primping and social striving most of the girls did. She didn't need it; her music and her plans for the future had been enough. They'd given her distance, kept her insulated from the storms of teenage social life. When her friends were worked up over a boy or a conflict with parents, Julia was always the first to jump in with a silly line to relieve the tension. She wore thrift store T-shirts and frayed corduroys and didn't try to be the prettiest or the smartest or the most popular, just didn't care that much about it.

But all of that was gone, that old life. She didn't talk to any of those people anymore. She'd gotten rid of her cell phone, tossed it into a lake, actually. Burial at sea.

Marcus had suggested they meet at two thirty, since the snack bar would be less crowded then, between lunch and dinner. As usual, Julia was early. She couldn't help it. She'd always been the type to arrive ten minutes before a meeting, and none of the tricks she pulled to delay herself ever seemed to work. If she were ever sentenced to execution, she'd probably arrive ten minutes early for that, just to get a good seat.

She tried to slow down, scraping her shoe soles on the dirt and rocks in the woods.

As a way to distract herself, she started thinking about how the date had come about. "You have this way about you," Marcus had said that night in the library, when they were working on the counterpoint project. "It's like you live in your own self-contained world. I've been wanting to know what's going on in there since the first time I saw you." After he said it, he smiled in a teasing way, and she wasn't sure if he was being genuine. She almost made a quick joke back, her habit. *Nothing going on in here. My world's in a budget crisis.* But then she noticed he was blushing, all the way from his ears down to the base of his neck. There was something reassuring about his discomfort. Seeing it, she'd felt a protective tenderness for him, the way you might watching a child pedal a bike up a steep hill.

"You want to get lunch on Thursday in the snack bar?" he'd said after that, so casually anyone listening would have thought he'd just tossed out the offer, not even caring what her answer would be. But he'd given a specific day. He'd mentioned the snack bar, as if an off-campus date would have been too much to ask.

"I'd love to," Julia had said. "But are you going to be there?"

And Marcus had smiled.

When she got to the top of the hill, where the woods ended, Julia heard a train clacking away from the station at the base of campus.

She checked her watch: ten minutes early. Of course. She walked onto the train platform, into the warm, bright sunshine.

That was when it happened, suddenly, in the midst of all that sparkling weather. It was as if someone had pulled the plug on the day, and all the excitement just drained out, like water from a tub.

She knew what it was, this feeling. She'd told El Doctor about it, these aftershocks, as she thought of them, reminders of events she couldn't change, events she would have preferred to snip out of the cloth of her memory. She closed her eyes, and there it was again, her brother's face, pale with shock at what he was witnessing, his lips opening and closing, making no sound, until finally he'd asked, "Is that mine?"

But she couldn't do this now, couldn't let herself get dragged under. If you want to move forward, you have to stop looking back. Positive thinking, positive results. She stood straight, pushed her shoulders back, breathed, fixed the strap of the messenger bag like a seat belt across her chest, and continued across the tracks, up the tree-lined path to campus.

Inside the snack bar, Julia couldn't spot Marcus. She looked around at all the tables and booths. Most were empty. At one table, two women in suits were smiling over something one of them had said, then they got up to leave, carrying stacks of paper. Inside a booth, three muscular-looking boys sat talking over empty plates and balled napkins.

They made Julia nervous, these people. The way they moved and talked and smiled seemed foreign, like they were all doing a dance she'd never learned. The thought surfaced again that maybe she wasn't fit to be here, at a college, so soon, no matter what El Doctor said.

But it's best not to overthink things. That's how you get yourself into trouble. When you stop and think about how vulnerable you are, or how strange the world is, it's easy to end up feeling confused and lonely.

In the corner, next to the doors where people walked in to order their sandwiches, a man in a red shirt and white apron was standing beside a trash can. Julia recognized him as the guy who usually made her sandwiches. She remembered thinking more than once that he was cute. He had shaggy brown hair, and could have passed for a student if he were a couple years younger. He always smiled when he saw Julia, and offered her an extra handful of chips or a second spear of pickle with her order. She didn't know if he did that for other girls, but it was such a simple and plainly sweet gesture that it charmed her. A pickle for your thoughts, my dear.

When she looked at him, though, smiling, ready to wave, he looked down, like he was embarrassed. She wasn't sure if maybe he didn't recognize her, or was surprised at meeting her without the lunch counter between them, or if he was just socially awkward, but whatever it was, she felt disappointed. She wanted to give him a signal that it was okay to be friendly, wave to her when she came in. *I won't bite.*

She didn't have a chance to do anything, though, because just as she was considering it, Marcus walked in.

CHAPTER 2
Sam

c—◆—◇

Although he was careful not to be vain about his appearance, Sam Blount didn't see a problem with being aware of it. In fact, at thirty-nine years old, it seemed perfectly natural to take a little extra time in the mornings. Who didn't want to keep a good thing going as long as he could?

Sam had light-brown hair, which he washed daily in a moisturizing shampoo and kept long, parted in the middle and feathered over his ears, in the style of so many of the boys on campus. Mornings he put in a good thirty minutes, shaving and moisturizing his face and combing his scalp for gray hairs, plucking them out at the roots. The gray hairs had cropped up after his mother's death, over a decade ago now, though in some ways it felt like it had hardly been a month. Loss worked on a different timetable than the rest of life, Sam knew, and there was no way to predict when it would come knocking on your door.

Sam lived in Marshallville, the town just south of Stradler College, where he worked. Despite the students' joking about Marshallville (which included lines about "martial law," "Stradler's welfare cousin," and even the title "Badler"), so far it had been a decent place to live. He had a private entrance to his apartment, up a set of damp-smelling, gray-carpeted steps. Below him lived a retired construction worker named Vic who never left his apartment and was so deaf he wouldn't know if the house were collapsing. The front porch of the house sagged, and paint chipped off the siding, but the neighborhood was quiet enough. No one had hassled Sam or stolen from him. He kept the van on the street—he couldn't bear to get rid of it, he'd gotten such a good bargain—and it hadn't even had a window broken.

After all, the apartment would need to last him a couple years at most. Sam wasn't the type to stay in a place for long. He had an itch for motion, action. He thought of himself as a wanderer, like Augie March, a spirit cut loose by circumstances and the desire to see the world. In the past eight years, he'd lived in California, Maryland, Iowa, Massachusetts, and now Pennsylvania. He held jobs for a year or two, rarely more, then moved on.

Since the previous summer, Sam had worked in the snack bar at Stradler. He'd had experience in food service, and he always tried to work in places frequented by college students. It was a great way to meet people, see what was going on in an area, and he found the students' energy and optimism sustaining. He'd never had the chance to go to college himself, but he liked books and would have enjoyed the chance to study them; this proximity was the next best thing. He wouldn't have wanted to be packed away in some stuffy restaurant folding cloth napkins and asking old people if they wanted another gin and tonic, even if it had paid double what he was making now.

Walking through the campus, Sam gave the impression of a man who smiled easily, was hesitant to disturb anyone, always apologized first whenever he bumped into another person in a crowded path. His boyish haircut and loose clothes suggested the good-natured ease of someone who didn't expect overly much from life. Only when he was alone did a certain restless intensity, usually hidden, emerge. But this shadowed part of himself, these darker thoughts, were aspects of his personality he chose not to share with the world. It was easy enough to grin and slam the door on that room of his mind.

Today, a humid morning at the end of September, Sam's workday started at five thirty, as it did most days, with a cup of herbal tea and a dry bagel left over from the night before, which he ate while sitting on an overturned milk crate in the snack bar's driveway. The light was gray, the sky beginning to brighten, like a movie screen before the film starts rolling. A breeze ruffled the tops of trees. The campus of this school was an arboretum, and everywhere you looked there were trees, tall and sturdy, short and spindly, smooth or furrowed, tasseled with pine needles or sleeved in fat, green leaves. This was the most attractive place he'd ever worked, and surrounded by this abundant beauty, Sam couldn't help but feel that something special was waiting for him here.

After breakfast, he got to work, sweeping the floors and wiping the counters. He restocked the refrigerator cases, the cereal shelves, the racks of potato chips, keeping a tally of the empty spaces so he didn't have to run up and down the stairs a dozen times. He took all these chores seriously, and it meant a lot to him when his manager noticed. "Spotless," Horacio had marveled last week, turning a juice glass under the light. "You're the only one who does it," he'd told Sam, almost tearfully, referring to the way Sam wiped out the glasses with a cloth after they came out of the dishwasher, to eliminate streaks.

By six thirty, the others were arriving. Horacio greeted Sam in his formal way. "Good morning, Sam. How are you?" Sam shook his manager's thick-fingered hand, their daily routine.

Downstairs, Lonnie was playing his metal music on the boom box.

"Same shit, different day, huh?" Lonnie said to Sam when they were putting on their aprons in the storage room.

"'S not so bad," Sam said.

"Fuck you."

"Maybe later."

Lonnie was grinning. His was a hard way of talking, a way that stamped out all the nuance and grace in the world. Sam didn't enjoy it much, but he was familiar enough with that way of seeing things to be able to answer back to people like Lonnie in the kitchens where he worked. If you don't adapt to your environment, people will single you out, give you trouble.

"Language, Lonnie," said Megan, the cashier, a single mother who'd lost a husband to a younger woman and found religion. She had the echo of a former prettiness in her features. Tall and broad in the hips, with heavy breasts, she was pined after by the men, though Sam couldn't fathom the appeal. To him she looked worn, with her colored hair, tired eyes ringed with makeup. He preferred a fresher look.

"I just can't heeeelp myself," Lonnie crooned.

"You're going to have to, if you want to be the cook here."

"Chef."

"Don't flatter yourself."

"Hey." Lonnie held up his palms, suddenly serious. "I'm the chef, and if you don't give me the proper respect, I'll stick my dick in the soup before you can say *boo*."

This was the refuge to which all of Lonnie's arguments fled. He looked around, satisfied with the point he'd made.

Megan shook her head. "You're the only sane one here," she said to Sam, and he offered a vague smile in return.

Breakfast was slow—maybe the warm weather—but lunch picked up. Sam worked the counter, taking orders and preparing sandwiches, jumping back to the grill when things got heavy on Lonnie.

"Slow down," Horacio told Sam, chuckling at his own joke. As he passed behind the counter, he placed a hand on Sam's shoulder in what seemed a fatherly gesture.

The line for sandwiches extended out the door, a typical lunch-time rush. Most of the people waiting were students, and Sam loved the snatches of conversation he overheard.

"What the hell was that question about angles?" a boy said, raising his palms and widening his eyes to emphasize the strangeness of the question about angles.

Another conversation picked up between two girls: "He *really* said that. I'm not even kidding. Right after he finished."

"You around next Friday, man?" a boy in line asked Sam, handing him a yellow flyer. "We're having some people over. You should come by."

"Sounds good," Sam said, stuffing the flyer in his apron. It was something that happened from time to time, getting invited to student parties, to smoke in their rooms, shoot baskets in the gym. The invitations were flattering, as if they considered Sam a member of their team, and Sam always showed up.

"What can I get you?" he asked the boy who'd given him the flyer, riding the wave of goodwill that swelled beneath him.

After the rush, the snack bar drained of people, giving Sam time to help the custodians sweep around the tables, toss out trash, straighten chairs. It was when he was changing the trash by the door to the dining area that he saw her, the girl.

He didn't know her name, but he'd been aware of her since the beginning of the school year, noticing her when she passed by him on the campus, and the fact that she was often alone, appearing lost in private thoughts. Sometimes he found it hard to speak when she got to the front of the line. If there'd been a door, he would have held it. If there'd been a chair, he would have pulled it out. For some reason—maybe because he imagined the type of fortunate, polite family she must have come from—she put him in mind of these old-fashioned gentlemanly gestures, that kind of innocent courtship.

When her eyes came to rest on him—she had large, lovely brown eyes—he looked down at the trash bag he was tying. He didn't mean to snub her, but she brought out the shyness in him.

Before he had a chance to fix it, she was waving and smiling at a tall boy with a long neck that pushed his head out in front of his body, coming in the side door. By the way she greeted him, Sam knew the boy was her boyfriend, and the thought of them together, kissing, holding hands, clamped a cold fist over his heart.

Sam took the trash outside, along with a slice of deli ham, and hurled the trash into the dumpster. There was a stray cat—a gray one with a white spot the size of a nickel over its eye—that hung around the door to the kitchen, and Sam fed it the piece of cold ham, then jogged back inside to the counter to take the girl's order.

"So you like it here?" he asked while he was making her turkey sandwich.

She looked up, clearly surprised by the question, since they'd never exchanged more than a few words. But she seemed pleased he was speaking to her. She had a broad forehead, round face, and small chin, a white scar halfway between her lips and nose.

"Oh, at Stradler? I like it. My classes are good. People are nice. No one's cursed me out yet." She looked at him for a second, then said, "Just kidding. I get cursed out all the time."

He smiled, registering the joke. The boyfriend was standing by the wall, toasting a bagel.

"Where are you living?" Sam asked. Though a disappointment, the news about the boyfriend had taken the edge off his shyness. It wasn't such a risk to talk to her.

"In Mannerleigh."

"That's a nice dorm. I visited someone there once. You like it?"

"It's pretty. I like the walk to campus. It's all girls, so the bathrooms are clean. I think it's a little quieter than some of the other dorms."

"That's a big thing for me, the quiet," Sam said. "I read a lot. Write a little bit. I can't concentrate when there's too much noise." He wanted to bring in some of these details about himself, give her a picture of what his life was like.

"What do you write?"

"Just stories. Some of them are things that happened to me. Some are things I made up. There's so much to write about in the world."

She smiled at that. If she ever asked to see some of his writing, he knew he could copy something from a book, make a few changes so she couldn't search it out. He just wanted to make a good impression, and he thought the writing might intrigue her.

"You're making friends, I guess." He looked down at the sandwich when he said that.

"A few. No one here knows about my time in the slammer."

She joked a lot. He hadn't realized that before. She always looked a little down when she was alone. And something else: maybe she and the tall boy weren't a couple yet. She didn't seem to want to acknowledge him.

"Anyway, that's good," Sam said. "You seem like someone who wouldn't have trouble making friends."

He caught her blushing after he said that. When he handed her the sandwich, the plate piled high with chips and extra pickles, she said, "I'm Julia."

The sound of her name, this offering, lit something inside him, the warmth rippling out to his limbs.

"Sam. A pleasure."

He removed his hand from the plastic glove and they shook. He noted the mention of the Mannerleigh dorm.

CHAPTER 3
The Woods

E arly again, Julia waited for Marcus on the train platform. It was a bright day in the first week of October and the air had that smoky-fresh smell that always signaled fall to her. The sky was a polished blue. Her breath fogged the air. The weather reminded her of chilly walks home from school with her brother when he talked about his life, the girl Hannah he liked, his favorite Coltrane albums, his plans to become a journalist and live in Spain. She'd teased him that in junior-year English the class had read his whole life story in a book by Hemingway.

It's okay to remember, she thought now, but don't dwell on it. It's too easy to get lost there, and then you'll never come back.

Julia saw Marcus approaching from the other end of the platform. He was wearing a burgundy sweater and corduroys that were too big for him. She liked the hodgepodge way he dressed, as if plucking outfits from a bin sale. A lack of concern for others' opinions had always been a draw for Julia.

"Hey," she said when he was close enough to hear.

He looked at her and didn't say anything for a few moments. Then, when he was almost near enough to whisper, he said, "Hey, Julia," in a detached way that made her think he was the type of guy who avoided getting excited about things, who worried about showing too much of himself.

"I like your sweater."

He looked down. "Are you sure?"

"You seem surprised."

"I don't think anyone's ever told me they liked what I'm wearing. Usually people ask if I need spare change."

"It would take more than change to fix that."

He glanced up and smiled a little.

Julia smiled back. "Ready to walk?"

"Why I'm here."

She started down the path, Marcus following. The ground was hard and veined with tree roots. There were smells of pine and dirt. The temperature dropped as soon as they got into the woods, and she felt the hair on her arms prickle beneath her sweater.

"I had no idea this was here," Marcus said, looking around with interest.

"It's a good place for any illicit transactions. Drug deals. Dead bodies. Whatever you've got."

He grinned. "How about clothing trafficking?"

"Don't dip into your own stash."

It was good, Julia thought, the way they were kidding. She was having fun. That kind of mild ribbing was always in her comfort zone with guys. It was the way she used to kid around with her friends' boyfriends, who often seemed to get closer to Julia than to their own girlfriends. She was the kind of girl that guys were friends with but didn't ask out. The fact that she was comfortable with them, didn't need or care to impress them, seemed to put them at ease.

While Julia and Marcus walked, she glanced over at him, and noticed he hunched a little, like he was apologizing for being so tall.

Before she'd talked to Marcus, she'd seen him only in class, or walking around campus with headphones on, like he was moving inside a bubble, disconnected from the people around him. A loner with a boner, her friend Danny used to joke about guys like him. But even though Marcus appeared distant, Julia had noticed there was an aspect of desperation to him, too. He'd called her three times this week, acting casual but then making sure to confirm their plans for the walk. The third time she'd said, "We're going for a walk?" and when he didn't respond, she told him she was just teasing.

"I heard that you play jazz piano," she said now.

"Who told you?"

"Hobbes." He taught the music-theory class they took together. "Was it a secret?"

"He walked in on me the other day in the practice room. Snuck in like a bandit. I didn't hear him at all. I would have stopped playing if I'd known he was there."

"You don't like to perform?"

He shook his head. "Hate it."

"Hobbes said you were really good."

"He hadn't plugged in his hearing aid."

"I'm pretty sure it's battery operated."

Marcus opened his mouth to speak, then closed it. It seemed like he'd wanted to make another sarcastic comment about himself, but maybe felt it would have been too much.

"How about you?" he said. "You have an instrument?"

Julia was going to say, *I used to play the trumpet*, just set it out there, lightly, test how it would feel. She hadn't wanted to make a secret of it, that history. She was thinking of trying to pick up the horn again sometime this year, maybe spring semester, play a few scales, see if the pain was manageable. The music had been her life in high school, not just a hobby but a kind of atmosphere she existed in, practicing three hours a day, the orchestra concerts and solo recitals. It was all she'd expected of her life, to do that one thing well enough to make a career of it. *A solid orchestra seat*, her teacher at Peabody had told her. *With enough work, maybe more.*

"No," she told Marcus. "I don't play anything."

The light in the woods was thin and clear, like light in an aquarium. Marcus slipped his arm into hers. It should have been nice, that first awkward touch, but the contact made Julia sad. Strange, the way her mind worked. Because in that moment, rather than enjoying the walk and being touched by a cute guy, what she thought of was her brother. The fact that she would never see him again. Never. The word astounded her. All our lives we walk around with a word like that nipping at our heels, and we don't so much as glance down at it.

"You okay?" Marcus said.

"Sure. Why?"

"You seemed like you were thinking about something."

"I'm sorry. I was just thinking about home."

"Do you miss it?"

"Sometimes. But usually I'm glad to have a break." She forced a smile.

Marcus was looking at Julia, and for a second she thought he was concerned. She didn't need that, another person worrying about her. Then she thought he might kiss her, which could have been nice. At least it would have kept her from making any more dumb jokes.

"Where'd you get that?" he asked, indicating the scar above her lip.

"Oh," Julia said, and before she knew it she'd pulled her arm from his and was covering her mouth with her hand. She saw Paul. Saw the snow swirling behind his head, his lips moving, no sound.

"Did I say something?" Marcus asked.

Breathe, she heard El Doctor say. *Breathe, Julia. You can't control your feelings.*

She took her hand down. "Sorry."

"You look upset. Are you feeling okay? We don't have to talk about it. I didn't mean to—"

"It's okay. Really. It's just not my favorite subject. I promise I won't have a panic attack."

He smiled. "No worries. Another time."

"It's ugly, isn't it. The scar."

"Not at all." He was looking at her, trying to make her see that he meant it.

"I feel like it marks up my whole face."

"I barely noticed it. I swear. And I like it. It's got character."

"I'm not sure my face needs any more character. But thanks."

The trail was descending, and she had to look away from him, concentrate on stepping slowly so she didn't twist an ankle. She was fine with stopping that conversation anyway. It wasn't going anywhere she needed to go on a date.

As Julia and Marcus walked down the slope, the hush of water got louder, the brush on both sides of them more vibrant. Sunlight coined the forest floor. They crossed a slatted wooden bridge, the boards sagging under their weight, then started up another hill, into the fresh scent of leaves and something spicy-sweet like cinnamon.

"Tell me what you were like when you were a kid," Julia said to Marcus. It was a question she was always interested in.

"Pretty serious," Marcus said. "Quiet. In all the pictures, I have this puzzled expression on my face, like I'm trying to work out a hard math problem."

She smiled at that image of him. Keep talking, she thought. "Where did you live?"

"In the country. Farmland. Horse farms all around us. The horses came out with blankets on their backs in winter. Lots of corn and animals and trees. Not many people. I'm used to being by myself."

"It sounds beautiful."

"I can take you sometime, if you want. It's just a couple hours from here."

She didn't say anything to that, wasn't sure yet what she wanted, there was too much bouncing around inside her head. She didn't know how close she could get to Marcus. If she let him share himself, he'd expect her to do the same.

The slope was flattening, and Julia could see a clearing ahead of them, a wide carpet of grass, blemished by sandy spots and piles of charred sticks where students had lit bonfires. She felt warm from the walk, and was breathing heavily.

They walked into the field, the luxurious sunlight. Marcus stopped. Julia turned toward him, and he was looking at her, a pensive expression on his face. It must have been the one he had in the old pictures he was describing, like he'd kept that scared child hidden inside himself all these years.

"I just wanted to tell you I've really enjoyed the time we've spent together," he said. He reached for her hand. When she touched him, his fingertips were cool. He leaned over and kissed her. Just like that, their lips were together. His mouth was warm, and his skin had a motherly smell, like toast. And Julia felt strangely outside it all, floating above it, and she was angry at herself for not feeling more and at the same time worried she would always be that way. A cold fish.

After their walk, she went back to the dorm, wondering how she could explain all this to Leanette, make a story of it. She knew there was a chance Leanette would tease her, and that the teasing would most likely run toward sexual strangeness, a topic Leanette was practically evangelical on. She might joke that Marcus was secretly a pervert, invited little girls to his room to play doctor. But a comment like that wouldn't bother Julia. She liked dark humor. She'd say she wondered why it was so easy to schedule a follow-up.

On the carpet, just inside the door when Julia walked into the room, was a yellow sheet of paper. She picked it up and saw it was some kind of advertisement for a party. At the top of the flyer, someone had scrawled a note: *Hey Julia, hope to see you there!*

Odd that the person had used her name. She couldn't explain it, but she had the feeling someone was watching her read the note. How do you ever know if feelings like that are instinct or paranoia?

She walked back into the hallway. Looked left and right.

No one was there.

⚬━┼━⚬

Sam got up from the chair in his living room and laid down the book he was trying to read, a collection of stories by an Irish writer named Trevor. It was still early, hardly past eight, but he had to get to sleep soon if he wanted a full seven hours. Normally, he didn't have trouble focusing on his nightly reading, which he did to keep his mind active, help him relax at the end of a day. He liked fiction best, the doors it opened into other people's lives, but he'd read almost anything, as long as it had a good story to it.

It was Marilyn, an ex-girlfriend, who'd gotten him started with the reading. An English major at Harvard, she'd told him all the best books. He would never have discovered *Jude the Obscure* on his own. His mom hadn't been much of a reader. Sometimes gossip magazines or dieting guides, but never real books. "I'd rather live it than read it," she'd told Sam, though she hardly left the house.

Tonight, though, he couldn't concentrate. Thoughts sloshed in his head. Why were these memories of past relationships harassing him now, disrupting what were usually the most peaceful hours of his day?

He knew the answer, if he was honest with himself. It was excitement that did it. Anxiety, too. About the girl, Julia. Worries about the future always led to nostalgia about the past. It was the way of the mind, Sam knew, mixing what was over and what was just beginning.

He knew she liked the tall boy, and that they were probably dating. But that could change. Those things often did. In some ways, having the boy in the picture could help Sam get to know her. There was always a risk of making a move too soon, and the boyfriend could be a useful reminder to keep the proper distance, take his time and chat with her.

He wasn't sure about the exclamation point. That's what was getting him now. It was the one aspect of the note he'd questioned while writing it. In general, he didn't like dramatic punctuation, but he thought it held a certain appeal on a party flyer. He hadn't signed his name. There wasn't any question about that. He'd wanted her to think a classmate had left the flyer, slipped it under her door when she wasn't in, forgotten to sign a name. Maybe the exclamation point contributed to that illusion.

CHAPTER 4
The Party

J ulia and Leanette were sitting on their beds, talking, textbooks splayed on their laps, in the sparsely furnished dorm room. Julia had once joked that the room was like a prison cell looking in the mirror at itself, with its perfect symmetry of steel-framed beds, faux-wooden desks, corkboards, cinder-block walls. The only difference was that Leanette's side was plastered with photos of her high school friends, standing in groups with their arms around each other. Julia hadn't put up any photos. Just a poster her brother had given her, a present when she'd gotten accepted to the Artistically Talented Youth program at Peabody. The poster showed Miles Davis playing the trumpet in a fog of cigarette smoke.

"So where do you usually get them?" Julia asked Leanette now, picking up on a conversation they'd been having.

"Why? You need condoms?" Leanette raised her eyebrows.

"Maybe sometime. I have an art project I'm thinking about."

Leanette put both her hands over her mouth and squealed, a sound that made Julia want to bite herself. When Leanette took her hands down, she asked, "Seriously, is this a 'just in case' thing? Or are we talking a specific guy?"

"Why do you assume it's a guy? It could be a small cucumber."

"Who is it, Julie? Really. You *have* to tell me. I *need* to know."

"He's in my music class. I don't think you'd know him. He's pretty quiet. Doesn't hang out a lot."

"Are we playing twenty questions? Even quiet people have names. And, besides, before I tell you where you're going to get your condoms, I think it's only appropriate for me to know whose sperm I'll be protecting you from."

"I'm going to let the condom do the protecting."

"Julie," Leanette said in a mock-stern voice that must have come from one of her parents. She was trying on a severe look. "Tell me now. I won't tolerate another second of your dillydallying."

"Okay, okay, his name's Marcus Broley. You probably don't—"

"Tall?"

Julia nodded.

"Ha! I know who he is." Leanette had pored over the online freshman directory, which featured high school photos of that year's entering class, with more rigor than she'd studied any of the textbooks she'd hauled back from the college bookstore. "I'll bet he has a long dick. Long and thin."

"That just sounds weird."

"If you go down on him, careful he doesn't poke your eye out."

"I'll wear my lab goggles."

Leanette snorted. "The drugstore's best, by the way. You can get condoms at the health center, but they only have the military-issue kind. Slimy as snails and they make your pussy smell like disinfectant."

"That's the perfume I douche with anyway. Eau de Lysol. It doesn't always attract guys, but I've never gotten a urinary tract infection."

They went on like this for a while, drifting further away from the subject of Marcus. After the kiss, Julia knew she was heading toward sex with him. They'd seen each other almost every day over the past week; Marcus made sure of it, always calling or dropping by. Sometimes they studied, other times "went for a walk," which was code for finding a place where they could make out, an activity Marcus seemed deeply invested in. Julia assumed sex was a given, the place any normal college relationship ended up.

"So when are you going to see him again?" Leanette asked.

"We're supposed to meet up at a party on Friday."

"What party?" Julia could tell that it bothered Leanette there was a party she hadn't been informed about.

"I don't know. I got this flyer." Julia took the yellow paper out of the desk drawer where she'd been keeping it and handed it to Leanette.

Leanette studied the invitation. "That's an *off*-campus party. Is that Marcus's handwriting?"

"No. It must have been from someone in one of my classes. Or a stalker."

"You have a lot of admirers."

"I don't think it's like that. Although I did douche recently."

Leanette was watching Julia as if she'd just spoken a fluent sentence in Turkish. It wasn't Julia's style to brag about a guy being interested in her, so she let the silence hang for a moment.

But Leanette broke it. "You know you're going to need a friend to accompany you to that," she said.

The party on Friday was in an apartment building nicknamed "The Barn," a ten-minute walk from campus. Most of the people who lived there, Leanette told Julia, were Stradler students or alumni who'd stayed in the area to take advantage of the school's social life. People with big plans, like joining a drumming circle or converting an old vacuum cleaner into a bong. Inside the building, the carpets reeked of beer and weed and cigarettes. The hallways were dark, and people crowded into corners and against walls, music throbbing from the apartments.

To Julia, it felt like unearthing some subterranean world, like any minute little mole men might come running out of the apartments. Part of this effect could have been a result of the four medicinal shots of rum Leanette had forced Julia to take with her around eleven, just before they left their room. It was the most Julia had ever taken, and the ground already rocked like a ship and sometimes she had to grab Leanette's arm to steady herself. She didn't know how she'd ever find Marcus in this chaos.

Julia and Leanette walked down the hall, toward a particularly crowded apartment. The open door was plugged with bodies. Julia felt herself being pushed forward, her breast crushed into the check-patterned shirt of the boy in front of her. Nice to meet you.

"Don't let him do that!" someone screamed from inside the apartment.

"There's no way!" someone else said.

Julia heard what sounded like a chicken clucking somewhere ahead of her. It was all so strange and dreamlike. And hot. She felt her stomach shift, and realized she was going to be sick if she didn't get out of this crowd.

"I gotta get some air!" she yelled to Leanette.

"I gotta see what's inside that apartment," a voice answered. Not Leanette's.

Julia shoved her way out of the crowd, thinking, *So this is what it feels like to be drunk.* The walls leaned in her vision. She felt like someone had thrown a blanket over her head, it was so hot and dark.

Outside, she felt better, with the wind against her face. It was warm for early October, but cooler than inside. The houses in the neighborhood were mostly dark, some with an upper window lit in a room where a couple sat reading or watching TV. Julia walked to the curb and bowed her head, trying to collect herself, to stop the pavement from rocking.

She didn't know how long she was like that before a hand touched her on the shoulder and a voice whispered, "Hey."

She stood up, regretting the fact that Marcus would see her in this condition. But when she looked up, the man in front of her was shorter than Marcus, with shaggy brown hair. He had a familiar face, good-looking, but for a second Julia had trouble placing it. She thought maybe he was a student, in his faded T-shirt and ragged jeans. But then her mind snapped the image into place, and she could picture him standing behind the sandwich counter at the snack bar.

"Sam," she said—a bit loudly, she realized—the name piped into her thoughts from some unknown place. She didn't know why, but she was happy to see him.

"How's it going, Julia?" He looked pleased that she'd remembered his name. "I saw you when I was coming up the street. It looked like you weren't feeling well."

"What makes you say that?"

He smiled, as if to acknowledge the joke but also to say that he really did want to know how she was doing. Like in the snack bar, she had the feeling that he didn't really respond to humor, or that maybe he saw through that kind of shield, saw through to her. It was disarming, realizing she couldn't crack a joke to protect herself.

"I'm doing better now, thanks," she said. "It was just really hot in there."

"I'll bet it's a madhouse. I was just stopping by because I promised someone I would."

She nodded. She couldn't tell how old he was. He looked like a guy who hadn't graduated too long ago, still wearing students' clothes, his hair disheveled. But there was something else in his face, a kind quality, but also a sadness, she thought, an experience in the world that the others in her classes hadn't lived through yet.

He must have noticed her studying him, because the next thing he said was, "I don't come to a lot of parties. I'm starting to grow out of it. But a little fun's good sometimes. Gets you out of yourself. Don't you think?"

Normally, she would have come back with some deadpan line about how she didn't like fun, it took up too much time. But she knew a line like that wouldn't have worked with him, that it would have seemed like an obstacle, some clutter in the way of a more genuine conversation they were supposed to have.

So she said, "I think it's important to try. Even if it's hard sometimes."

His face changed when she said that. Something softened around his eyes, and she could tell he understood what she was saying, that he could relate to it.

"What do you think makes it hard?" he said.

"I guess things that happen to you. Things you can't control. The world. All that." She didn't know if it was the alcohol that was making her talk like this, so earnestly, with so little armor, but she didn't mind. When you've been holding something in with all your strength as long as she had, maybe what you really want, more than anything, is to let it go.

"Were there things that happened to you?" He was looking at her, focusing on her in a way she'd never been focused on before. It was as if she were a mystery he needed to solve. Julia could tell that he truly wanted to hear from her, hear everything she had to say. His eyes alone told her that.

"There was one thing. A thing I don't really like talking about."

She thought he'd tell her it was okay, she could talk to him. That's what people usually say when they want to be sympathetic. She could hear the words even before he said them.

But instead, he said, "My mom passed away last year. I still can't even tell some of my friends about it. It's just so unbelievably hard. I feel like I'm going to cry every time I mention it."

She'd never imagined this, talking so openly with someone about these sad subjects. She'd figured it was a part of life, a part of herself she'd always have to hide. But it touched her how honestly he shared his feelings, and so she told him, "I lost someone, too. My brother, actually."

"I'm so sorry," he said. "I'm so sorry, Julia." He put his hand on her shoulder. He didn't try to ask her about it, to get her to talk more, which was what El Doctor would have done. He was simply there with her, and he seemed to respect her grief.

Without thinking about it, Julia put her hand on his. They stayed like that for a little while. She was usually hesitant to touch anyone, but just then she didn't feel uncomfortable about it. In fact, she felt something else, something slippery and warm, a kind of animal need for him.

He must have sensed how she felt, because he seemed to lean forward slightly, and then, without thinking about it, Julia pressed her mouth against his. She didn't know if it was the alcohol, she truly didn't, or if she just wanted him, wanted someone, but she couldn't even remember what had led up to kissing him. It was like a film had been cut to that precise instant, everything before it black. And here she was, not stopping, not pulling away. She'd never lost control like this before. She didn't know what it meant, or whether it was good or bad or where it was headed, only that she'd crossed a threshold.

She couldn't say how long it lasted—seconds or minutes maybe, her sense of time was so disturbed—but at some point she pulled back and looked at him. And that was when she saw, over Sam's shoulder, that Marcus was standing on the sidewalk, watching them.

CHAPTER 5
The Dump

S am had the day off. Most weeks he got only one day, now that Horacio had changed the schedule, but he didn't mind that. He wasn't the type to count the minutes left until the end of a shift, the days until a vacation. He liked work, liked the structure it provided; it helped him stay positive and productive. Without the structure, there was a risk of feeling aimless, adrift in his own freedom.

For that reason, Sam always set chores for himself on his days off. Today, he was hauling a load of trash in his van to a landfill seventy miles west of Marshallville. He enjoyed the drive. The spell of good weather had extended over a week, and now Sam was riding beneath a lake of cloudless sky.

Doing mindless work was the best way to clear his head, especially after a big event like what had happened the night before. He hadn't even imagined giving Julia his number, let alone kissing her for several minutes in the street. At best, he'd thought he would say hi, strike up a little conversation, and say something interesting that would get her attention. But when he saw her practically stumbling into the road, he'd known it was his responsibility to go to her, make sure she was all right, and when he found out she was, he couldn't help but view it as a small opportunity to advance his cause.

The landfill was surrounded by a chain-link fence that must have been twelve feet high, topped with a healthy stitching of barbed wire. Sam pulled up to the booth at the front gate. Inside, a plump red-haired man with pouchy cheeks sat watching a TV. He was wearing thick glasses, the kind that sit way down on your nose, and he was leaning toward the TV like it was hard to see. When Sam stopped the van, the man pulled a tissue out of a box next to the TV, and with a slightly sickened look, as if he were disposing of a large insect, he used the tissue to slide open the window of the booth.

"Help you?" the man said to Sam.

"I have some bags to dump." Sam held out the money for the fee.

But the man held up his hand. While Sam waited, the man removed a pair of rubber gloves from his desk drawer and pulled them on with a look of relief.

"Can't be too careful," he said, taking the money. "All the germs out there."

"Tough place to work if you're sensitive to it."

The man shrugged. "Don't always get your first."

Sam nodded. There was a framed picture of a woman on the man's desk. When the man handed Sam his change, Sam said, "That your wife?"

The man looked at the picture, then back at Sam, an anxious expression on his face. "Why? You seen her around?"

"No." Sam smiled to show the question was harmless. "Just asking."

"Oh." The man looked relieved. "Well, that's her." He took off his gloves and showed the photo to Sam. The woman was over sixty, with a pleated chin and penciled-on eyebrows, a helmet of bobbed blond hair.

"Nice," Sam said.

"It's not easy," the man said, shaking his head. "People think it's fun having a pretty wife. But try it for a week. It's a burden. Sometimes I wish she was plain. Have to watch her everywhere I go. With a *hawk's* eye." He pointed at one of the thick lenses of his glasses.

"I can see the problem," Sam said. "But I hope you get time with her on the weekends. You get normal weekends, right?"

"We're closed Sundays. Saturdays I come in late. I also get Tuesdays."

"You have to work early?"

"Five on a normal day. Six on Saturdays."

"Tough schedule. How late do you stay?"

"Two o'clock. Get back while it's light out. Enjoy the day."

"Not sure I could do it. I'm thinking about a change of work, is why I ask."

The man put the photo back on his desk. "What line are you in?"

"I work with children."

"That's tough, in its way."

"It has its rewards. Anyway, nice talking to you." Sam reached his hand out to shake.

But the man held up his palm again and waved to Sam. "Can't be too careful. All the bacteria out there. No way to know what you've been touching before you got here."

"All good stuff," Sam said, and waved, driving on through the gate, up the dirt path between the piles of litter. When he was out of the man's line of sight, he took out a pen and a piece of paper and wrote down the following information: *Mon, Wed, Thurs, Fri @ 5am-2pm. Sat @ 6am-2pm(?).*

The man in the booth this morning was a nice guy, and Sam had enjoyed talking to him, wanted to make sure he'd have the opportunity again. He liked hearing about other people's lives, the routines that swept them through their days. That was why he'd told the lie about his job; it kept the conversation going. Sometimes you had to invent details to keep things lively. It was why he'd told Julia that his mom had died only last year. What did it really matter if it was last year or eleven years ago? The feeling was the same. And it helped Julia to understand his sensitivity and to open up to him a little. Sam didn't believe there was anything wrong with fiction if it was interesting and helped you get to the truth about a person.

People were usually pretty open with Sam. More than once, someone had told him he had a quality that made you trust in his good intentions. One of his ex-girlfriends, Alyssa, had told him he had "boyish eyes," a phrase Sam had stored away among the sweeter moments of his life.

The landfill was a desert of refuse and dusty trails, the wind gusting a sour smell at Sam when he climbed out of the van. The workers piled dirt over the rubbish every day or two, Sam had learned, making the waste of people's lives disappear. Some fat brown birds swooped and beaked at the trash, the bottles and cartons and smears of food, the bags like the ones Sam had brought.

As he unloaded the trash, Sam's mind returned to the memory of kissing Julia, which he'd been carrying around all day as he did his chores. Her lips were salty and cool against his, and they split like a ripe fruit at his tongue's pressure, exposing the wet cavern of her mouth. He couldn't have imagined a lovelier way to spend his time than kissing her, and he wished it had gone on for hours, even days. After she'd pulled back, though, after she'd seen the tall boy standing there, Sam knew it was best for him to leave. He didn't want to get in a fight with the boy, or upset Julia any more. So he wrote his cell number on a piece of paper—it wasn't listed anywhere—pushed the number into her hand, and said she could call him anytime if she wanted to talk.

Things were moving so quickly with her, Sam thought as he tossed the trash bags onto the hills of refuse. It wasn't like him to be this eager, this aggressive, but he felt an urgency with her. He'd known she was special, a kind and sensitive person, since the first time he'd seen her, and he couldn't bear the idea of a relationship not working out between them.

And maybe something else. Maybe it was the birthday he had coming up, his fortieth, a great beast of a birthday whose shadow fell over every day of this final week of Sam's youth, as he thought of it.

Whatever it was, he wanted more than anything to be with Julia, and he knew it was going to happen. Sam was an optimist, and when he fixed an image in his mind, like the image of himself with Julia, it always came true. He could see it just ahead of him, like headlights approaching on a long, straight road.

CHAPTER 6
Two Conversations

S he called Marcus the morning after the party, left a message asking him to call her, saying she wanted to talk about what happened. He didn't call back that day, and she tried him again the next day, Sunday, then six more times on Monday. She sent him an email saying, *Please call me*. Then she left a couple more phone messages, saying she was sorry, she wanted a chance to explain, she felt horrible.

And that was all true. Julia was ashamed of what she'd done to Marcus. She wasn't usually an impulsive person, and she didn't know what had come over her that night with Sam.

She called Marcus one more time, saying she understood he needed time to think things over, but that she'd like to go for a walk with him on Friday if he'd consider it. She told him they could head off after their music class, around four. She hoped he'd be up for it. "I'll buy you a coffee," she added. "Any size you want. Except large or medium. Just kidding. Bye."

Leanette walked in while Julia was leaving this last message, and when Julia hung up, Leanette said, "I wouldn't worry about it so much. Sam is *much* cuter anyway."

"Well, in that case."

Leanette laughed. "It's not that big a deal."

"I'm just not the type to kiss a guy behind someone's back. I'm not the type to kiss a guy at all, really. I'm supposed to be in the library or putting zit cream on my nose or playing Scrabble in my pajamas. I think I made a mistake."

"What mistake? Kissing a hot guy who could probably teach you every position in the *Kama Sutra*? Anyone would have done it. *I* would have done it."

"I acted too fast," Julia said. "Marcus is a sensitive guy. I know how much something like this would hurt him. I didn't need to jump on Sam at the party. I'm not that horny. That one little kiss is causing a huge mess for everyone."

"First of all, as far as I could tell, that wasn't a little kiss. I think he had his tongue on your spleen when I walked outside. Second of all, it's not a mess. You're free to jump on anyone you want."

"I jumped and I landed on my face."

"That's fine, too. The question is whether Sam will be landing there also. Why don't you call him and see what he's up to this weekend?"

But Julia held off. It seemed like it was only right to put some distance between herself and that night. The thought of picking up the phone and dialing Sam made her light-headed. She didn't know why his sympathy, his need, had stirred her feelings so much. At the party she'd wanted him in a desperate way she was almost afraid of.

She'd hoped to catch Marcus in music class on Wednesday, to ask again about the walk, but he didn't show up. When she got home, her phone was ringing. She dropped her bag and ran across the room. She wouldn't have admitted it to herself then, but she was hoping it was Sam, that he'd looked up her number and decided to call.

She picked up. "Hello?"

"Hi, sweetheart." It was a man's voice, high and a little too gentle.

"Dad. Hi. What's going on?"

"Nothing, honey. Everything's fine." He always started their conversations this way, like he was calming a child. "I thought I'd see what's going on with you. It's just been a while."

"It's only been a week. They haven't even changed the milk in the dining hall. Everything's the same."

He chuckled. "That's good. That's great. Say, how's the weather out there?"

"Probably the same as in Baltimore."

He chuckled again, choosing to take it as a joke, even though Julia could hear the sharpness in her voice.

He asked about her classes, the dorm, the food, all the mundane stuff she knew he couldn't really care about.

"You ever pick up the horn and give it a shot?" he said.

"No, I haven't."

There was a pause, and Julia could tell he was waiting for her to say more.

Finally, he said, "Maybe it's worth a try. Might be getting better."

"Dad, please. You know I can't."

"I'm not pressuring. I just thought maybe you'd healed and—"

"I don't want to talk about it."

"Okay, no problemo. Hey, by the way, did you ever get in touch with that doc?"

He hadn't used words like *doc* before the accident. He hadn't said things like, *Betcha got a good sleep last night*, hokey phrases that made him sound like Mr. Rogers on Quaaludes.

"No, I haven't," she said. "Why are you bringing that up?"

"You think you might want to give him a buzz? I told him you'd call."

"I'm busy, Dad. I have a lot of work. It turns out my crack habit leaves plenty of time for studying."

He didn't laugh at that. Instead, he said, "Dr. Heder recommended him. He's supposed to be a good guy. This is important, Jul."

"Don't call me that."

"I'm sorry."

"Why didn't Mom call? Why didn't *she* think it was so important?"

"She wanted to call. She's just getting home so late and—"

"Sounds tough."

"Julia."

"Please, Dad. Please don't bother me about this anymore. When I tell you I haven't picked up the trumpet, you go right into the doctor speech. I'm not playing because I can't. It doesn't mean anything else, so don't take it as a sign of my demise."

"Why are you so angry?"

That's what did it, what popped the bubble. "Stop!" she screamed into the phone.

"Julia. Honey. Please."

"What is it with you? Why do you need to push so much? What the hell does it matter to you? I'm not bothering you. I have a scholarship. I hardly cost you anything."

"It's not about money. You're my daughter."

For some reason, that got her. The anger drained away, and she just felt tired. Like she could sleep for days.

"I'm sorry, Dad. I just need a little more space. It'll work out. No mug shots in the paper, I promise. Unless my philosophy midterm goes really bad."

"I worry about you."

"I'll be okay. I'll call you soon."

"Please do that."

When she put down the phone, her hands were shaking. She didn't want to be alone. She picked up the receiver and dialed Sam.

CHAPTER 7
Dinner Date

They were supposed to meet at six on Thursday. Sam had recommended the restaurant, an Italian place called Minelli's, which he'd driven by in Shady Grove, a town north of Stradler. He'd chosen the location because students from the college hardly ever went up there. It was better for them to have their privacy, he thought, to be able to really talk and get to know each other. Sam wasn't sure if the food was any good. Restaurants weren't a big attraction for him, and he wouldn't have known whom to ask. The menu was affordable enough, and, truthfully, Sam didn't care much about food.

On the phone, Julia had asked how he was going to get there, which Sam knew was her way of asking about a ride. He would have liked to offer it, and under other circumstances would have carried her on his shoulders if necessary, but it didn't seem appropriate for people to see him, an older man, picking her up and dropping her off on the campus. He thought a little distance would be prudent. So he told her he was coming from an errand north of the restaurant, and asked if she'd be okay with the bus.

He arrived forty minutes early and found parking a block from the restaurant, giving him time to stroll along Main Street. The stores, which belonged to another era—a pharmacy, a variety shop, a shoe repair—were all closed, the merchandise cloaked in shadows. There was a feeling of unreality to these moments before the date. He could hardly believe that in a few minutes he'd be sitting across from her in a restaurant. *The world is a remarkable place*, he thought.

Claire, another ex, had said that to him once. She could surprise him that way, with a comment that felt too romantic for a girl who dyed her hair black and wore black lipstick and powdered her face a deathly white. She listened to bands with names like "Blood River" and "Holiday Massacre," but she was one of the sweetest and gentlest people he'd met in his life. She wrote poetry and went to church every week. She was the first girl he'd slept with, and there was always a special feeling about that. He still remembered the denim jacket she'd been wearing the day she'd said that.

When Sam walked into the restaurant, intentionally arriving about fifteen minutes late so she'd be the one waiting, Julia was standing in the dim alcove at the front. She was wearing a blue dress, with a thin black sweater that she'd left unbuttoned. He could see by the glow of her cheeks that she had on makeup, and he felt underdressed in his jeans. Looking down at his sweater, he noticed there was a tear in one of the arms and could hardly believe he'd worn such a tatty piece of clothing. He smiled, as a way to greet Julia, but also at how beautiful she looked, how lucky he felt himself to be.

They said hi, hugging lightly. Sam pulled open the inner door and they went inside. The restaurant was empty of customers, and a bald waiter held out a hand, indicating they could sit anywhere they'd like, and then eyed them as they made their way to a table by the wall. On the table was a checkered cloth and a flickering candle in a red globe. Sam had expected music, but the place was filled with an airy silence, a suggestion of neglect. He wasn't sure if Julia would have liked something livelier. He should have looked inside the restaurant before he'd proposed it.

After they'd gotten their menus, had their waters poured, and bread placed down in front of them, Sam said, "I'm sorry, this place is a little quiet."

"It's great. It's nice to be away from campus."

"I don't go out much," he explained. "I don't really know all the places."

"Don't worry about it. I like empty restaurants. You get a lot of attention."

Sam noticed the bald waiter was still watching them and saw him whisper something to the busboy, who looked at Sam and smiled.

"Sure?" Sam asked Julia. "We can go somewhere else."

"I'm sure. I wouldn't know what to do in a trendy place. I'd spill someone's mojito on myself. I'm glad we'll get the chance to talk."

"Me too, Julia. I'm really happy about that, too."

His excitement was like a pressure inside him, and in order to release some of it, he reached across the table and placed his hand on hers. Her fingers were damp—was she nervous?—and when he squeezed them, she squeezed back.

The waiter came to take their orders, eyeing Sam in that suspicious way. Sam removed his hand from Julia's. They both pointed to dishes, and Sam asked Julia if she'd like a glass of wine, partly out of politeness, and partly to tell the nosy waiter she was plenty old enough. Sam never drank alcohol himself, but he wasn't one to discourage its use in others.

Julia said she was fine with water. The waiter took their menus and left.

After a minute, Sam thought about reaching for Julia's hand again, but before he could do it, she asked, "Would you be up for telling me about what happened to your mother? I know it's a bad topic to start with. And we don't have to talk about it if you don't want."

The question caught him by surprise, the forwardness, and he remembered the story he'd told about his mom passing away the year before. It made sense that Julia was particularly interested in this topic, because of what had happened with her brother. The landscape of loss was one they were both familiar with, like travelers who'd visited a remote city, and the tales they brought back were a way they could relate to each other. The experiences connected them in some fundamental way.

"There's not much to tell," Sam said. "She'd been sick for a while." He shook his head and released a breath. "Awful thing to watch."

"What did she have?"

"Cancer. In her bones." He mentioned the part about the bones because he knew those details were what made a story sympathetic, helped people relate to it, understand what you'd been through. He'd learned that much from his reading.

"Were you working at Stradler then?"

"We were living in Pittsburgh. Lived there my whole life until she died. In fact, I've never left Pennsylvania."

He didn't know why he said that. Sometimes he just got on a roll with something and ended up telling a story because it sounded better than the truth. He thought she'd ask more about his living arrangements. He'd driven through Pittsburgh a couple times, on his way to other places, and he felt confident he could say some believable things about the city.

But instead Julia asked, "How long did it go on? Your mom's illness."

"Over a year. It's hard to remember exactly. The time just blurred together after a while. When you're taking care of someone, all your thoughts go into the person and the chores you're doing for them. The bathing and the feeding and giving the pills. You forget about yourself."

This last piece seemed to weigh on her, and Sam thought he saw her eyes gleam in the candlelight. She blinked the emotion away, though, and Sam was aware how important it was to her to stay in control of her feelings. He admired that bravery and restraint, and was touched by her reaction to the portrait he'd painted of himself.

"It must have been horrible having it drawn out like that," Julia said.

He sensed she wanted to talk about her own experience. "Was it very sudden with the person you knew? Your brother, you said it was?"

She nodded. "Very."

"An accident?"

Again, a bobbing of her chin. He could tell it was difficult for her to talk about this. Her face had changed completely. She'd lost the quickness, the wittiness, and it seemed to have been replaced by a darkness that had rested just below the surface.

The waiter brought their plates of pasta, setting them down on the table. He asked if there was anything else he could get for them, and they both shook their heads.

After a few bites, Sam said, "I won't ask you about your brother, if you don't like to discuss it. I understand it's hard to talk about those things."

Julia put down her fork. "It's okay. I don't usually talk like this, believe me. But for some reason I trust you. I feel like I can be more real with you."

It flooded him, the warmth of what she'd said. "That means a lot to me, Julia."

She smiled with her lips pressed together, and he got the feeling she was holding something behind them. He was about to tell her she looked pretty, thinking it was time to do that, when she said, "I was picking him up at the airport. After his first semester at college."

"He was older, I guess?"

She nodded. "A year and a half. He was coming in on a red-eye from California. He didn't even have on a coat. Just a sweater and an ugly pair of yellow gloves I'd given him for his birthday a few years before.

"My parents didn't want me to pick him up. They were going to get a cab for him. But it would have cost a lot of money, and I really wanted to see him. I played the trumpet, and I had an audition the next day for a spot at Juilliard, this big conservatory, and I wanted to tell him about it. I was scared and excited and he knew about all I'd gone through to get to that point. How important it was to me. I didn't tell a lot of people about that part of my life. But I always shared it with him. He was my best friend. I was kind of the sidekick in my family, and he always did well in school and sports and had girlfriends, but I just felt like he understood me."

"That's how I felt about my mom," Sam said. "Like she knew me better than anyone."

Julia watched him, waiting for him to say more. He realized the interruption was ill timed.

"But keep going. I'm sorry to interrupt."

"It's okay. My parents agreed to let me pick him up. It was really early. Five or six in the morning. Some crazy hour. They weren't even going to be awake when I left. But the night before I was supposed to pick him up, my friend Danny called and she wanted me to go to this party with her. I told her I couldn't, I had to get sleep for my audition, but there was a guy she liked and she said she needed me to go with her, and I always did that kind of thing for my friends, played the wingman. So I told her I'd go for an hour.

"At the party I kept telling Danny I had to leave, but she wouldn't let me, and everyone else kept telling me to stay. They were drinking a lot, and I knew I'd have to give them rides. It kept getting later and later, and finally I got to that point where it felt like it was more trouble to go home than just to stay out.

"So I didn't end up sleeping. I went to pick up my brother. I was worried things would be different when I saw him, that he'd be this adult all of a sudden and I'd still be a little kid. But it wasn't like that. When I got out of the car he picked me up and hugged me in front of the airport. He said he'd heard a trumpet star was coming to pick him up. It was cheesy, but I laughed.

"When we were driving back home, he just kept telling me how great college was, all the subjects he was studying and the people he was meeting. Then, after a little while, he fell asleep. He hadn't slept more than a couple hours all week, because of finals. I was driving and looking over and watching him sleep, and I loved that, seeing him that way. We were the only car on the highway. The whole thing was peaceful, you know?

"I don't know when it happened, but I fell asleep for a second. It must have been just a second, because when I opened my eyes, I saw the median strip coming at me. I swerved, and then I was heading toward the guardrail. I swerved again, and then everything was tumbling and we were both screaming.

"The car landed on his side. It must have knocked him out, because when I looked over, he was sleeping again, but even more still than before. That was the weirdest thing. How still he looked. His window was cracked and his arm was sticking through it.

"My lip was bleeding, all over my face and my neck, and it felt like someone was pressing a hot iron on my mouth, but I got my seat belt off and opened my door, and I crawled out and went around to his side. I was so scared, but when I shook his arm he woke up. He didn't say anything, but his eyes were open.

"I took his hand and I started pulling. I didn't know what I was doing. I just wanted to get him out of the car, and I thought if he was away from it he'd be okay. He was pinned there. I probably could have tried to get him out through my side, but I wasn't thinking. I had blood all over my shirt. There was glass everywhere and it was dark because the headlights had gotten knocked out.

"I pulled as hard as I could, trying to tug him out of there, and finally his glove popped off in my hand and I just fell back on the ground. I already knew something was wrong because the glove was soaking wet. Right then, while I was sitting on the ground, a car came up the highway and suddenly everything got bright from the headlights.

"I was looking at the glove, and I saw he was looking at it, too, and both of us were shocked because it wasn't yellow anymore, but this dark brown color, like mud, and it was dripping on the ground.

"It looked like he was trying to talk. His lips were moving. But there wasn't any sound coming out. That's what I keep remembering.

Him trying to talk and no sound. Like a TV on mute. And then finally he said to me in this high, scared voice, 'Is that mine?' That was the last thing he ever said to me. It was like he was there with me one second, and the next he was gone. Completely gone."

When Julia finished speaking, her cheeks were glowing, and her eyes shined. She was breathing heavily, the thin sweater rising and falling, and Sam could tell she'd been transported to the accident, to the cold air and the wet glove in her hand. She stayed like that, breathing, remembering. Sam had stopped eating while she told her story, and now he waited for her to collect herself.

"You're an amazing person, Julia. We haven't known each other for long, but I can tell you're a strong and good person."

She was looking at the table, shaking her head. "I don't think so. I think I'm a pretty wretched bitch."

"Don't say that. You shouldn't think that about yourself."

"It's best to be honest."

"It's not the truth. I'm not going to try to convince you, but I don't want you to try to convince me either. I can believe what I want. You've told me everything, and I don't think that about you."

She looked up at him with an expression Sam could only describe as puzzlement, and again he reached across the table, this time pushing the hair from her eyes with his fingertips, no longer caring what the bald waiter would think. He felt the way she leaned into his touch, her cheek against his hand, and he said to her, "Would it be okay if I kept my good opinion of you?"

She nodded, and he felt her skin brushing his fingers.

CHAPTER 8
Going Home

It was like a dream, the whole evening. The way she'd let go, told him the story about the accident. Why did he bring that kind of talk out in her? She felt like she was leaving a therapy session every time she finished a conversation with him.

But she hadn't told him everything. Once she'd gotten off the bus, walking down the tree-lined path to her dorm, she thought about what had happened after the accident. She hadn't told Sam about how she'd stopped playing the trumpet, because it was too painful after injuring her lip, her embouchure was too weak from the muscle damage, and it was depressing how much she'd lost, it made her sick, filled her with a bitter soup of regret and anger and shame.

And she hadn't told him about how she'd had to give up her audition at Juilliard; how she'd cut off all her friends because she blamed them for keeping her at the party; how she'd thrown her cell phone into a lake so they wouldn't call anymore; how she'd screamed and cursed at her dad when he told her it wasn't her fault; how her mom stayed silent during these fights, staring at Julia with a look on her face like she'd drunk sour milk; how she'd stopped doing work, stopped going to school, stopped listening to music, stopped caring at all about anything, curled up on her bed like a dying animal.

And she hadn't told Sam about how her parents had sent her to that place. Aster House. Where they sat in circles and Dr. Heder, El Doctor, as she liked to call him, made them *talk about themselves*. They cut all your food, because they didn't trust you with a knife. That's for your steak, not your wrists, sweetheart. The biggest surprise was that the walls were blue. She'd thought they would be white. And El Doctor wore sneakers and jeans, no lab coat. Julia had her own room, and when she wasn't in therapy, she stayed there doing work for her high school classes. She'd left her trumpet at home.

Even though it was a weird place, she was actually happy at Aster House. She'd always liked blue, and it saved her time not having to cut her food. Since the accident, Julia had been having trouble getting her feelings straight, and whenever the sadness lifted for a moment and she began to enjoy something simple, like listening to a Clifford Brown album or taking a walk in the woods, she started feeling horrible about herself and guilty because she didn't deserve any of it. It was all a scramble in her head. So it was a relief at Aster House to not have to work so hard to pretend she was normal, pretend she liked eating and watching TV and going to the mall, pretend she wasn't all fucked up inside. When they told her it was time to go, that she could keep her scholarship to Stradler—the school she'd applied to as a backup, which had a decent music program—Julia asked if it would be okay to stay at Aster House a little longer.

The thing, though, about being in a place like Aster House, is that it marks you. After she was back in the world, Julia felt humiliated about it, because being in a place like that means you've failed, not just at grief, but at life. You're a dud. Put her back in the box and ask for a refund. You have something broken inside you, and no matter how much you try to be normal, there's really no way to know if the broken thing got fixed.

Now Julia walked alongside the other students coming back from the library, backpacks strapped to their shoulders, textbooks hugged to their chests. She was thinking about how generous Sam had been, listening to her story about Paul. It was the first time she'd been able to describe the whole accident to anyone except El Doctor. There was a quality in Sam—in his silence, his eyes—that made Julia feel he'd understand. You can never know for sure if someone understands you. But sometimes you sense when someone feels the world the way you do.

When she got back to the dorm, Leanette was out. Julia noticed that the red light on her phone was blinking, which meant she had a message. She thought of Sam calling to make sure she'd gotten home safely, and she liked the idea of that.

But when Julia dialed her code, the message she heard was:

"Hey, Julia, it's Marcus. I've been thinking about what happened. The other night was kind of rough for me, and I've been trying to decide what to do. I was thinking for a while of just dropping it. But I don't know, I couldn't. I guess what I'm saying is, I still like you and I want to talk to you. Let's do that walk after class tomorrow. I think it's still possible to work things out. I know you feel bad about what happened, and everyone makes mistakes. I think that's the main point of college parties. Anyway, see you then. Bye."

CHAPTER 9
The Talk

⚬━✦━⚬

J ulia had another message when she got back from lunch the next day:

"Hey, Julie, it's your dad. Just givin' you a call to see how things are going. Hey, if you have a sec, give us a buzz back and let us know what's happening. I tried calling you last night a couple times, but I couldn't reach you. Just wanted to make sure you weren't miffed at me from our call the other night. Give us a buzz when you can. Talk to ya soon. Bye."

Julia was late for class, and didn't have time to return the call. She rushed off to Hobbes's music class, and still didn't get there until ten minutes after it had started.

After class, Julia and Marcus walked outside together. They didn't say much as they left the building. The air was sharp, the sky frosted with clouds. They walked up a gravel path to a bench in the middle of a courtyard. Around them, students hustled to their classes, their feet crunching the gravel. It seemed like neither of them had the energy for a walk, so they sat on the bench.

"It's good to see you," Marcus said.

"Really?"

He nodded.

"You got your hair cut," Julia said. She could see his sideburns were uneven, which meant that he'd probably gotten it done at the place in town the students called "the chop shop."

"That's never a good thing, when someone says that. It means you look like you got attacked with gardening shears."

"What you do in your free time is your business."

He smiled, that half grin of his.

"Anyway, I appreciate your calling," Marcus said. "I'm sorry I didn't call back sooner. It's been really busy. I'm studying for that Rackoff psych midterm that got pushed back. He's not giving it until almost Thanksgiving."

"I heard that class was impossible."

"Pretty much. Anyway, I'm sorry. It was just—I needed time."

"You shouldn't be sorry. I did an awful thing. You had every right."

His expression shifted when she said that. His eyes seemed to widen, and Julia thought she noticed the twitch of a smile at the edge of his mouth. It was a weird reaction, and for a second she wondered if he'd heard her right.

"I just want to tell you I'm still up for hanging out." He was speaking quickly. "If you want to give it another try—"

"Marcus." She had to stop him. She could see where he was going. "I wanted to meet you, because I felt I owed it to you. What I did was wrong. Inconsiderate. I want to apologize."

"I told you," he said, agitated this time, "I forgive you and—"

"But I can't be with you."

When she said that, something happened in his face. More than one thing, really; it was like a whole story took place there. All the excitement dropped out of his expression, and for a moment it was blank. Then the excitement was replaced by something else, something fierce that could have been fear or panic or even anger, Julia couldn't tell. He just looked deeply upset.

"Why?" he said, appearing to strain to keep his voice in check.

"Because I'm with Sam. The guy from the party. We're dating now."

Marcus leaned toward Julia, as if he were having trouble seeing her, and she couldn't help shifting back an inch on the bench. "Are you," he said, "*really?*"

"I'm sorry I handled it in such a shitty way." She was speaking quickly herself now, wanting this to be over. "I feel horrible about it. I really do. I should have talked to you before anything happened with Sam."

Marcus was still squinting like he couldn't make out what was in front of him. Then he finally said, "You're making a huge mistake."

"Okay," Julia said.

But Marcus kept looking at her. "There's something off about him."

"Don't do this. Come on."

"He's not normal. He's got something wrong with him."

"Please *stop*. He's a kind person. You shouldn't talk about him."

"You don't know what you're getting yourself into. He's twice your age, Julia."

"Please don't lecture me, *Marcus*."

They stared at each other for a moment, both openly angry.

"You're completely wrong, by the way," she said, more coolly now. "And the jealousy is ugly. It doesn't suit your new haircut."

"Oh, thanks so much."

She got up. "I'm sorry, but I don't think this talk is going anywhere helpful."

Before he could say anything else, she started walking away. The scene had shaken her up. She'd never seen that aggressive side of Marcus.

Back in her room, the message light was flashing. Julia didn't even check it. She picked up the phone and dialed Sam.

"Hello?" he said when he picked up.

"It's Julia. I was just wondering, would you be up for hanging out at your place later?" The words just spilled out.

There was a pause. Then he said, "What time were you thinking?"

"How about now?"

After he gave her directions, she hung up, suddenly nervous. She changed into her good jeans, the ones that pushed everything into place. Checked her hair. Put on more foundation. Some blush. At that moment it seemed very important to look good for him, like she couldn't afford to disappoint him. She packed a toothbrush and an extra pair of underwear in her purse. Just in case.

Then she was ready. She picked up the purse and opened the door.

Outside, in the hallway, Julia could hardly believe what she saw. Standing there, in a black sweatshirt with the word "Orioles" written across the front, was her father. He was looking at the floor, pinching the bridge of his nose between his thumb and finger.

When he took his hand down, Julia could see his eyes were red. He looked up at her and whispered, "Thank God."

"What are you *doing* here?"

"You're coming home with me," he told her, his voice so low she could barely hear. Then something cracked in him and he started to sob in the middle of the hallway.

CHAPTER 10
The Preservationist

B irthdays were always tough times for Sam, clouded by loss, but this year's was worse than most. Forty years old. He could hardly believe such a number could be associated with him. To Sam it was the end of youth. The trail had narrowed in his thirties, the pavement giving way to dusty tracks, but now he'd found the true end point, the edge of the cliff.

The plan had been to spend the night in his mom's chair, reading a novel and sipping a protein shake, which was what he substituted for meals when he wasn't at work. He thought it would be nice to start his fifth decade in someone else's skin, wrapped in a fictional character's hopes and disappointments. It was the way Sam relaxed, getting out of himself.

But when Julia had called, he'd been yanked right back into his own body, his wishes for the relationship that had been striding along so smoothly. She'd said she was coming over right away. Even if he didn't pick her up at the bus stop, the trip would take less than an hour.

Which meant he had to get ready now. There was the plucking, the shaving, the washing and moisturizing. He tweezed his nose and eyebrows, which seemed particularly thick tonight (was he imagining that?), and even used the whitening strips on his teeth. He considered giving himself a quick shave on his chest and the top of his back—something he did once in a while before a big night to feel lighter and more youthful—but worried he might have razor burn when she arrived. Everyone had ways to stave off the glums, as his mom had called them, and these rituals were the best method Sam had found.

He glanced at his fingernails, which were in need of a good filing. That was something his mom had impressed on him, the importance of neat fingernails. As a kid, Sam had bitten his nails from morning till night. His mom had told him it was an ugly habit, that people couldn't trust a nail-biter, but he couldn't help it.

As he began clipping his nails, Sam remembered the morning—he must have been twelve or thirteen—when he'd woken up in their house in San Diego and started chewing on his thumbnail, the way he always did, but there'd been something different. The nail tasted bitter, ammoniacal. The taste filled his mouth, and he ran to the bathroom sink and started spitting.

After a few minutes, he noticed his mom was standing in the doorway, watching him. He looked up at her.

"Pee," she said, then chuckled, watching Sam like he might join in laughing with her. It turned out she'd taken an old nail-polish brush and painted the urine on his fingernails while he'd slept. She'd had to pee into a cup.

Later on, after he'd washed his mouth with Listerine and scrubbed his nails with lemon juice, his mom had said to him, "You won't do that again."

Which was true. He never put a fingernail in his mouth from that day forward, remembering the taste of it. That was the thing about his mom, she got results. And she did it for Sam. He wouldn't have learned how to act properly without her.

After he clipped his nails, Sam started on the filing, rounding the edges the way he liked them. His mom had been a friend to him. When he was a boy—in fact, all the way until his dad died—Sam had lived in a kind of isolated dream world with her. She was in her late thirties by the time she had Sam, and only later did it occur to him that she might not have intended to have kids at all. But at the time, she was a benevolent spirit, whisking in and out of rooms with food, toys, affection. If Sam was bullied at school, as was often the case, his mom would rush to his defense, insulting or even slapping the kids who'd done it. She was so loyal that after a while Sam stopped telling her when he was being picked on, for fear of what would happen to the bullies.

Sam remembered the way they used to talk, he and his mom, the closeness they'd shared, a feeling he'd never quite found again with another woman. She'd tell him everything about herself, even the things you weren't supposed to tell children, just because she loved him and trusted him.

"I just feel it's best to be honest," she said to him once. "That's the problem with most relationships, Sam. Not enough honesty. People are always hiding things. I don't want to do that with you. I want to give you an idea of how the world really is."

And part of that idea must have been the glums, the days when she stayed under the covers and didn't make meals and talked about when she used to be pretty. If Sam said he was hungry, she'd tell him, "You can find something for yourself, can't you? That's an important lesson in life, taking care of yourself. You can't depend on others to do it all the time."

He was five years old. He asked her why he had to learn that.

"Because today is a day when I would like to kill myself," his mom announced, pulling the sheets over her head to block out the sun from the window.

But she never did. She wouldn't have left Sam like that, even if she felt that way some days.

The glums usually came on Fridays, the day after Sam's dad, Herbert, visited. Herbert had a limp and a bushy orange mustache, and every Thursday night he drove up to Sam's house after dinner, reeking of what Sam later recognized as cheap whiskey. The house was on a mountain overlooking the city of El Cajon (which Sam's dad referred to as "cojones," getting a laugh each time he said it). The few times Sam had made the drive with his father, he'd ended up feeling sick from the way the little green Mazda lurched and swerved, sometimes bringing Sam only inches from a drop off the mountain, or a collision with a cliff face. It seemed that Sam's dad sped the car in proportion to the thickness of the whiskey smell emanating from his body; on the nights he stumbled and slurred his speech, you could hear the car—tires screeching and motor revving—from half a mile away.

On Thursday nights Herbert arrived at Sam's house with pocketfuls of candy. He loved candy, the messiest, stickiest varieties: anything coated in caramel or rolled in sugar or sprinkled with nuts. For the first ten years of his life, Sam thought his father's business was candy. (In fact, he was a janitor at the Jewish Community Center.) He'd hand the candies to Sam, warmed from his pockets and already adhering to the wrappers, while Herbert went into the bedroom with Sam's mom and shut the door.

Sam never ate the candy. He took it outside with him, and fed it to squirrels, or the occasional stray dog or cat that passed through his yard. There were a number of strays in the neighborhood, and Sam enjoyed stroking their heads once they'd grown to trust him.

Sam had learned it was best not to ask his mom about his dad. When he did that, she came back with comments like, "I feel like you're judging me. And I don't approve of that, Sam. Judgmentalism is a poor quality in a person, and I don't know where you're getting that from."

So he stayed quiet about these visits. Of course Sam figured out pretty soon what his mom and Herbert were doing in there, he wasn't stupid. His dad was never at the house for more than an hour.

Sam finished filing his nails, surprised at how long it had taken. Amazing where your mind wandered when you didn't hold the leash on it. Julia would be there any minute. It had already been an hour since she'd called.

He went into the living room to straighten up before she arrived. He'd never invited anyone to this apartment, so he wanted to make sure it was clean for his visitor. He did a quick sweep over the floors, a little dusting on the shelves and counters. He fixed the cushions on his mother's chair.

Looking at the apartment—the sputtering radiators, the warped floorboards, the cracked windowpanes—he could imagine the way a girl like Julia, who probably came from a rich family, would see it. She'd think it was a mess. Most of the furnishings were inherited from Sam's mom. He had her chair, her faded rug, her framed Eiffel Tower poster, and in drawers he kept her clothes and photos, plates and silverware.

Sam hated throwing things away, that was the truth of it. The apartment was cluttered with all the stuff he couldn't bring himself to let go of, some of it his mom's, some of it mementos he'd picked up during his wandering. Each time he moved, he brought these possessions with him, and the familiar objects were a reassurance to him when he was starting out in a new place.

Where was Julia? That was the question that kept poking its head into his thoughts. She'd called almost an hour and a half ago. There was no way it could have taken her this long to get here, even if she'd walked the whole way from the school. It was evening practically; the thinnest gray light strained through the clouds.

And now Sam's thoughts turned a corner, headed down a familiar dark street. There was a good chance Julia had changed her mind, decided not to come at all. That had happened before, a girl having second thoughts, pulling back. Patrice had seemed so eager with Sam at first. She was studying environmental biology at Southampton. Sam had found out she was a vegan, and was thinking of cooking a meal for her.

But he didn't want to let himself go there, it wasn't worth it. He'd had a great relationship with Patrice, as he'd had with other women, and as he was having now (at least until tonight) with Julia. There wasn't any use thinking about the missteps and the problems, the eventual partings. What was there in the world that didn't finally come to an end?

As a way to comfort himself, in the shadowy entryway to his forty-first year, as these worries over Julia roiled inside him, Sam went into his closet and brought out the shoebox. It was what he always turned to in these toughest moments, what helped level him out. He placed the box on the kitchen table, sat down, and opened the lid. Inside the box was a small collection of keepsakes, items that reminded him of past relationships, of places he'd lived. The objects were so obscure—a ticket stub, a pebble from the beach—that another person would have mistaken them for garbage. But they were all Sam needed to be enveloped again. Sometimes just the sight of these objects could make his throat tighten, his eyes ache.

He was a preservationist. That was how he put it to himself, the word he used for the particular way he got by. He'd never been able to let go of things easily. He understood there was a quirkiness to it, the kind of trait people might scoff at, like they would at someone who'd learned to play the mandolin or darned his own socks. *A hoarder*, those people might call him, if they wanted to paint it in a disparaging light. They were the same types of people who called him "simple Sam" in high school, like the boy Reese, who'd told Sam he couldn't get into a college even if he fucked the dean. Sam didn't care about those people. The pleasure he got out of preserving ran too deep for someone so ignorant to touch.

As he examined the contents of the box, fingering the items briefly, he thought about running into Reese now, how sorry he would feel for him. Sam could imagine what Reese looked like, belly sagging over his belt, face pitted with acne scars, slumping home every day to a wife who smelled like pencil shavings and whom you couldn't have paid Sam to touch. The thought alone was nauseating to Sam. He would have taken his loneliness any day over the rewards of a beer with friends, or a family holiday. What Sam got out of life was so much richer than any of those consolation prizes.

As he turned over the possibility of a meeting with Reese (who would be a man now, over forty years old himself), Sam heard something that caused him to stop what he was doing, close the lid on the shoebox. He listened again, and, yes, there it was, a creaking outside the apartment, footsteps on the stairs.

The noise got louder, closer, and then, like a hand shaking him from a dream, three sharp knocks.

Sam got up from the table and went to the door. He opened it with a smile on his face.

She was there, Julia, his girl. She'd come to him. She looked up at him with those large, lovely eyes, and Sam could see she was in distress. He thought he saw her hand tremble when she let it fall by her side.

"I just had an awful day," she told Sam.

"I'm sorry. What happened?"

But instead of answering, she said, "Anyway, I'm here now. Lucky you."

He smiled and told her to come inside.

CHAPTER II
The Bedroom

It would have been natural to sit down at the kitchen table, but the shoebox was there, and he didn't feel comfortable showing that to her now. It would seem overly sentimental, and she'd get the wrong impression about him, think he was a sad person, lost in the past. So he took her into the living room, let her sit on his mom's chair while Sam sat on the hard chair he'd pulled out from the kitchen table. He could see her looking around, taking the place in, the furnishings, the way he lived. He guessed it was new for her, these cracked windowpanes, these water-stained floors. Not the ordered rooms and polished surfaces she'd grown up around.

"I like your place," Julia said. He could tell it took some effort. "There's a lot of room."

"I'm still filling it out, straightening things up. But I think it'll be a good place. You can just feel when something's right for you. You know?"

She nodded, eyes drifting. He could tell she was still thinking over the events of that evening.

"So tell me what happened," Sam said. "You mentioned you had a bad day."

She took a breath. "My dad showed up. Completely out of the blue. Just as I was leaving to meet you."

It wasn't what Sam had expected. He'd been thinking of grades, or slipping on the tiles of the dining hall in front of some other students. He should have known that someone who'd been through what Julia had wouldn't have overdramatized such minor events.

"What did he want?"

"He said he wanted to take me home. He'd called me a couple times and I hadn't picked up. He even sent an email, and he never touches the computer. I didn't know he could turn it on. We'd gotten in a little fight last time he called. He said he didn't think I was ready to be on my own."

"Why would he think that?" Sam was looking over Julia's shoulder at the shoebox as they talked, thinking of how he was going to get Julia away from it. She'd laugh at him if she saw it. But the only other room in the apartment was the bedroom.

"There's something I didn't tell you. Something about my past."

"What is it? You know you can tell me anything."

He saw the way she looked when he said that, like she was weighing each word. Sam got the sense she was on the edge of an important revelation.

"I was in a place," she finally said. "After my brother died. A kind of institution, I guess. I needed some time away from everything."

"Is that all?" In fact, he could have told her, he liked the idea of it a good deal. "You thought that would matter to me?"

"It's not the kind of thing I like talking about on a first date."

"That doesn't affect me at all. Something like that can't change the way I feel about you, Julia. It's completely natural that you'd need some time to get over what you went through."

He could see how clearly she relaxed after he said that, and he was happy to have put her at ease. If he got her into the bedroom, they could stay there for the rest of the night. If she needed food, he'd call for delivery and bring it back to her. He could move the box when he did that, or when she went to sleep, or when she went home, whichever came first. It was just a question of how to say it to her, since there was only the bed in there, and he knew the suggestion might put her off.

"So what did you say to your dad?"

"I told him I wouldn't go with him. I said I was going to my boyfriend's instead. Actually, I told him I was going to my pimp's house for drug money, then I took it back and said it was just my boyfriend. I know he thinks I'm going to do something crazy."

"Really?" Sam hadn't imagined she'd tell her parents she had a boyfriend so soon. It was always better to wade into a relationship, test the water before inviting others in. But with Julia he'd been reckless, dived headfirst.

"He didn't want me to come here. He said I was making a mistake getting in a relationship. I wasn't ready. But he can't control my life anymore. I'm eighteen. I said he needed to leave or else I couldn't keep my relationship with him."

"That sounds hard."

"I felt bad about it. That's the thing, I know he cares. He started crying again, which was too sad. And he started saying, 'Julia. Please. Don't do this. Please.' And I felt so bad for him, because he's really the only one who cares. My mom would be happy to never see me again. With my dad, it's that all his worrying just smothers me. It makes me angry and then I feel bad about being angry, because he isn't really doing anything wrong.

"So I told him I'd be okay, he had to leave, he had to understand he was making everything harder. I was about to cry myself, but I held it back. I told him he had to trust me and know I'd be okay, but I just needed a little more distance from him, that it was too much pressure to have him worrying all the time."

"How did he react to that?"

"He just stood there. Didn't know what to say. He wasn't really crying anymore. Just looking at me. And tears were still coming out of his eyes, but he wasn't shaking or sobbing or anything. He was still in the doorway. I hadn't even let him in the room. I told him again I was sorry, and then I closed my door and locked it and left."

"Sounds awful," Sam said. He'd realized that offering these small, supportive comments helped keep her going, confiding in him.

She pushed a loose strand of hair behind her ear, and he thought he saw her fingers trembling again. It gave him an idea.

"You're shivering."

"Oh. I'm fine."

"No, really. You look like you're freezing."

"Maybe a little. I didn't even think about a coat, and then when I was outside I couldn't go back. I didn't know if he was still there."

"I understand. But listen, I have some of my mom's sweaters in the bedroom closet. They're just sitting there, no good use for them, except I couldn't let them go. Come and pick one out."

CHAPTER 12
The Kitchen

———◆———

S he didn't know what time it was. Eleven, possibly. Maybe midnight. She didn't have any way to know, since there were no clocks in the bedroom, and she hadn't brought a watch. It was so dark Julia couldn't see her hand when she held it in front of her face. She heard Sam breathing in a regular rhythm next to her. He'd fallen asleep just after they'd finished, so quickly it was like he'd been drugged.

But she hadn't fallen off herself. Each time she got close, it was as if a hand pulled her back from the edge.

Maybe it was because this had been her first time, something she'd told Sam right before he'd entered her. He seemed to hold her just a little more gently after she said it, almost like he was afraid of breaking her. It didn't hurt as much as Julia had expected. He was careful, and when she felt that pinch between her legs and sucked in air, he slowed down and reassured her. In the end, she couldn't say the experience was pleasurable, but it was like he'd shown her a room where later on there might be a party.

Afterward, she felt a strange blend of relief and disappointment. Relief, she thought, because it was finally over, that silly act she'd dreamed and worried so much about. It was so basic she could have laughed. But then the disappointment came, not because Sam wasn't good at sex, but because nothing had really changed. Her old self clung to her, like a scent she couldn't wash off.

As she lay there, feeling the pain and tingling between her legs, the one image that kept coming back to Julia was the way he'd looked at her. She'd never been looked at that way before, with that peculiar mix of intensity and distance. She didn't know why, but it bothered her, that kind of attention. Maybe she was just self-conscious. But his interest felt like something more than lust, something different. When they were having sex, she'd kept going, kept fucking, in part because she had the idea that when he finished, he might stop looking at her that way. Not a good thought. Not a healthy view of sex, Dr. Ruth.

And something else. During sex was the first time she'd really watched Sam. Of course she'd looked at him before, across the counter at the snack bar, on the sidewalk outside the party, across the table at the restaurant; but this was the first time she'd really *seen* him. She still thought he was handsome, but something uncomfortable she noticed was that Marcus had been right, Sam was older than she'd thought, into his thirties at least. And she couldn't pin it down, but there was something else. He was so attentive to her that it was like he wasn't even aware of his own body. She'd noticed it when they talked, too, like he was floating above the conversation. Maybe he was just a little eccentric. That was okay. She had her own quirks.

Julia was thirsty. Her throat was dry and it felt hot in the room. The radiator by the window kept clanging. She didn't think she'd get to sleep very soon. She listened again to Sam, to see if he was awake, but his breathing was steady and slow.

She decided to get some water. She sat up and slid out of bed, replacing the covers gently, so she wouldn't disturb him. Julia was in her underwear and couldn't see anything. She had to feel around for her jeans and the sweater she'd borrowed, and then for the door. When she got everything on, she left the room.

It was so much brighter here in the living room, where the windows were covered by normal shades rather than the thick drapes in the bedroom. Sam had told Julia he'd inherited the drapes from his mom. It seemed like he'd gotten a lot of his furnishings from her.

Julia walked into the kitchen, opened the cabinet above the sink, and took down an old jelly glass that must have been another hand-me-down. She opened the refrigerator. When the light popped on, she was a little confused by what she saw inside. Filed in neat rows, like items in a vending machine, were a couple dozen bottles of weight-loss shakes. Nothing else. Both shelves were full of them. They must have been all he ate or drank. He didn't even have a bottle of ketchup or a half dozen eggs in there.

She shut the door, shaking her head. Was he on a diet? Loss does strange things to people. She needed to get him to eat. She went to the sink, turned on the tap, and filled her glass. Then she sat down with it at the kitchen table.

On the table was a shoebox, a brown one with a striped pattern Julia didn't recognize from any brand she'd ever seen. The box looked old, worn at the corners, the colors faded. She remembered it had been there when she came in, but she didn't have a chance to ask about it because they'd gone right into the living room. She thought maybe it was some receipts he was saving for his taxes, or some old music, or maybe some of the writing he'd talked to her about one time.

Julia felt a little funny about looking at his personal things, and she told herself it wouldn't be right to peek inside the box. But it never works when you tell yourself things like that. Curiosity won out. She reached for the box.

Before she could open the lid, though, she heard Sam's voice.

"Hey," he said, "I didn't realize you were still up. What are you up to?"

Julia put her hand back down on the table. He was standing in the doorway to the bedroom. She wasn't sure how long he'd been there, and now she felt a rush of guilt. Sneaky bitch. Can't leave your wallet lying around that girl.

"Just getting a glass of water," Julia said. "I was thirsty."

"I could have gotten it for you. Just ask me next time."

"It's okay, I didn't want to wake you."

"Were you having trouble sleeping?"

"A little. I'm always like that in a new place. No worries."

He smiled. "I guess you'll get used to it."

"Or you'll get sick of being woken up and stick me on the couch."

He smiled. "That's a possibility, too. You need anything else?"

She shook her head. "I think I'm getting tired now."

"Should we go back?"

She joined him in the doorway. He put his arm around her, and they walked back to the bedroom.

In the morning, when she came back into the kitchen, the shoebox was no longer on the table.

CHAPTER 13
Marcus

Marcus went running. It's what he usually did when he was facing some emotional difficulty, some news he wasn't yet ready to accept. There's something direct and clarifying about physical pain, and that was what he needed. He chose to go to the track, not caring about the fact that his thighs were numb from the cold, or that his knees ached from pounding the hard surface, or that all he saw for lap after lap was the field house and then the bleachers, like some revolving display. He wanted dullness and pain, a blankness filling his vision, whiting everything out.

He'd had the talk with Julia two days ago, the talk where she revealed that she'd chosen that man, Sam. Marcus had done everything possible to convince her, win her over. He hadn't liked Sam from the moment he'd seen him. He was too old for Julia, and that didn't sit right with Marcus. Sam wasn't a good fit. Her judgment was flawed, very flawed, and Marcus wanted to correct it. He worked over the possibilities.

Don't fuck this up. You better not fuck this up.

As he circled the track, Marcus's mind wandered a familiar path, back to the other girl, Tree. She'd been like Julia in a lot of ways, almost uncannily, with those wide eyes and the way she looked you over that let you know she was always thinking, thinking. That was why Marcus had been drawn to Julia, not just because of who she was but also because of what she suggested, that bridge to his past, a place he thought he could never go again.

Remember that. You're finished with all that.

No one here would find out about Tree. He'd never mention her. That history had been buried, over a year ago now, and he was a new person.

Pounding and pounding, circling and circling, until his calves quivered, the impact of the pavement rippling up his legs, his spine, all the way to his teeth. He was running so hard that old cavities ached, that his eyes seemed to wobble in their sockets. It was full dark, after eight, and he could hardly see the lines on the track. And then finally he couldn't run anymore, his legs just gave out, and he collapsed onto the pavement, shredding his palms. Good. Done. He'd gone seventeen miles.

Walking back to his dorm, his body so numb it didn't even feel the cold, he thought about food. Again, he'd forgotten to eat. It was getting to be a habit with him.

Now it was too late to go to the dining hall, so he turned down the path toward the snack bar.

He got there too late. It was closed, the gate padlocked. He'd have to eat chips from the vending machine in the dorm basement. Which was fine. He did that a lot of nights. He didn't really care.

Heading back up the path to his dorm, Marcus could see the back of Slade Hall, the building that housed the snack bar. He looked over where the dumpsters were, and that was when he noticed it. At first he wasn't sure that what he thought he was seeing was accurate, but he looked a bit harder, and then, yes, he was right, that's who it was. Sam. And that cat, the stray that was always hanging around the dumpsters.

Marcus watched the man and the cat. He studied them like a painting, something slightly abstract that he couldn't quite understand the meaning of. And then, at once, he did. He knew what he needed to do, how he could persuade her. It was all coming together. Sam, the cat, Julia. He just wasn't quite sure yet how he would do it, and when.

CHAPTER 14
An Encounter

c———⚔———o

It was late afternoon, the end of Sam's shift, and he was closing the deli case, wrapping meats in plastic and putting them back in the refrigerator. Lonnie was cleaning the grill. Megan was closing out the register. Horacio kept ducking in and out of his office, sometimes with the excuse that he'd forgotten something, other times plainly watching them work.

It had been four days since Julia had spent the night at Sam's apartment. He hadn't slept while she'd been there, but just after they'd had sex, he'd almost nodded off. He'd felt so peaceful with her that he'd nearly forgotten about the shoebox on the table. Then he'd heard her getting up from the bed. By the time he'd spoken to her, she was about to open the lid.

Which was only natural. Most people would be curious about a box sitting on a table in front of them. The fact that she'd tried to open it didn't change his opinion of her; it simply reminded him to be a little more careful. If he came off as too weird, too nostalgic, with all his collections, it would spoil the relationship. He knew he was quirky, and he knew that people—even Julia—might judge him for that, at least until they really got to know him.

"Sammy, whatcha doin' tonight?" Lonnie asked him.

"Meeting up with a friend."

"That sounds fun. Let me ask you, is this friend gonna let you in the front door? Or does she prefer to open up the *back*?"

"Lonnie, don't start that dirty crud tonight," Megan said. "I'm going home to my daughter in twenty minutes."

"Hope she lets you in the front," Lonnie whispered to Sam, and Sam smiled, knowing that if he didn't, Lonnie would just say it louder.

In the past four days, Sam had called Julia three times, but talked to her only once, and that time she'd been rushing out to the library to finish a paper so she couldn't stay on. He wasn't sure what the trouble was, why she seemed a little distant, but he was beginning to worry. He thought maybe she'd swing by the snack bar to see him—not his favorite idea, though he could have handled it—but no luck. Sam tried to shore up his mind against gloomy predictions, but somehow they kept squeezing in.

"Hey, Megan," Lonnie said, "let me know when your daughter's ready for me to call her."

"If you get within fifty feet of her, I'll shove a knife in your crotch."

"Shove it where?"

"In your organ, Lonnie."

"Oh baby, I luuuv how you say *organ*."

"Hey, Sam," Megan said, "do you think they'll hire that new cook soon?"

Sam smiled.

"Chef," Lonnie said.

"I think the position said 'cook.' I'm pretty sure that's all it was."

"Megan, I'll stick my dick in that soup so hard your daughter'll taste my pubes."

After he said that, Lonnie looked back and forth between Megan and Sam, then nodded, concluding his argument.

The part that Sam's mind kept getting caught on was the sweater. Julia had worn it home with her when she'd left Sam's apartment the morning after they'd been together. Which was fine with him. In fact, he was happy to see her in it. His mom would have liked that. But he'd gone to so much trouble to help Julia out, to comfort her when she needed it, and now she didn't even have the time to give him a quick call, thank him, and let him know when she'd be coming by again to return the sweater? It was hard not to be disturbed by it.

Just as he was thinking about how sorely he'd been treated, the honey ham he was wrapping slipped out of his hands and fell to the floor, smacking the tiles. The ham bounced to a disconcerting height, and Sam watched it, hardly believing what he'd done. He'd never dropped a food item at work in his life.

"Hey, Sam," Horacio said, coming out of his office, "what the fuck?"

Sam looked down at the ham, then over at Horacio, who had an expression more of disappointment than anger at the ham wobbling on the floor.

"I'm sorry," Sam said. "I'll wash it."

"I can't serve that," Horacio said. "Put it in the trash."

"I'll take it," Lonnie whispered.

Sam shook his head. He brought the ham out to the dumpster, and was about to toss it in when he saw the gray cat with the white spot above its eye. He decided to leave the ham next to the dumpster. The cat walked over and began to lick it.

That was when Sam realized he was being watched. He turned around. A tall boy was standing about thirty feet behind him, in the grass beside the pavement. Sam recognized him immediately. It was the boy Julia had met for lunch. The boy who'd seen Sam kiss her at the party. He was standing there, watching Sam, with what looked like a small grin on his face.

"Hey," Sam said. "We're closed. Were you coming to get a sandwich or something?" The path from some of the dorms passed by the dumpsters on the way to the snack bar's front entrance, so it was possible the boy had been coming that way. But still, it was weird that he'd stopped.

The boy shook his head. He started walking toward Sam. "I kind of wanted to talk to you."

Sam didn't know why, but he felt nervous as the boy approached. "What is it?" he said, hoping to get it over as quickly as possible.

When the boy was only a couple feet from Sam, he stopped and said, "I think Julia's a great girl. You're lucky."

Sam nodded, offering a tight smile. He didn't want to betray anything about his situation—the good or the bad—and he hoped Lonnie, who had just emptied the pans of uneaten fries into the trash, wouldn't come outside with the bags and catch them talking.

After a few seconds, the boy continued, "I just wanted to say I hope you're nice to her. I'm looking out for her." He blushed when he said that, and Sam could see he'd been working up to it.

Sam nodded again, charged by an emotion he couldn't identify. He didn't know if it was anxiety or just stress, but he wanted to end the encounter. All of this was new, and difficult, and he couldn't make out what the boy had in mind. Sam had never had a relationship that had caused so many disturbances. First Julia's dad. Now this boy. Every day there were more people involved.

"That all you wanted to say?" Sam asked.

"That's it," the boy said. He leaned down to scratch the gray cat on the head, but the cat hissed, guarding the ham, and the boy pulled back. "I'll leave you alone," the boy muttered, and walked away.

CHAPTER 15
The Window

⁂

"So how was it?" Leanette asked Julia as they were walking back from the dining hall. It was the third week of October, steely cold, and the air had a scoured smell. Leaves had fallen from the trees and then been swept up, and now the campus had a bare, trimmed look.

"How was what?"

"The sex. His cock. Come on, I know you didn't spend the night over there and end up watching *The Golden Girls.*"

"Don't judge my tastes in entertainment," Julia said, trying to buy enough time to figure out how she was going to answer. She wasn't sure how to explain what had happened, what kind of spin to put on it, or if the questions she had about Sam were the normal ones. Julia didn't want to say anything that would leave Leanette wondering about her.

"It was nice," Julia finally said.

"Nice? Are we in the nineteenth century? Did you have to remove your chastity belt? Come on, did he go down on you?"

"We only touched through a hole in a bedsheet."

"Seriously. What positions did you try? Is he more of a classic or a contemporary?"

"I'd say he's kind of an avant-garde." Julia paused. "But, seriously, it was a little weird for me."

"Weird how? Did he make you dress up like a cave woman? Or slap his ass with a riding crop?"

Julia laughed. How could she even start to explain? She would have felt bad saying anything negative about Sam, who'd been so nice to her, who listened to her in a way no one else did. It wasn't worth risking that.

"Nothing like that," Julia said. "Just different than I expected."

"You mean you didn't come? I wouldn't hold your breath for that. I come maybe one in three times with Drew, and we do it twice a day."

Drew was the guy Leanette had been seeing lately. She spent a few nights a week at his place. He was on the Frisbee team, had a shaved head, and was always overly nice to Julia, like she was the secret to winning over Leanette.

"Not just that," Julia said. "It's like he seemed a little distant, like he wasn't totally there with me. Maybe I need practice. I was pretty nervous."

"That's just how guys are. It's like their brains go to the tips of their penises and stay there. I can't even tell you how many times I've told Drew to look at me while we're having sex. *Focus*, I tell him. And then he finishes and I'm left trying to get off on a wet noodle."

"Spaghetti or rigatoni?"

"Macaroni."

"Actually," Julia said, "the truth is he was looking at me the whole time, was the thing. It was like auditioning for *American Idol*."

Leanette laughed now, too. "All I can say is that the first time is horrifying. You can't get around it. I mean, imagine, if it wasn't in our genes, the idea of a guy stabbing that thing into you over and over. It's *traumatic*."

They walked along the curved path, past the hedges in front of the athletic center, the grove of trees where the dreadlocked kids played their drums. On the way, Leanette waved to several people she knew from her classes.

"I think another thing was that I'd just had this fight with my dad," Julia said, "right before I went over to Sam's. Did I tell you my dad drove all the way up here because I hadn't returned a couple phone messages?"

Leanette shook her head. "That's ridiculous."

"He was practically having a breakdown. I told him he had to give me some space."

"I think that's totally reasonable."

Julia still hadn't told Leanette about her brother, her time in Aster House, her dreams of being a professional musician. She avoided these topics whenever they got close to them in conversation. Julia knew they couldn't really talk about her life without mentioning that stuff, but she didn't want to crack the lid on those subjects.

"And I also feel weird about what happened with Marcus," Julia said. "I know you think it's stupid. But when I told him about Sam, he went a little nuts. He got this angry look on his face and started saying all this mean stuff about Sam."

"What did you do?"

"I kicked him in the nuts and called him a sissy."

"That's perfect."

"No, I got up and left. But I felt bad. I mean, even if he didn't react well, I shouldn't have put him through that."

"Look." Leanette grabbed Julia's wrist, turning Julia to face her. "Marcus has his right hand, so he's going to be just fine. He's jealous, but he'll get over it. Your dad is a grown man, and he has your mom. Why don't you stop feeling guilty about everyone and look out for yourself?"

"I know. You're right. I just hate when I'm the cause of people getting hurt."

"You're not the cause of them getting hurt."

When Leanette said that, Julia saw her brother's pale lips opening and closing on words she couldn't hear. Don't do this, she told herself. Don't go there.

"Thanks," she said to Leanette.

"Whatever. It's just my opinion."

Julia opened the door to their room, and right away she knew something was off. It was as cold inside as it had been outside. She flipped on the light. Both their beds were made, their desks arranged in the usual way, Julia's neat, Leanette's messy. Julia looked across the room and noticed the window was open. Their room faced a cement walkway and a patch of scrubby grass. You never saw a single person there, and for that reason, Leanette sometimes hopped onto the ledge, opened the window, and smoked cigarettes.

"Did you leave that open?" Julia asked.

"I don't think so. But maybe. You didn't have it open for anything?"

"I never open it."

They walked into the room. Julia shut the door. Leanette closed the window. They both checked in their desks, under their beds, in their closets. Nothing was missing or out of place.

"I wouldn't worry about it," Leanette said. "I probably left it open. Or maybe the wind blew it."

CHAPTER 16
A Conversation

I t was dark in Sam's apartment, only a couple reading lamps bright-
ening the room. Outside, the wind whistled in the street, and from
time to time a car passed, light spreading in the window.

They'd just gotten back from dinner, a couple slices of pizza at
a place in Marshallville, and now they were both reading, Julia a
philosophy textbook, Sam a novel he was enjoying about a man
named Zuckerman who was a writer and seemed to have a gift
for imagining the lives of other people. Julia was sitting on the
sofa, Sam on his mom's chair. He kept a little distance sometimes,
gave her space, for fear she might think him too aggressive. And
there was something nice about taking his time with her, sitting
together and reading or talking. In truth, he preferred it to the
physical affection.

Julia had started coming by again after her midterms were over,
thanking him for the sweater and apologizing for not returning it
sooner. The exams were what had kept her away, Sam reassured

himself, not any hesitation about the relationship. He didn't know why he'd panicked. People get busy, he told himself. It doesn't mean she hates you or wants to break things off. But still, his mind had trouble letting go of the worry. Maybe he would never get over this insecurity; it always came back to bite him in a relationship.

Most nights when she visited they read like this, or just sat and talked. They could really talk. That was the great thing about their relationship. Julia shared everything with him, about her parents and her former friends and her love of music and the dreams she still had about her brother. She didn't see the need to joke with Sam as much anymore, and he took it as a sign that she was getting more comfortable with him. Sam could see what a relief it was to her to be able to unburden herself to someone, and he encouraged it with his own small revelations.

Tonight, there was a subject Sam hoped to discuss with her. He wanted to talk to her about the tall boy, the encounter they'd had by the dumpster that day when Sam was feeding the stray cat. Something didn't feel right about it, the way the boy had been watching him, that small grin when Sam turned around.

"You know," Sam said now, "a friend of yours came by to talk to me last week."

"Who?"

"A tall guy. Actually, I think he was the one who saw us kissing that time outside the party." Sam gave a small laugh after he said that. He wasn't sure how strong Julia's tie to the boy was.

"Marcus? What did he want?"

"I'm not really sure. He started telling me what a nice person you are, and how he was looking out for you. I wasn't sure how to take it."

She let out a sigh. "Was he messing with you?"

"It didn't feel like that. Why?"

She shrugged. "I actually had a talk with him, too. I told him I was seeing you now, and he was kind of upset. I probably should have told you about it before."

"Did he say anything about me?"

There was a brief pause. Then Julia said, "No." He wasn't sure if she was telling the truth.

They went back to their books. A few minutes later, Sam was still thinking about the boy when Julia said, "I'm kind of tired. Do you want to go to sleep soon?"

"I'm not tired. But you go ahead." He kept thinking about the strange expression on the boy's face. It was probably nothing to worry about.

It was only when Sam looked up and saw Julia, flushed with embarrassment, that he realized the mistake he'd made. She wasn't asking if he was tired. She was asking him to go to bed with her. He didn't know why he always missed these cues.

"Actually, I'm ready," he said. He got up and took her hand, helping her up from the couch, into an embrace. "I'm sorry I'm so distracted."

When they got into the bedroom, Sam turned on the light. He sat on the bed, waiting for Julia to come to him. But she'd stopped in the doorway, looking at something.

"What is it?" Sam asked.

She pointed behind his head. "Was it like that before?"

He turned, and immediately saw what she was talking about, the broken windowpane, glass teeth glittering around a dark hole, like the mouth of a person who'd been surprised. He looked down. On the floor, surrounded by more chips of glass, was a small stone.

"Come here. Look at this," Sam said, waving Julia over to the stone.

After she saw it, she looked up at Sam. "Someone threw it. It must have been before we got back. Who do you think—"

"It's not a great neighborhood," Sam said quickly, not wanting her to be afraid. "I'm sure it was just some kids playing around. It happens. We should just be careful."

She kept looking at him, and he wanted to say something more to reassure her, but the truth was, it had scared him, too.

CHAPTER 17
An Errand

J ulia was walking into town. There was an errand she needed
to take care of, something she'd been worried about for a week
or so, and she couldn't wait any longer. It was a Tuesday in the
middle of November, a gray afternoon. Icy rain prickled her face.

She'd gotten her grades from midterms the week before, and
she'd done okay. She probably wasn't going to be Phi Beta Kappa,
but she'd pulled in an A in music theory and an A-minus in English.
Her relationship with Sam definitely wasn't getting in the way
of school. They spent most evenings reading. He seemed to like
staying in. A couple times the thought crossed Julia's mind that
he was embarrassed of her, but she shook it out of her head. She
could see why it would be awkward for him to take her around.
There was the age difference, and his job, and people would have
given them looks.

The privacy was comfortable for Julia, too, she had to admit. It felt
pretty adult to be running off to her boyfriend's place after dinner,

and she liked keeping it a secret from other students. Her little affair. Leanette was the only one who knew.

With her head down against the drizzle, Julia walked past the big stone houses that lined the street. They all looked dark, seated behind hedges so thick you could lose a small dog in them.

In the last month, her dad had actually given Julia the distance she'd asked for. He'd called only a few times, maybe once a week, and always with little family news items, a leak in the shower tiles that had bled under the wall and soaked the carpet in the hallway, an operation Julia's aunt needed on a bunion. He hadn't mentioned "the doc," and he wasn't asking Julia how she was feeling in such a prying way anymore. Once, he put her mom on the phone, and after a few questions about the weather, Julia's mom said she had to hang up because she was expecting another call. They didn't discuss Thanksgiving, which was coming up in two weeks, the first time they'd be celebrating the holiday without Paul.

Leanette was spending a lot of nights at Drew's now, and some weeks Julia hardly saw her. It felt like they didn't even live together anymore. They'd bump into each other in the room, like strangers, when Julia was coming back from the library and Leanette was packing clothes or taking a smoke break. Julia missed her. She missed the conversations, the joking, the way they could vent about what was going on in their lives. As much as Julia liked her talks with Sam, they were never funny, never light. Julia would have told Leanette about the reason for this trip to town. It would have been nice to be able to share it with someone, maybe even laugh about it.

The situation with Marcus seemed to have gotten better. They said hi on the way in to music class, and it didn't feel awkward. Once in a while they spoke for a minute after class, asked each other how it was going, what did you think of the homework, that kind of stuff. If anything, he seemed to be making an effort to be nice to Julia. He always had a smile fixed on his face when she saw him, almost like he'd been practicing it.

The lawns gave way to pavement, the stone houses to brick walls. Julia passed the hardware store, the bank, the "chop shop," the toy store with its sad display of deflated rubber balls and faded stuffed animals. Were they even trying? She was heading for the drugstore on the corner, and she glanced around to see if anyone she knew was on the street, but it looked like the town was empty, probably because of the weather.

Julia pushed open the door of the drugstore, ringing the little bell tied to the hinge with a shoestring. At the pharmacy counter, a white-haired lady in a ratty brown sweater was holding a bottle of pills and talking to the pharmacist. Julia turned down the first aisle, hoping they wouldn't notice her.

She walked down the aisle, scanning shelves. There were cold medicines and laxatives and Q-tips, but she couldn't find what she was looking for. She turned the corner and started up the next aisle so quickly she almost tripped over something. She stopped short. In front of her, a boy with an angry case of acne and thick, dark hair like a bathing cap on his head was crouched on the floor, loading soap from a cardboard box onto a shelf.

"Can I help you find something?" he asked, his voice unsettlingly deep.

Julia almost lost her nerve then, almost said no, she was fine, just looking. She could feel her face getting hot.

But then some invisible hand nudged her forward and she said, "Could you tell me where the pregnancy tests are?"

His eyes flicked away. He pointed over his shoulder and said, "Aisle two."

Five minutes later, Julia was leaving the store with the brown-paper package under her arm, cheeks burning with shame. She felt like all her nerves were jangling, and it was so hard to think that she called out, "Thank you" to the boy as she walked out, feeling like an idiot and wondering if it was possible to avoid ever going into that store again.

The test was just a precaution. She knew there was something with the lines—one line if she was pregnant, or maybe two, or maybe just the word *Bozo* written in big red letters—but she couldn't imagine it would come back positive. It was just too absurd for her life to take that particular turn right now. Funny little Julia all grown-up.

When she got back, the room was cold. She flipped on the lights and saw that Leanette had left the window open again. She must have come back for a cigarette before her afternoon class. Usually it wouldn't have bothered Julia, but today the rain had gotten in the window, and the ledge was soaked. It could have gotten on her computer. She needed to ask Leanette to be more careful.

Julia crossed the room to close the window, dropping the package with the pregnancy test in it on her bed. It was right after she shut the window, when she was turning back toward the bed, that she saw it.

It was next to the wall, shielded by the side of the desk, which was why she hadn't seen it from the door. At first she couldn't make out what it was. It looked like a spilled tray of food or a ruined children's toy.

Then it came into focus. The fur. The ears. The one good eye staring into space, like it was looking at something not in the room. It was a cat, a real one. Or at least it had been. Now it was a mangled pile of gray fur, sitting in a brown puddle that stained the carpet. The fur on the cat's body was matted and caked with blood, and its face looked like it had been slashed or chewed on, the flesh around its nose and mouth scraped raw. One of its paws was missing, torn like a wing from a cooked chicken. In place of one of its eyes, there was simply a bloody socket. Above where that eye had been, Julia noticed a white spot the size of a bottle cap.

That was when she screamed.

Ten minutes later, the R.A., a girl named Wynn, had her arm around Julia and was rubbing her shoulder and saying it was all right. There was a campus security officer in the room, a crackling walkie-talkie hooked to his belt, and he was pointing out the trail of blood dotting the carpet, the wisps of blood on the window ledge, which Julia hadn't noticed before. It must have been a much worse mess before the rain had washed it away.

The officer said that the cat was probably attacked by a raccoon, or maybe a rabid fox. As it was dying, it escaped and found shelter in Julia's room, since her window was the only one open in the whole dorm, because of the rain. He told Julia not to touch the cat, that they'd get someone with proper protection to clean it up.

Julia wanted to ask him if it was possible for one animal to do this to another. The attack seemed too brutal, too merciless. But of course she didn't ask that question. She understood it was outside the campus security officer's domain.

"It's just bad luck," he said. "But hopefully your roommate will remember to close that window next time."

Part Two

TROUBLE ON CAMPUS

CHAPTER 18
News

———◆———

It should have been a good month. Probably the best of his life. Here he was, dating Julia Stilwell, the girl he loved, the girl he honestly believed he would spend the rest of his life with. In all his loneliness, he never could have imagined a relationship so perfectly beautiful. He should have felt peaceful. And yet, he was anxious all the time.

The trouble had something to do with the possibility of losing Julia, his nagging insecurity that he wasn't good enough, and also the encounter with the tall boy and the shattered window and the story Julia had told him, crying, about the bloody animal that had dragged itself into her room. Were all these events related? They seemed to be, in that they each projected failure, loss, the ebb of everything that had flowed to him in recent weeks. It wasn't like him to be so negative, but his confidence kept getting shaken.

"What's the deal, Sammy?" Lonnie said to him the week before Thanksgiving. They were in the stockroom, putting on their aprons before the breakfast run. "You look tense. Lady trouble?"

Sam shook his head. "Just busy. Nothing special."

"Listen, get your lady to give your horn a toot, and you'll be good to go. Nothing relaxes me like a good blow job."

"Good to know."

"Hey, I didn't offer to let you blow me. Speaking of which . . ."

Megan was walking into the room, holding up a newspaper folded open to an article she must have been reading. Sam expected her to say something about Lonnie's language, but instead she held up the newspaper and shook it. "D'you all see this?"

"Give it another shake, Megan. I like that."

"Lonnie, can you stop your filth for ten minutes? A girl got raped last night on the campus. I'm reading about it. It sounds horrible."

"Was she hot?" Lonnie asked. He looked to Sam, who closed his eyes and shook his head. He wasn't going to risk encouraging Lonnie on that tack.

"What's the girl's name?" Sam asked, suddenly terrified it could be Julia.

"They don't say."

"What does it say about her?"

"They found her unconscious. Clothes all torn. One of her fingers broken. It sounds savage."

"Did he do her while she was conscious or un?" Lonnie asked.

"What the *fuck* does it matter, Lonnie?" Megan shot at him.

It seemed even Lonnie knew it was time to quit with the jokes. He folded his arms over his chest and said, "I didn't know you cussed."

"They find the guy?" Sam asked.

"No," Megan said. "And it's scary. I have to walk all the way across campus every day to my car. It's dark out in the morning, and it's starting to get dark when I go home."

"I'll protect you, if you want," Lonnie said.

"I'll pass."

"Offer's always open."

"Everything else is closed," Megan said.

Sam tried to call Julia as soon as he got a break, but she didn't pick up. He had to remind himself she was in class, as she always was at this time, and she would have called him by now if she'd been the one who was attacked. That day, while Sam stocked the coolers and wiped the counters and made sandwiches, he kept thinking about what Megan had said. *A girl. Raped. Horrible. They found her unconscious.* The thought of someone like that, roaming the campus, brushing past Julia on her way to classes, hiding in the bushes at night—it made his palms sweat. He was worried Julia could be in danger. He had to keep shaking himself back to the present, telling himself to focus so he didn't screw up in front of Horacio again.

After work, Sam felt more tired than he'd been at the end of a day in a long time. On the way out, he picked up two newspapers, the Westbury daily, as well as the student paper, *The Tattler*, and as soon as he was outside in the parking lot, he began to read.

Both papers had stories on the rape. Neither released the girl's name, only that she was a student at the college. She'd been coming back late from the library. The attacker had been walking behind her, and at some point he'd asked the victim a question about an exam she was supposed to take the following morning. When she slowed down, he grabbed her.

She was beaten around the sides of her face, and had been pretty scratched up when she was found by the train tracks, early that morning, by a student returning from his girlfriend's dorm. The victim appeared to have struggled with the attacker, but it wasn't clear in the articles if her injuries were the result of resistance or just the whim of the rapist. The article in the student paper suggested that perhaps the assailant would have scratches from the attack somewhere on his body, probably around his face or hands. He was described as Caucasian, in his late teens to early thirties, with a thin build, and both articles said he was tall.

Sam folded up the papers and put them in his jacket pocket. Back in his apartment, he showered and shaved, nicking himself on the cheek, because he was preoccupied. Waiting for the time when

Julia usually got back from dinner, he tried to read some fiction, but couldn't keep his mind in that world, and so he got up and paced the apartment for a while, thinking.

He called Julia. Listened to the ringing in the line, hoping it would be cut short by her voice, but it just kept trilling until the voice mail picked up.

After the beep, Sam said, "Hey, Julia, it's Sam. I heard about this attack on campus and I wanted to call to make sure you were all right. I know you have your music study group tonight, but if you have a chance to give me a call before or after, I'd appreciate it. I just want to make sure you're being careful. Bye."

After he hung up, he realized how worn out he was from the day. He was beginning to get a headache. He thought he might be coming down with something, and decided to go to bed early, try to sleep it off.

He pulled the shades and turned off the lights, got into bed, but it was so early that he had a hard time finding sleep. After a half hour, he was about to give up, but just before he turned on the lights, his phone started to ring. Once, twice, braying into the dark room. Sam's first thought was of Julia, some trouble, or possibly just the assurance he'd asked for that she was all right. He picked up the phone. It displayed a call from a private number, which was how all the college numbers were listed.

He flipped open his phone. "Hello?"

"Hello, Sam." The voice was not Julia's. It was breathy and high, a strained whisper, and Sam got the sense that whoever was on the other end didn't want him to know who it was.

"Yeah. Who is it?"

"I know who you are," the voice said. It wasn't clear whether it was male or female. "You're not fooling me."

"I don't have any idea what you're talking about."

"I know you did this."

"Did what?"

"Raped that girl. The one at the college."

"What? Is this a joke?" Sam almost laughed, but wasn't sure if that was what the caller wanted. "Are you messing with me?"

"I'm watching you, Sam. You're going to slip up. And I'll make sure I'm there."

The caller hung up, and Sam placed the phone down, shaking his head because it really had been a strange day.

CHAPTER 19
Advice

S he'd taken three tests. The second two she'd bought at the drug-store in Harmonyville, since she was afraid to go back to the Stradler pharmacy and run into that boy with the deep voice. The Barry White of home pregnancy testing. Two of the tests had shown a red plus sign, which was supposed to mean she was pregnant. The third wound up in the trash when she heard Leanette's key in the door while she was waiting for the results. She dug it out later, and had a hopeful few minutes when the test looked negative, but the line was so faint that even someone as desperate as Julia couldn't convince herself for long that it was accurate.

She avoided Sam that week. She told him she was busy working on a project for her music class, and she was all ready to explain the details if he asked. But he didn't. He never questioned her stories. He asked when they'd get to see each other next, and Julia told him they'd plan something before she went home for Thanksgiving.

On the Friday before Thanksgiving, Julia sat on her bed, waiting for Leanette to come home and pack her clothes for the weekend. Julia had it in her mind that Leanette would be a good person to talk to about all this. She seemed to know a lot about what girls went through when they had sex, and Julia was hoping Leanette could reassure her that this was all normal and nothing to worry about.

Around six, Leanette came in and slung her backpack on the bed, sitting down next to it.

"Next year my boyfriend is living in the same dorm," she said. "I don't care who it is, as long as I can walk down the hall to fuck him."

"Are you going to let Drew know about this plan?"

"It's going to be a test of his love." She smiled. "Anyway, what are you up to this weekend? Seeing Sam?"

"I don't know. Maybe. I actually talked to some friends from home today." This was the lie Julia had thought of to start the conversation. "I found out one of the girls from my high school got pregnant."

"No! At college?"

Julia nodded, watching Leanette's reaction. Her plan was to tell the story of this imaginary girl, feeling out Leanette's views and advice, then mention that Julia had a few worries of her own that something similar might have happened with Sam. It seemed like the easiest way to work up to it. She wouldn't mention the pregnancy tests. She thought she'd wait a week, see a doctor first.

"Yeah, it's crazy. Just really strange," Julia went on. "I was thinking about what it would be like if that happened to a girl at Stradler."

"You mean, what she would do?"

Julia forced a smile. "Yeah."

"A girl would have to be a fucking moron to get pregnant in college." Leanette spoke like she'd thought about the issue before, and had developed strong views on it. "I mean, there's thirty kinds of birth control you can use. I'm on the pill and Drew and I use condoms every time, just in case. I can't believe anyone would be dumb enough to get pregnant nowadays if you didn't want to."

As Leanette talked, Julia's mind traveled back to that first night she'd had sex with Sam, the night it must have happened. It had been cold in his apartment, and they'd done everything under the covers. Julia felt his hands down there, beneath the sheets, working, and she just assumed he was putting on a condom. She was too nervous to really know what was going on. He was so quiet, and she took his silence as a sign of confidence, which was what she must have needed. Somewhere inside herself, she had to have known there was a chance Sam wasn't being safe, but she was too scared to question him. In that moment, the risk of pregnancy or disease seemed more bearable than making a fool of herself. Leanette was right. Pretty dumb. A fucking moron.

"The only way I could understand it happening," Leanette went on, "is if a girl got raped."

Leanette must have been thinking about the girl on campus, whom Julia had read about in *The Tattler*. After the story had come out, Sam had left a concerned message on Julia's voice mail. Then he'd called back another time just to make sure she was okay, and to tell her to be extra careful, that he was worried about her.

"Are they telling people who it was?" Julia asked Leanette. "I mean, who got attacked."

"Not officially. But it's Marcy Ogman."

Leanette wasn't going to be upstaged on any campus gossip, no matter how gruesome.

CHAPTER 20
A Phone Call

⚬━✦━⚬

He couldn't leave another message. He'd already left two, and a third would begin to seem desperate. Now he just called and let it ring until the machine came on, then hung up. Early on, Sam had liked the fact that Julia didn't have a cell phone, found it quaint and old-fashioned, but now he couldn't help being irked by how difficult it was to get in touch with her.

What was happening to their relationship? She'd said clearly to him that they'd get together before the Thanksgiving break, and here it was, Monday afternoon, and they hadn't even made plans. Was she avoiding him? It felt to Sam as if a wave of bad fortune—the rape on campus, the animal in Julia's room, the prank call he'd received—had struck them both, damaged their bond irreparably.

He dialed one more time. It was four o'clock, and he thought she was probably in class. The phone rang three times. Then someone picked up.

"Hello?" Julia's voice.

"Julia, it's Sam. I was worried about you. I hadn't heard from you all weekend, and we were supposed to do something. I'm not upset about that, but I just wondered how you were doing."

"Oh. I'm doing fine. You?"

Sam had wanted to tell Julia about the prank caller, the shock it had given him, but the mood didn't feel right. He wondered if it would have been too much for her, all this strange news. She might start to see him as tarnished, bad luck. So he decided to keep it to himself.

"Honestly," he said. "It's been a tough couple days. My mom's birthday was on Saturday." He jotted down a note to remember the date he'd made up for that. "I don't mean to drag you into all of it. But this was the first one I'd spent without her."

"I'm sorry. That must have been awful."

"Not my favorite day. It was a little rough. I thought maybe you and I would go for a coffee or something."

"You should have told me. I would have—"

"I didn't want to lay all that on you in a message. You seem so busy."

He left that hanging, wanting to see if she'd grab for it.

But she said, "I had my music project this weekend. I've barely been in my room. Remember I told you?"

"I understand, Julia. I know you have a lot of responsibilities on you. I just thought we said we'd get together, and I cleared my schedule for it."

She didn't respond to that. For a few seconds he listened to the wash of static in the line.

"But listen," he finally said, "if you're around tonight, maybe we could catch a movie together."

"I don't think I can. I told my roommate I'd meet up with her later."

"What about tomorrow? We could have dinner. Or just hang out. I'll drop you back off on campus." He hadn't meant to offer this last bit, but he thought that maybe her hesitation was about taking the bus, or the schedule being inconvenient, or getting home too late if she needed to get up for a morning class. He could deal with having people see them together if the ride meant that much to her.

"I don't know. I just have so much to do before I leave. I'm sorry I didn't realize it earlier. I need a calendar. Actually, I need to start using the one I have."

"Is something wrong?"

"What do you mean?"

"When am I going to see you?"

"After I get back. I told you. We'll make plans." There was a pause. And then: "I don't want to disappoint you. I guess I didn't realize you had so many expectations."

"I don't have any expectations," he said, and knew how it sounded, could hear the sourness in his voice.

"I don't mean that. Look, I'm tired and I'm not thinking straight. It just feels like things are moving a little fast. Or maybe I'm just slow."

"We can slow things down, Julia. We can go as slowly as you want."

More static, like wind in an empty street.

"I think I'm just stressed," Julia said. "I wouldn't be that fun tonight anyway."

"That's fine. You shouldn't worry. Let's just relax and we'll hang out when you come back."

It took a little while, but at last she said, "Sounds good," in a distant voice that somehow scared him.

They wished each other a happy Thanksgiving. Then the line went dead.

Sam held the phone to his ear, as if he were still talking to her.

CHAPTER 21
The Health Center

Julia had had her blood drawn on Monday, and she'd gotten the first appointment with the doctor, 7:15 A.M., the day before Thanksgiving. The receptionist had called and said the doctor wanted to speak to her in person about her results.

At first, when she said that, Julia assumed it meant she was pregnant. But then she reasoned that it could have meant she wasn't, that she had some hormonal problem, and the doctor wanted to speak to her about her condition, or give her a lecture about safe sex. She'd take that, no problem. Then she told herself that that was ridiculous and she was definitely pregnant. When you have very little knowledge and a lot of fear, it's easy to convince yourself of almost anything.

The waiting room was empty. It looked dirty in the early-morning sunlight. Julia checked in with the nurse, who told her, "Head down to that first door on your left. He'll be a couple minutes. He's just dealing with something that came up."

On her way down the hall, Julia saw a girl sitting in a chair by a small desk. The desk was blocked off from the rest of the waiting room by one of those tall gray dividers you see in offices. She recognized the girl as Claudia Ortiz, one of the students in her freshman orientation group. Julia tried to give her a friendly look, the kind you give to tell someone that everything's okay, but Claudia didn't see her and Julia realized that what she really wanted was for someone to tell *her* it was okay.

In the exam room, she sat on the cold metal table. The tissue paper they'd laid out crinkled beneath her. She heard voices in the hall, but couldn't make out what they were saying.

Dr. Wayne walked in. He was holding a clipboard, and Julia thought that in his big white coat he looked younger than she was. He had ginger-colored hair, and very white skin that was stippled with little red marks, like he was learning to shave. When she'd come in to get her blood drawn, she'd discovered that he played basketball on Saturday mornings with the Student Christian Association, and that he blushed when he talked about sex, which he always called "relations."

He sat in the wheeling chair in the corner and rolled up to the exam table where Julia was sitting. "Um," he began, looking at the clipboard, "I have some news for you."

"I'm allergic to wheat."

She didn't know why she said it, but he just shook his head, then said, "You're pregnant." He glanced up from the clipboard, then down again, as if to double-check his results. "This isn't a hundred percent, but it's pretty accurate. I'd take it as a pretty sure thing."

She had no idea how she looked. For some reason, at that moment she thought it was very important to stare at the white tissue paper on the table, where it bordered the metal surface. She kept telling herself she'd always remember that: it was what she was looking at when she found out she was pregnant.

"I wanted you to come in because I had a few things I'd like to, um, go over with you. Some reminders." It was all so funny, two people who looked like them having this conversation. It felt like they were rehearsing a high school play.

Julia couldn't hear much else of what he said. Later she remembered him blushing and telling her about diet and moderate exercise and some appointments she needed to make.

When he finished, she said, "You seem like a nice person. The way you said all that. It was very clear."

"What?"

She shook her head. Her thoughts weren't coming the right way. She asked him, "Is it okay if I tell my parents myself?"

"We're not going to call anyone. You're eighteen, it's up to you. But it's probably a good idea to get them involved. Can I ask you who is the, uh, father?"

"My high school boyfriend," Julia lied.

"So you've been having, um, relations for a while?"

"On and off. He lives pretty far away. Actually, he travels. Professionally. So we can't see each other that much."

"And he knows about"—he made a sweeping gesture with his hand, to indicate the health center, the pregnancy test—"all this?"

Julia nodded. She was starting to feel weak. She didn't know if she had the energy to talk anymore.

"That's good. That's the right thing."

She nodded again.

"Well, there's one other thing I wanted to mention to you. Which is that if you should decide you want to terminate the pregnancy, you need to do that in the first trimester, twelve weeks after conception. You're five weeks along, so that gives you less than two months to make up your mind. I just wanted you to be aware of your options."

She could see it was a struggle for him to say that. On Saturday he'd have to play basketball with a group of people who wouldn't like the idea of him bringing up these options. She had the strange impulse to take him in her arms, hold him and tell him he was a good person and smooth the back of his head with her hand.

But that would be creepy, so all she said was, "Thanks."

After the appointment, Julia was hoping to be alone for a while, but when she got back to her dorm room, she could hear through the door that Leanette was in the room, opening and shutting her desk drawers. Julia took a breath, bracing herself. She was going to have to pretend everything was fine. She was going to have to smile.

But when she opened the door, it wasn't Leanette in the room. It was a doughy-faced boy with a shaved head. He was wearing gym shorts and a hooded gray sweatshirt, like he'd just come from a workout. And he hadn't been opening Leanette's drawers; he'd been rummaging through Julia's.

It was Drew, Leanette's boyfriend. He stopped what he was doing. Looked up from the drawer he'd been digging in.

"Oh," he said, like he hadn't expected Julia back so soon. "Hey, Julia."

"What are you doing?"

"I'm sorry. Is this your desk? I'm just realizing that this doesn't look like Leanette's stuff."

"Yeah, it's mine." Julia stayed where she was, in the open doorway.

"I feel really bad," he said, shutting the drawer. "Leanette gave me her key and asked me to get her camera. I couldn't even remember which desk was hers." He gave her a friendly smile, the way he always did with Julia, and she wasn't sure how to take it. It felt almost like he was trying to calm her down. He was always so gentle and attentive to her, and for the first time Julia wondered why. Once Leanette had told her that Drew said Julia was cute, and joked that he'd be up for a threesome. At the time Julia had thought it was just one of those comments horny guys make at college.

He went over to Leanette's desk, opened a drawer, and looked inside. But he gave the contents only a quick glance, like he didn't expect to find what he was looking for.

"I'll be out in one second," he said. "I have to catch up on my reading for that Rackoff class. It's hell."

"Okay."

"You can come in. You don't have to stand in the door."

"I'm fine here."

"Are you all right?"

"Fine. Just tired. Did you find the camera?"

"Nope." He shrugged and shut the drawer. Julia flinched at the sound, but did her best not to show it. "Are you sure you're all right?"

"Positive."

"I have no idea where she put it," he said. He looked at her for another second, as if waiting to see whether she'd come in the room. When she didn't move, he said, "I'll leave you alone. You probably want to take a nap."

"Thanks."

He started out of the room, and Julia had to move from the doorway to let him through. As he passed, for some reason she noticed that his shorts and sweatshirt didn't have any pockets.

In the hallway, he waved, and Julia waved back. Only when she shut the door did she realize why she'd noticed he didn't have pockets. She'd been looking for a place where he could have been holding the key to their room. She hadn't seen it in his hand.

CHAPTER 22
The Courtyard

The story in the Tuesday edition of the Westbury daily had more details. A second girl had come forward, a nineteen-year-old, saying she'd been assaulted in Harmonyville, one stop over from Stradler, on the evening of October the twelfth, around 6:00 P.M. She'd screamed and fought and had been able to get free of the attacker and run away. A police report had been filed.

Originally, the crime had been written about in the Harmonyville paper, but now Westbury police were acknowledging that the attack shared certain details with the Stradler rape. In both cases, the rapist attacked from behind, wearing a hood and ski mask, and only speaking in a whispery voice that made it impossible to know what his real voice sounded like. Again, he was described as tall. Both victims were told not to look at his face or else he would stab them. In the Stradler case, the girl had tried to tear the ski mask from his face, but he'd prevented her from doing it and broken her finger. It was now believed that both victims were assaulted by the same man.

The article gave a few more details about the Stradler rape. It printed the victim's recollection of the words the attacker had said to her before he'd grabbed her. "You ready?" he had asked. And when the girl had asked, "For what?" he'd said, "The Rackoff midterm," which was the exam she had been studying for. Police said the conversation showed knowledge of the victim.

There were fewer specific details about the Harmonyville attack, but for some reason, the date—October the twelfth—sounded familiar to Sam. He searched the files of his mind, brushing his thoughts along the events of the past month or so, but couldn't come up with anything.

He decided to visit Julia. Since the rape they'd only spoken that one time on the phone, and now he kept wondering if she was all right, if she was scared, if she was taking the proper precautions against this criminal, locking her door and not walking by herself at night. He hadn't seen her in over a week, and he couldn't bear to go another week with the vacation almost here. His distance from her felt unfair, considering the energy he'd put into the relationship.

He waited in the courtyard of her dorm for her, knowing she came back on Tuesdays around this time. He stood, hands in pockets, chin tucked into his collar. The courtyard was nearly bare of vegetation now, a few stripped vines climbing the trellis. He would have sat on the cement bench, but it was too cold. Several girls walked by as Sam stood there, and when one threw a suspicious glance in his direction, he smiled and waved, so she'd know he was harmless.

When Julia came up the path, Sam watched her, and he could see the quick, nervous movements when she noticed a man was waiting for her, the glances over her shoulders, a twitching in her mouth. It was nearly dusk, and she must have had trouble making out who he was.

Then she recognized him. Sam saw her let out a sigh of relief. Or was it disappointment?

"Hey, Julia," he said when she was close.

They kissed quickly, neither of them much for public displays.

"What are you doing here?" she said.

"I just came to see you. I missed you. I wanted to catch up before the holiday."

"I told you, I—"

"I was worried about you," he said, trying to hold his voice steady. "I've been hearing all these reports. I wanted to make sure you were okay."

"I'm fine. Really. You don't need to check up on me. I'm very safe." There was a new sharpness when she spoke to him.

"I do it because I care about you, Julia. No other reason. You know that. I'm concerned. I love you."

He wasn't sure, but it looked as if she shifted an inch back when he said that. Was it too much? He never knew when to let it drop. Her lips were barely parted, and there was a breath of pause before she said, "I understand. I know you're worried about me. I just need some space."

"Don't you think I'd give it to you if I could?"

After he said that, she seemed to deflate a little. He hated what he was doing to her, causing her pain. If he didn't love her so much, he would have called it off in an instant.

"I don't know," Julia said. "I can't know what's in your mind." She hesitated for a second, as if contemplating how to deliver her next words. Then she said, "But I do know that I don't feel the same way. I'm sorry. I'm just not ready for this kind of relationship."

"What are you saying?"

"I want to break up."

The words struck him with an almost physical force. Unbelievable, that life could sneak up behind him and slap him with this news. He felt utterly stunned.

But she wasn't finished. "Please don't call me," she went on. "Please don't come visit me on campus. It'll be too hard for both of us. I think you're a great person. But we need to just let this go."

Great person. She kept looking at him after she said that, as if to make sure it had registered. It was that look that hurt him more than anything. It was a measure of the space that had opened up between them, a reminder of loss, not just of her, but of his mother and of Patrice and Alyssa and others he'd loved. The idea of feeling that way about someone and no longer being able to be close to her, touch her, express these emotions—it was unfathomably cruel.

He didn't know what to say to Julia. But before he could find any words, she said again, "I'm sorry," and walked past him.

Later, in his apartment, Sam looked in the mirror. He combed through his hair and noticed there were tufts of gray, impossible to uproot without creating a bald spot. They'd hidden in there, nearly unnoticeable, like dead grass in a field, but now he could see every one of them. He didn't know how he'd fooled himself. And his eyes. There were lines around them, like cracks in ice, spreading when he squinted. It was crazy that until his fortieth birthday he'd thought of himself as young, as someone who could give love and receive it as freely as a teenager. Who would have believed that?

Still, he spent an hour in the bathroom, with his creams and washes and tweezers, and when he emerged, he felt better, lighter and more hopeful. What Julia had said to him wasn't irrevocable. The relationship wasn't doomed. They were in a rough patch, which happened when you were in love. They were both good people who cared about each other, and that was what mattered.

The phone started to ring. Sam saw it was a private number. Julia, calling to apologize, to explain how she'd been stressed over her school work and hoping that maybe he'd have a coffee with her and talk it over.

Sam picked up. "Hello-o."

"I know you tried to rape that other girl, too," the caller said. Sam recognized the voice, that strained whisper that wasn't male or female, the one that had spoken to him in his darkened bedroom the other night, accusing him of a horrible crime.

"What are you talking about?"

"The one in Harmonyville. In the paper this morning. The one that happened in October. You thought you'd get away with it, that no one would ever know, but I knew right away when I read it. And everyone else will, too."

"This is getting ridiculous," Sam said. And then he remembered something. October the twelfth. It was the night he'd had dinner with Julia in Shady Grove. "I was having dinner with my girlfriend in an Italian restaurant. Minelli's, if you want to know. So maybe you should stop this whole—"

"We'll see," the caller said, leaving the issue hanging. Sam didn't understand why this person would keep up the joke. He was about to tell whoever it was that he didn't have time for this when the caller continued, "I saw that scratch on your face, by the way. I know what that's from. I read about that, too. The girl at Stradler tried to tear your mask off. You broke her finger."

"What scratch? " Then he remembered. "I got that scratch from shaving. It happened *after* the girl was attacked. You can ask anyone at my work."

"We'll see," the caller said again. "I don't care about all that. I know the truth about you. It's all going to come out. You just watch."

After they hung up—a mutual decision—Sam dialed the operator to see if he could retrieve the caller's name and number, but when he told the operator he wanted an unlisted number, the operator told him she couldn't give it to him. Sam was about to tell her that the caller was harassing him, but thought it better not to bring in other people, so he let it go.

And there was another reason. As he was talking to the operator, he remembered something else. The day the tall boy had come to talk to him, behind the snack bar where the dumpster was, the day Sam had dropped the ham. *I'm looking out for her*, the boy had said. It wasn't exactly a threat, but it was close to one.

Sam hadn't seen the cat since that day. There were a number of strays on campus, but Julia had told Sam that the bloody animal that had crawled into her room was a cat. And the rock had been thrown in Sam's window around that time, too.

It would have been easy for the boy to swipe Sam's number from Julia, if he wanted to harass him. The boy—Marcus, Sam thought his name was—could have seen the scratch on Sam's face one day when he came into the snack bar, or when Sam was walking across the campus to his van.

Sam needed to have a talk with the boy.

CHAPTER 23
Midnight

J ulia woke up in the music library, just before midnight. She had on a pair of headphones, but no sound was coming out. She'd been working on an analysis of a Brahms piano concerto, trying to go on exactly as she would have if she hadn't found out that morning that she was pregnant. She didn't know another way to deal with the information, since it was news she wasn't ready to accept, so she figured the best thing was to block it out.

Running through her mind was the scene of the breakup with Sam, but the details were so faint it felt like it had happened in a dream. She didn't know why his appearance in the courtyard bothered her so much, but when she saw him, she knew she wasn't ready to tell him about the pregnancy, and the only other choice was to break up with him. How could she keep something like that hidden from her boyfriend? She needed time to think, to decide what she wanted to do, and this was the only way. If she had a baby, the idea of picking up the trumpet again, of working through the pain and maybe even getting enough strength back to be in an orchestra would be impossible, a fantasy.

It was almost midnight. Julia needed to get back to her dorm. There'd been another story about the rapist that morning, and campus security had posted announcements that women shouldn't walk alone after ten. There was a number you could call if you wanted an officer to escort you back to your room. But calling and waiting for an officer seemed like a lot of fuss. She could rush across campus in ten minutes, and there wasn't much chance she'd meet anyone along the way.

She started out into the white bloom of the street lamps. The campus was quiet. Julia was in the center of a quad of academic buildings, all dark now, but the path was well lit. Beyond the buildings, darkness hung like a curtain. It was cold, probably close to freezing, and her breath smoked the air. She looked around and saw that all the paths were empty. She didn't hear anything but her own footsteps and the occasional gust of wind.

Crossing the quad, she looked around. She thought maybe she'd catch another student coming back from a study session or a late night visit to a boyfriend's room, but there was no one. It was only two days before the holiday. Maybe people were in their rooms packing. Julia hadn't even started doing that yet.

She walked through the space between Dwyer Hall and Panagakos, hurrying because there was a place where the path narrowed. She thought she heard a scraping sound, like someone's shoes on the pavement, but it could have been her imagination, which had been churning since the cat and the doctor's visit. And the drowsiness didn't help. Julia felt like her mind was walking a step behind reality, unable to catch up. Probably a symptom of anxiety. El Doctor could have diagnosed it, she was sure.

In front of her, the path sloped down the main lawn of campus, lit by more street lamps. There was a long open stretch to the train station, then a couple blocks through town, since her dorm was just off campus. She'd made the walk several hundred times in the past couple months, at every hour of day and night, but for the first time she was scared. She thought about turning back, but the music library would have been closed and she wouldn't have had anywhere to go.

Julia started down the hill, listening to her pants chirp with each step, her shoes clicking the pavement. The rape had been by the train tracks, she remembered, and that was where she was looking when she first heard the sound. It was a rustling in the grass, beyond the lights and the trees, far into the darkness where she couldn't see. She kept her breathing and footsteps quiet, and she heard it again, out there in the solid dark, something moving in the grass.

It could have been an animal. The campus was surrounded by woods, and some mornings she'd seen deer nibbling at the shrubs in the courtyard. It could have been a raccoon or a squirrel or a fox, dashing through a field for the cover of a tree.

She kept on, more quickly now, listening to the swishing grass. Whatever it was, it seemed to be keeping pace with her. When she sped up, the rustling got louder, and she thought she heard foot-steps, but wasn't sure if they were animal or human. It all seemed too strange to be happening. She listened for breathing or barking or a call in the darkness, but there was nothing except the rustling, trailing her to the station.

"Hey!" Julia yelled, thinking she could scare whatever it was into a response.

But she only heard more rustling.

She was halfway down the slope when she started to run, clutching her bag and pumping her arms. She couldn't hear the rus-tling anymore, just her pant legs brushing against each other and her footsteps and her own breathing. She was watching the lights ahead of her, down by the train station, thinking that if she got that far she could at least see what was chasing her. It was too bright down there for anything to stay hidden in the shadows.

She kept running, not even knowing if she was tired. She wanted to get away, but also to make sense of the thing that was chasing her, give it a shape, a body, a voice. Julia hadn't run like this, with all her energy, since she was a kid. She wasn't even sure anymore if she'd actually heard anything rustling in the grass, if she'd sensed the shadow that she'd thought was just beyond the reach of the lamps, or if it had been only in her mind.

But she couldn't take the chance. She ran past the train station, through the town, up the street to her dorm. When she got to the door, panting, sweating, maybe even crying, she couldn't tell, she tried to pull the door open, but it was locked, like always. She dug out her keys, fumbled with them, and then dropped them on the cement in front of the door.

It was a good opportunity to grab her.

But when Julia reached down for the keys, she saw Vanessa, a girl from her hall, walking into the entryway.

"Are you okay?" Vanessa said when she opened the door. "I heard you trying to open the door. What happened?"

"I don't know," Julia said between breaths. "I just got scared."

"Everyone feels that way. It's awful. You shouldn't be walking alone at night."

Julia nodded, coming inside. "I don't know what I was thinking."

When she got back to her room, Julia saw that Leanette had gone to Drew's. She'd put a note on Julia's desk saying, "Have a great break!" with a smiley face instead of a dot under the exclamation point. She was going to visit Drew's family in New Hampshire for the vacation. Julia remembered that she'd wanted to ask Leanette about whether she'd given Drew the key to the room earlier, but hadn't had the chance. She figured she'd do it when she got back.

Seeing Leanette's note, their desks and chairs, the ugly gray carpet, the too-bright ceiling light, Julia felt calmed by these familiar harmless objects, and silly about her panic during the walk home. She had too much on her mind, and it was making her edgy. Hardly a month pregnant and her mood was already swinging like a pendulum. Now she felt the overwhelming need to sleep, and decided she would do that right away, without even brushing her teeth.

As she was drifting off, she thought about Aster House. It had been pretty nice to have every minute of her day scheduled for her, so she didn't have to make any choices. It wouldn't be such a bad thing to end up in a place like that. You could do some gardening, catch up on reading, and you wouldn't have any of the responsibilities that weighed people down. No balancing a checkbook or grocery shopping or preparing for interviews. Kind of a vacation, if you looked at it the right way. If you felt sad or anxious or couldn't sleep or had a headache, they'd give you a pill and you'd feel better in an hour.

Julia must have fallen asleep while she was thinking like that. When she opened her eyes, something about the quiet made it feel like it was very early in the morning. It was cold in the room, colder than it should have been.

She was probably one of the only students in the dorm. Most of them had left that afternoon, Julia realized, getting a jump on the vacation. The hall outside her room was silent, her window dark. She wondered if maybe they'd shut off the heat.

Then she heard a noise.

It wasn't exactly talking, and it wasn't whispering either. It was a kind of high, strained singing, light and breathy, like when people hum while they're doing chores. She didn't recognize the melody, and she couldn't make out the words. It took her a minute in the dark to figure it out, but she realized the singing was coming from her window, which was open, and there seemed to be the shadow of a man outside it.

Her breath caught in her throat. She sat up. The singing—which had been so faint she could hardly hear it, and she wasn't sure if maybe all this was in her mind—had already stopped. She thought of screaming, but wasn't sure if anyone was around to hear, and she didn't want to make things worse with the man outside her window. If she ran, she didn't know how far she could get before he caught up with her.

Julia looked at the window again, and it was hard to tell if the shadow was really a man or just the way the night looked. If it was a man, he hadn't moved in a while, at least since she sat up in bed, and maybe that was a good sign. Maybe he'd gotten scared and run away when he realized she wasn't asleep.

She sat there, breathing, thinking. Nothing seemed to change.

She was still sitting there when the shadow began to move.

CHAPTER 24
The Parking Lot

A second girl had been attacked on the campus. There was no article in *The Tattler*, since the students were heading out on Thanksgiving break, but the article in the Westbury daily revealed the victim was a freshman. No name had been released. She'd been coming back from baking bread in a friend's dorm for a student organization. The details were all the same: a man in a hood and ski mask, approaching from behind, telling her not to look at him or he'd stab her.

It was a brief article, since the crime had been committed early Tuesday morning, and now Sam was finishing up his shift on Wednesday afternoon, the day before Thanksgiving. He had plans for when he finished work, early today because of the holiday. Sam knew that the tall boy, Marcus, had his music seminar with Julia that afternoon, and he planned to catch him at his dorm before he went home for vacation. It had been easy to find out where he lived. He was the only Marcus in the freshman class, and the online directory gave all his information.

Sam was anxious about the meeting. He hadn't slept well the night before, thinking about it, and that afternoon he'd drunk a large coffee to stay alert. Normally, Sam didn't drink anything with caffeine, preferring to rely on the energy his sleep provided, and now he felt shaky and light-headed, not quite himself.

"Hey, Sammy, d'you hear about that other girl?" Lonnie said to him when they were sweeping behind the counter. "Looks like this guy is having a ball."

"Sounds bad," Sam said. "He'll probably get put away for a long time."

"If you think with your executive branch, the judicial branch'll smack you down."

Sam nodded, hoping to put an end to it.

But Lonnie kept on. "I tell you, I'm a man who thinks only with my executive branch. Sometimes I consult the treasury—you know, the family jewels—but the executive is in charge. He's gotten me in a lot of trouble."

It was odd to Sam how insistently Lonnie joked about these tragic events. It seemed almost like a necessity, like it relieved him of a burden.

Megan was glancing up from the register, frowning at Sam and Lonnie. She must have sensed the way Lonnie was talking, even if she didn't hear all the words. Sam couldn't deal with another scene between them, and he thought the easiest way to quiet Lonnie was to tell a joke, show him you were on his side.

So Sam said, "Next time I'm baking bread, I'll stay far away from you."

He looked at Lonnie after he said that, thinking he'd see that satisfied grin, that glimmer of approval—but instead Lonnie's eyes were big and his lips parted to show his teeth, a face like he'd dropped something fragile. Sam watched him for a second before realizing Lonnie was looking over Sam's shoulder. Sam turned around.

Behind him, Horacio was watching Sam with an expression of naked rage. "What did you say?"

"What?" Sam asked.

"What did you say about that girl? The one who was baking bread?"

"I was just—we were just—"

"What the *fuck* is wrong with you, Sam? That girl is my *fucking* niece, you asshole. This is going to destroy her life. I went to see her in the health center yesterday morning, and she can't even look me in the face. She's devastated. I don't get your fucking jokes, but I can tell you that your work has been for shit lately. You're on the edge, Sam. I'm watching the fuck out of you."

"I'm sorry."

Horacio waved him off, the apology seeming to anger more than assuage him. He walked back to his office.

"Disgusting," Megan said to Sam and Lonnie. "Both of you."

Lonnie watched Horacio's door, and when he heard it slam, he said, "Megan, I will stick my executive branch so far in your soup . . ."

After work, Sam walked to Marcus's dorm. What was happening felt unreal—his floundering at work, the caller's absurd accusations, Julia slipping away from him. A couple months ago, when his relationship with Julia was beginning, he couldn't have imagined his life taking such an unfortunate turn. He'd envisioned them together during the Christmas holiday, in a secluded ski lodge, watching a fire in a cold room, reading books and sharing the parts they liked with each other. The vision was so clear and pleasing it had seemed impossible for it not to happen. He didn't know how he'd turned onto the path that had led him here, on the way to interrogate a college freshman.

Sam waited in the parking lot behind Langhorn Hall, which the boy would need to walk through when he came back from the music building. Marcus was late, and the thought crossed Sam's mind that maybe he'd left early for the break, that he wouldn't be coming back to his dorm today.

Sam was nearly ready to call it off—he was so tired, and his hands were trembling—when he saw the boy approaching from the quad.

He was by himself, his backpack strapped to his shoulders so that it rode high on his back. Sam noticed he hunched a little, and wondered again what Julia could have seen in him.

The boy seemed to be in his own head, humming a song, and he didn't notice Sam until he'd entered the parking lot, fewer than fifteen feet from where Sam stood. The boy stopped, watching Sam for a moment with a look of mild curiosity on his face.

Then Marcus said, "What do you want?"

Sam looked around to see if anyone was watching them, and when he saw that they were alone, he walked up to Marcus. He could tell the boy was uncomfortable, but Marcus held his ground. Maybe he wasn't so easily frightened.

"How did you get my number?" Sam asked.

"What are you talking about?" The boy's eyes squinted, in a way that might have been mocking.

"How did you find my cell number? It's not listed. You must have stolen it from Julia."

The boy heard him that time, because a smile tugged the corner of his mouth. "I have no idea what you mean."

Marcus took a step forward, as if to walk around Sam, but Sam held his arm out and said, "Wait."

The boy stopped. Sam dropped his arm.

"I don't know what you're trying to pull," Sam went on, "but it's going to stop. I'm onto you. I can see you're jealous. But the fact is that Julia chose me. That's the end of it. Don't mess with her anymore. And don't mess with me."

"First of all, I hardly talk to Julia anymore," Marcus said. "We say hi outside class. Sometimes I ask her what she thought of the homework. Second of all, I don't have any interest in *messing* with you."

Sam couldn't tell if the boy was angry, or simply impatient. He looked like a misbehaving child held at detention, with that self-satisfied grin.

"I don't believe you. I just don't believe you. I'm not saying you hurt that cat, but I wouldn't put it past you. And I wouldn't be surprised if you threw that rock at my window a few weeks ago either. I know you're trying to upset her, turn her against me. And if you mess this up for me, I'm not going to forget it."

"I honestly have no idea what you're talking about. And your relationship is all yours. It's not mine to mess up."

Sam wasn't sure if these ambiguous phrases were a mind game the boy was playing, a way to use his education against Sam. He felt frustrated, unable to break through the barrier Marcus had erected.

Now Sam reached out and grabbed the boy by the throat, lightly, to show him he was serious.

"If you ever call me again," Sam said, glancing to his left and right, "you're going to regret it."

After he said that, Sam gave the boy a shake, and he heard something land on the pavement. Marcus swallowed, and Sam felt the boy's Adam's apple bob against his palm. Even so, Marcus just smiled, waiting for Sam to let go. His face was getting red, but he didn't try to push Sam's hand away. And he didn't confirm or deny what Sam was saying.

Sam let go. He might have been holding the boy's throat more tightly than he'd meant to, because now the boy coughed and gasped for air. There was a red mark where Sam's hand had been. When the boy recovered, he looked at Sam in a pitying way, still grinning, and said, "Are you finished?"

"Yeah," Sam said.

Marcus took a step back, looking at the ground. Sam remembered something dropping just after he'd shaken Marcus. Now Marcus seemed to spot what he was looking for. He leaned over and picked up a small metal object from the asphalt. His cell phone. Marcus placed it in the pouch of his backpack where it must have fallen from, then walked away.

Sam felt cold. He was wearing a T-shirt and a sweater, and he realized he'd sweated through both shirts.

CHAPTER 25
After the Encounter

❦

On his way back to the dorm, Marcus thought about what Sam had just done. His hand on Marcus's throat. Unbelievable. Marcus hadn't even touched Sam, which was what was so amazing about it. It was assault, really. No one would be able to argue with that.

Marcus looked around, on the off chance that he'd been fortunate enough to have a witness. But there was no one near the parking lot.

Sam was slipping. Marcus could see it. That would be the best way, to have Sam bury himself. Marcus might not even have to get involved, because Sam was doing all the work. Marcus would just stand by and watch it happen.

Of course, there was a chance Sam could really lose it. For a moment, Marcus had thought Sam might actually hurt him when he had his hand on Marcus's throat. But then he realized it was just a show; he didn't mean to do anything other than scare him.

Marcus walked inside the dorm. In his room, alone, he took a deep breath, then let it go, sitting down on his bed. It was going just how he'd predicted. There was no way Julia would stay with Sam if she'd seen what had just happened. And it would keep happening. No question about that.

The best thing was to keep his distance. Now Marcus just needed to wait, to watch. Sam would ruin his own chances. Marcus didn't need to do anything else. Just pick the right moment to have a talk with Julia, and she would come around, see Sam the way Marcus wanted her to.

And then, without knowing how he'd gotten there, Marcus was thinking about Tree. He lay facedown on the bed, eyes closed, and in his mind he was lying on top of her. *Hey baby.*

It wouldn't be long.

CHAPTER 26
Thanksgiving

T he shadow kept moving toward the window, and Julia could hear the man, the rapist, whatever he was, climbing in to get her, the soles of his boots rattling the window casing. She got up from the bed, too scared to scream, worried it might make him attack more quickly and not even knowing if there was anyone around to hear. She ran toward the door, unlocking it and rushing out of the room, not even closing it behind her. She could hear the man as he jumped down from the window, his boots smacking the floor, and his footsteps as he began to run after her.

Julia looked both ways down the hall. There was no one here. She started to run toward the fire exit at the far end of the dorm, through the curving hallway. She didn't scream, couldn't see the point of it, and she didn't want the man to know which way she'd run. But she could hear his boots on the carpet the whole time, and that strange, high singing.

She was thinking that maybe there'd be some people in the lounge, but no one was there. The TV was off, the cushions piled on the couch. So Julia kept on down the hall, hearing him, the shadow, getting closer. She hadn't gotten a good look at him, and she was afraid she'd never be able to identify him if she made it out alive. She wasn't sure if she'd be able to get to the fire exit. It sounded like he was gaining on her, like he was just around the last corner.

The bathroom was on her right. She figured she could duck in there, just to get out of the hallway, and maybe the man would keep running past her. If she had a minute to catch her breath, maybe she could think of something, or sneak away while he retraced his steps.

She opened the bathroom door, walked in, and shut it behind her.

Inside, the bathroom was dark. The students were asked to keep the lights off at night to save energy. She leaned back against the door, trying to control her breathing. She heard the man's footsteps running past the door, and when the footsteps quieted and it seemed like he was far enough away, Julia let herself take a breath and turned on the light.

Right away, when the lights flickered awake, she knew something was wrong. The room wasn't supposed to look this way, with dark smears on the walls. When the lights came fully on, she could tell what it was, that red-brown liquid with the metallic smell. It was everywhere, smeared on the toilet stalls, the mirror above the sinks, the shower curtains. She had no idea what had happened in here, but the sight of it made her whole body go cold.

And she heard something. Outside the door. His boots on the carpet. The singing, that high, sad singing. It sounded barely human.

She pushed open the door of the second toilet stall, thinking this was her only chance, to hide in here. The stall door opened, and she saw the toilet was filled with the dark liquid she knew was blood. And then the bathroom door swung open and she could hear the singing...

Julia started awake. Here she was, on the train, curled up by the window, green hills and fields rushing past. It had been a dream, of course. She hadn't been chased by a homicidal shadow. It was a bad dream.

She was on her way home. It was Thursday morning, Thanksgiving day. She hadn't slept much in her dorm since she'd woken up to the shadow in her window and that singing, and when she had fallen asleep, dreams like this usually woke her.

It was a strange thing, because now she didn't even know if she'd heard that singing in the real world, or if it had been only in her dream. After Julia had heard it, she'd gotten up and turned on the light. But with the light on, she could tell the window wasn't open. She was all ready to call campus security, but standing there in the light, the whole story felt dramatic and possibly untrue. Julia had walked to the window and seen that no one was standing outside it.

In that moment, it felt like the dream world and the real world had blurred together, and she had the sick feeling that she was the type of person who could lose her mind. She didn't want to tell anyone about the man who followed her home, who sang outside her window, because she knew there was a chance she'd made it all up.

When you've been in a place like Aster House, it's easy to question yourself. She knew girls there who believed in the wildest fantasies: that dead people were still alive, or that they were being spied on or chased, or that they were the secret children of dictators. She didn't know where the switch was that turned you from one kind of person into the other, but she felt that she had it in herself. And when you worried about it, what you were really doing was inching closer to it.

As the landscape streamed by, Julia held her arms around her knees, thinking.

She needed to talk to her parents. She needed to tell them about the pregnancy. It was too much to bear by herself, and the stress must have had something to do with these dreams. In her mind she kept hearing what Dr. Wayne had said about the first trimester, how she had only seven weeks to make up her mind about the baby. Julia was trying to avoid calling it that, because even the word made it feel more real.

This was the first Thanksgiving without her brother. Julia didn't know what to expect, because she'd never been the only child at a family holiday like this. When she was growing up, she'd always had the sense of being a sideshow to Paul, an odd but passable kid, enjoyable enough if you didn't stare too hard. And that had been comfortable. She didn't need the attention.

Normally her brother had done the cooking, but this year Julia's dad said he'd make the dinner. Back at her parents' house, she slept most of the afternoon, figuring she wouldn't bring up her news until after they'd gotten through the meal. She woke up only as her parents were putting the food on the table.

"I have to acknowledge," Julia's dad said before they started eating, "that it's a tough night. We're sad not having Paul here to share this with us, but I know this is what he'd want us to do. And we're all thankful for the family we have."

Julia's mom looked at the table while he talked, and Julia had the sense that her mom was lonely. Above them, the skylight was slicked with rain, showing a blurry view of tree branches like a TV with bad reception.

"Now let's see if my cooking is as bad as everyone expects it to be," her dad said, then made a barking sound that probably was meant to be a laugh.

They all started serving themselves. Julia listened to the clink of plates and silverware in the quiet house. She missed the sounds Paul used to make, his music, his jokes, his door slamming. She could still hear all of them in her mind, and their absence made her realize both how thin and how solid the line is between past and present, life and death.

She knew she had to share her news. But she thought it could wait a minute, that it would be too much just now.

Julia's dad still had on his chef's apron. As they ate, he talked about the challenges of cooking the different dishes, referring to the bird as the "toykey." Julia had to make an effort to laugh. He seemed so tired, but he just kept talking, kept asking Julia and her mom if they wanted more potatoes or veggies or stuffing, kept making his jokes. Julia got the feeling he was terrified of what would happen if he stopped, of the silence that would fill the house.

"So how are things with your beau?" her dad asked.

Julia hadn't expected any questions about Sam. She'd almost forgotten that she'd told her dad about him that night outside her dorm room.

"We're not seeing each other anymore," she said, looking at her plate.

"That's too bad," her mom broke in. "Did you have different interests?"

Julia looked up from her plate. Her mom was smiling for the first time that evening. Julia could see there was real pleasure in her expression, and the idea struck her that her mom actually enjoyed Julia's pain, that it gave her relief. It's an awful thing to realize that your unhappiness can give your parent satisfaction, but pain has a way of spilling over. Julia didn't blame her for it. She didn't even think her mom hated her. Actually, Julia believed her mom needed her.

"I've just gotten busy with school," Julia told her mom. Another time, before all this, she would have said that the problem was actually that their interests were too similar, they were both sadists and they had no one to play the masochist. But she couldn't say something like that now.

"Well, it's good you found out," her dad said, chuckling, trying to smooth over the tension. After the night he'd shown up at Julia's dorm, he'd stopped questioning her, doubling his efforts to stay positive and cheerful. He must have been afraid that if he didn't, he'd lose Julia.

When they opened the second bottle of wine Julia realized that she and her dad hadn't even touched their glasses, which had only a couple sips in them anyway. Her mom was quieter than usual, and she laughed at some of Julia's dad's jokes, then sat silent during others, as if she hadn't heard what he'd said. It seemed at times like she wasn't there with them at the table, like she was locked in some dark room inside herself.

When her dad made tea to have with the pumpkin pie, he asked her mom if she wanted sugar, and her mom said, "I prefer honey." Her tone was so sharp that her dad looked like he'd been slapped. Underneath her words, she seemed to be saying, *How is it possible that you don't know that simple fact about me after twenty-two years of marriage?* Then she laughed, as if to say she'd just been kidding.

Julia wanted to talk to both her parents about the pregnancy, but as soon as the meal was over, her dad got up from the table and said, "I'm tuckered out. I think I'm going to hit the hay." He looked on the verge of collapsing. "I love you both," he said to Julia and her mom, "but would you two mind scrubbing up a few dishes for me?"

"I thought you'd never ask," Julia said, and forced a smile.

She started washing, since too much of the soap irritated her mom's hands, and her mom dried. Julia figured it would be impossible to talk to her parents tonight, so she'd put it off until tomorrow. She could see her mom wouldn't even have the energy to react.

But a funny thing happened. As they washed and dried, Julia began to feel a pressure building inside her. She tried to dampen it, but the more she resisted, the stronger the pressure became. She began to feel as if she needed to tell her mom everything, to hear what her response would be. Julia couldn't wait for the morning, for her dad and his nervous joking, his gentle reassurances. Maybe she wanted her mom's anger. Maybe she needed it.

So, when her mom asked her if there was anything new at school, Julia said, "Actually, there's one thing I wanted to talk to you about."

"Mm?" her mom said.

"I wanted to ask your advice about something."

"Would it be okay if we did it another time?" her mom said, looking out the window behind the sink, into the darkness in the yard.

Julia should have stopped there, but that thing kept expanding in her, that compulsion, and she said, "It's kind of important. Really important, actually. I just didn't know when to bring it up."

Her mom's expression changed when Julia said that. She stopped looking dreamily out the window, and her eyes snapped into focus on Julia's face. It was like her mom had been waiting all night for this moment.

"Are you serious?" her mom said. "Are you really serious?"

"Mom—"

"Do you have any idea what this day is like for me?" She stopped drying the dish she was holding, just looking at Julia. "I can't believe you'd come in this house and start pestering us about whatever little problems you're having with your boyfriend or your roommate or your school friends. Do you have a clue what it's like to be missing a child? Do you have any notion?"

"I'm sorry, I—"

"Listen to me, Julia." Her mom dropped the towel on the counter and grabbed Julia's wrist. She was squeezing so hard Julia thought she might break something. "I didn't want your father to go up there to get you. I told him to stay. I told him to let you do what you were going to do. Do you understand me?"

Julia nodded.

"But he wanted to make the trip. He said he had to do it. He couldn't bear the thought of something happening to you. So I let him. I said okay. And then when he came back, I can't even explain to you the state he was in. What you did to him. He cried and muttered to himself. He couldn't go to work. I had to call in and say he had the flu."

"I didn't—"

"What I'm saying is that you've done enough damage. Between your dad and me and your brother, *you've done enough damage!*" This last part she shrieked. The plate dropped from her hand and shattered on the floor.

"Don't come to us with your problems now," her mom said. "Don't drag your dad back into it. You've done too much to him. To all of us. We can see each other and play nice on the holidays, but don't be so fucking selfish as to think everything goes back to normal when you want it to."

Julia's mom let go of her wrist. Pain flooded Julia's arm. Her mom had her hands on the counter and she was leaning over the sink with tears in her eyes. Seeing it, a strange relief came over Julia, a kind of cold satisfaction. So we're here now, she thought.

Her dad came out of his room then. He was wearing boxers and a yellowed undershirt, and he looked older than Julia had ever seen him. He had that eager, merry look on his face. "I heard a little somethin' drop, and wasn't sure if you two needed a couple extra hands to sweep it up."

Julia's mom didn't even look at him. She stared into the sink.

"No, Dad," Julia said. "It's all right. Don't worry. Something just slipped."

"You sure?" He kept looking at them, like he was waiting to be released.

"You trusted the wrong people with your dishes," Julia said.

He smiled. She could see he was relieved. "It's a tough night for everyone," he said. "Maybe we should all hit the sack a little early."

Julia looked at her mom. "I'm sorry if I said anything to upset you."

Her mom shook her head.

"I'm heading back up to school in the morning," Julia told them. "That was all I wanted to ask you about, Mom. I just have a lot of work I need to finish before finals. I wanted to know if it would be all right if I went back a little early."

CHAPTER 27
An Unwelcome Visitor

S ince his mom's death, Sam always ate his Thanksgiving dinner alone. It was the one day of the year when he cooked an actual meal for himself, rather than just opening a protein shake. He'd made a small turkey and some sweet potatoes and had opened a can of jellied cranberry sauce, the kind his mom had always bought for the holidays. He had his mom's Jean Raeburn cassette playing. Jean was singing "The Quiet House," and Sam hummed along to the melody.

He felt good about the confrontation with Marcus. It had been the right thing to do. The boy probably just wanted to make a little trouble, and the incident with the cat was most likely a coincidence. Marcus didn't seem like the type of guy who would really hurt another person. Sam had done just enough to calm Marcus down, let him know it couldn't go any further.

Now that Marcus was out of the way, Sam had a clear path to Julia. She'd probably be calling him soon, maybe even tonight, wanting to apologize, tell Sam she'd been wrong about everything. He could imagine her relief, and his own.

Sam listened to Jean's voice skipping across the melody, singing, "If ever there's a time you need me/Just say the word and love will lead me . . ." It was such a beautiful song, so bright and pure and hopeful. It was how Sam saw the world. There were a few precious things—Julia, his collections, his job at the college—which were all he needed to be happy, and there was no reason he couldn't have those things. As long as he worked and stayed focused, it would all come together for him in the end. Even Julia. Sam was glad he'd kept his mom's old cassette player, since none of the new stereos had tape decks. It was the player they'd had all those years ago in the house in San Diego, the exact same one, still working like new, probably because Sam used it only on holidays and special occasions. His mom had always played the Jean Raeburn tape on Thanksgiving. It was her favorite holiday, since it fell on a Thursday, which meant that Herbert, Sam's father, would join them for dinner. His mom played the tape and sang along and cooked, a bigger meal than she ever served when she and Sam were the only ones at the table.

She'd been playing that tape on Herbert's last Thanksgiving, Sam remembered it well. He was fourteen, still short for his age and only beginning to fill out in the shoulders and chest. He didn't shave, didn't have a need to, but that was okay with him, since he liked the smooth feel of his skin and he got the sense that a baby face endeared him to women. Herbert teased him about it sometimes, telling Sam that when he sprouted a few whiskers he'd show him how to hold a razor, though Sam didn't have any interest in learning to shave from Herbert, who had a mustache so bushy that food got stuck in it.

Herbert had gotten meaner as he'd aged. The drinking had gotten worse, too. Oftentimes he stumbled up the steps of the house, lurching, grabbing hold of the doorframe. For a long time Sam hadn't understood why his mom put up with it, but he was becoming aware that love wasn't something you could turn on and off like a faucet.

As Herbert drank more, he ran his Camaro—he'd gotten a new car after being promoted to supervisor—even harder up the mountain to Sam's house. Sam had told his mom he wouldn't ride with Herbert anymore, because he feared for his life, and Sam's mom had laughed, saying, "He's not that bad," but had never pressed Sam on the issue. She must have known he was dangerous. In addition to the drinking and the speeding, Herbert had also gotten rougher with Sam's mom. Some Thursday nights, when they were locked in the bedroom together, Sam heard them screaming at each other, horrible things, words he'd never heard before, and once, after Sam's mom had shouted that Herbert was a "fucking liar and a maniac," Sam had heard a crisp slap.

He had walked into the bedroom. His mom was bent over the bed, hands on her face, sobbing. Herbert was standing next to her, taking deep breaths and looking halfway between rage and misery. Sam expected Herbert to throw him out of the room. He wanted that, looked forward to the opportunity to use his hands to defend himself, even though he knew Herbert had twice his strength.

But his mom was the one who spoke to Sam. She lifted her face from her hands, and Sam saw the red welt forming on her cheek, the blood on her lip, and she said, "Get *out* of here! You know this is none of your business!"

Sam left the room and shut the door behind him. He took an old metal bucket from under the sink in their utility room, then went outside with the bucket and a packet of marshmallows Herbert had given him. He walked around the neighborhood for twenty minutes until he found a squirrel on the sidewalk next to an abandoned lot.

It took some time, but the squirrel finally came forward to sniff the candy. Sam let it eat, then offered another marshmallow. He'd become practiced at this. At last, when the squirrel began to accept the food more readily, Sam clamped the bucket over it. He'd always had sharp reflexes. He heard the squirrel scrabbling at the bucket's walls.

He just held it for a little while, thinking of it as a pet, talking to it, trying to calm it down. Sam only wanted the company. To sit for a minute with a little companionship. He'd always loved animals. Soon he lifted the bucket and let it go.

That year, when Sam was fourteen, Herbert had shown up to the house for Thanksgiving so drunk he could hardly walk and needed to yank himself up the stairs by the doorframe. Sam's mom offered him a beer when he came in—it was a way to minimize his drinking, since otherwise he would have drunk whiskey—but Herbert asked for a tall whiskey, one ice cube, and told Sam's mom to leave the bottle on the table.

That night Herbert had already eaten one Thanksgiving dinner at his other girlfriend's house, since he knew Sam's mom wasn't a great cook. He didn't eat much anymore anyway. He had a beer when he needed nutrition, saying the barley was good for him. Sam remembered watching Herbert doze and lean in his chair as he and his mom ate. Herbert had brought dessert, of course, some kind of pie with crumbled cookies and caramel and drizzled chocolate on top, and he said he was saving room for that.

When the tape clicked off, Sam's mom got up to change it. But when she walked past Herbert, his eyelids opened and his pupils focused. He grabbed a handful of her shirt. He had an animal look in his eyes, and he asked Sam's mom if she'd like to join him in the bedroom.

She giggled, glancing at Sam. "We couldn't. We're in the middle of dinner."

But Sam said, "It's fine. I wanted to take a walk before dessert." He didn't want to deal with their flirting all night anyway.

They went into the bedroom, and Sam poured himself a glass of water. He went outside with it, sipping as he walked.

After a while, Herbert came out of the room with Sam's mom. She was humming "The Quiet House," and Herbert looked clear-eyed, almost sober. Sam nudged the whiskey bottle closer to his glass. But Herbert didn't want any more to drink. He didn't even want his slice of gooey pie, and before Sam's mom could serve it, he was saying he had to get going, had to be at work at six. (That couldn't have been true, since the Jewish Community Center must have celebrated Thanksgiving.) Herbert said he'd enjoyed the dinner, and gave Sam a scratch on the head like you'd give a dog. Sam forced a smile, thinking he'd wash his hair before he got into bed.

Herbert's car started, and he pulled out of the driveway, tires shrieking.

Later, Sam would wonder if it was possible to want something badly enough that the world could make it happen. He'd wished for things many times, but never as feverishly as what he wished for that night.

It was Monday that he found out. Sam came home from school, and his mom wasn't in the house. She didn't work anymore, having inherited the house from her deceased parents, and was living partly off their money, partly off Herbert's, and partly from the earnings of a previous career she'd hinted at but was obviously ashamed of. Sam fixed himself a snack—two breakfast sausages wrapped in a tortilla, his usual—and sat down on the couch, turning on the TV. He flipped through, looking for a good sit-com, mostly getting soaps and talk shows.

Then he clicked over to a local cable station, and on the screen, unbelievably, was a grainy picture of Herbert, who'd been missing for three days. Sam could hardly believe it. He guessed that no one had called his mom because Herbert hadn't told anyone about her.

All of a sudden, Sam was filled with an emotion he'd never experienced before. The best way he could describe it was as a kind of lightness, like he'd been filled with helium all the way to the tips of his fingers. He seemed to be floating an inch above the couch, and nothing in the room felt real.

His mom came in. The newscaster was still talking, but Herbert's picture was no longer on the screen.

"What are you watching?" Sam's mom asked.

Even now, sitting alone with his Thanksgiving dinner, listening to his Jean Raeburn tape, waiting for Julia to call, it didn't feel real to Sam, his dad's death. It seemed like something out of a book, or a dream, not his own life. In the days following that TV news report, Sam and his mom learned that Herbert's Camaro had been found. He'd been speeding down the mountain on Thursday night—it must have been on his way back from visiting Sam and his mom—and he'd lost control on a curve, hopped a guardrail, and dropped right off the cliff. The car exploded in flames. It was burned so badly it took the police four days to identify the body, finally linking it with reports of a missing janitorial supervisor. They had to identify him by his teeth. The police questioned Sam and his mom, and they both admitted Herbert had been drinking.

Sam thought he'd go to bed early tonight. It was silly to think Julia would call on a holiday. She was home with her parents, sitting at the table. She must have wanted to get up and give Sam a buzz, but it would have been impossible to do it with her family around, especially since her dad knew about a boyfriend and probably hated the idea of it. That was okay. Sam could win him over later, once Julia had made up her mind.

The song was ending, and Sam heard those final words he loved: "One day you'll find me waiting/As the light is slowly fading/In a quiet house that's built for two/And one is me and one is you." How could you say it better than that? Who could sing it with more feeling than Jean?

He was still lost in those last phrases when the knocking started, three solid raps on Sam's door, startling him from daydreaming. He put down his fork. Who would visit him on a holiday? His downstairs neighbor Vic hadn't even once come to say hi. No one at work knew where he lived. The only possibility was Julia. She must have gotten in a fight with her parents over Sam, told them she couldn't stay in the house with them if they didn't accept the man she planned to marry, and then stormed out.

She'd taken the train all the way back to Stradler, was standing now at Sam's door.

Three more knocks. Sam got up from his chair, trying to calm his breathing, and walked to the door. Before he opened it, he looked into the peephole.

It wasn't Julia standing on his welcome mat; it was a man in a police uniform.

CHAPTER 28
The Dining Hall

❦

The atmosphere on campus had gotten tense. For the past two weeks, since the second rape, Julia had seen it posted in the library that campus security was on "high alert." Stradler had instituted a "safe walk" policy, which required women to walk with at least one other person after 10:00 P.M. There were volunteer student patrol groups that went out every night with flashlights, looking for suspicious men. Campus security cars drove along the footpaths, shining their high beams into pockets of darkness. Julia heard girls in her classes talking about carrying pepper spray or razor blades. It felt like the campus was under siege. She probably wasn't the only one having nightmares.

Julia had ended up leaving her parents' house early on Thanksgiving weekend, but she was too afraid to come back to campus during the holiday, so she rented a cheap motel room where she found a grease stain and several long, curly hairs on her sheets. Charming place. Still, it was better than being by herself in the dorm.

The trip gave her time to think about whom she could go to for advice. Not Leanette. Not her parents. Not her high school friends. Who was left?

She didn't want to have a child, not now, maybe not ever. A baby wouldn't nap during trumpet practice. You couldn't leave a baby for three weeks while your orchestra went on tour. Somehow, even though Julia hadn't been able to pick up her horn in nearly a year, she couldn't imagine a future without music. It had always been the destination toward which her life traveled. She remembered the first time she'd heard Rafael Méndez on an old record, the sound of his horn so sharp and hot it seemed to cut through the static, the ticking needle, the poor recording, even time itself. The beauty was so intense that it felt close to pain. It had filled her eyes with tears. She'd wanted nothing more from life than to make that sound.

What about Sam? Could she tell him about the pregnancy? He was a pretty big part of this, too. If she didn't have the baby, could she ask him for help? Help to get rid of it? She didn't know what Sam would want her to do. Julia didn't think he'd want a baby any more than she did, but there was always a chance he'd fight with her, tell her to have it, that it was his baby, too.

She didn't love Sam, never could love Sam, she knew it now. He was a sweet person, a sympathetic listener, and she'd appreciated being able to share her darker self with him, but the pregnancy had made it clear to Julia that they'd never end up together. Their worlds were too different, too distant, and she'd never really be able to joke with him. As much as they talked, she felt that they both kept equally much to themselves.

So maybe it was better to hold off from telling him. What could he really do that Julia couldn't? Maybe it was better to take care of this herself without anyone ever knowing. To go on exactly as if it hadn't happened. Plenty of people did that, and they got by just fine.

In the weeks after Thanksgiving, Julia spent most of her time by herself. She'd hardly seen Leanette, who was basically living with Drew now. It seemed like Thanksgiving break had gone well.

Leanette said that Drew's parents had invited her to join them on a trip to France over the summer.

"They were so *liberal*," Leanette said, one time when Julia bumped into her in the room. "They let me sleep in the guest bed with Drew the first night I got there, no questions asked."

"What kind of questions were you expecting?"

"Oh, I don't know. What high school did you go to? Who's your hero? When was the last time you got tested for herpes? I have no idea. I've never done this before. I know *my* parents would have asked for a Breathalyzer and a full résumé with cover letter."

"How about references? That could be awkward."

"They'd be calling his third-grade girlfriend, asking if he slipped her the tongue."

They talked like that for a bit, and Julia enjoyed sliding back into their old routine. After a few minutes, she thought of something she needed to ask.

"By the way," Julia said, "I saw Drew the other day. Right before break. He was getting your camera. He said you gave him the key."

Leanette frowned, thinking about it. "I don't think so. But I guess it's possible. Honestly, I can't remember. I asked him to do about fifty different things before we left. I almost feel bad. But it's probably better he knows what the future holds."

"He didn't say he ran into me?"

Leanette shook her head. "And it's weird. Because he's always asking about you. If I wasn't so secure, I'd almost think he had a crush."

Julia was going to mention that he'd been looking in her desk, but before she could, Leanette said she had to run and slipped out the door.

Since Leanette was so busy, Julia was eating most of her meals alone. She liked going to the dining hall at unpopular times, ten thirty in the morning, three in the afternoon, when almost no students were there. She just wasn't up for a lot of small talk. Once, in the last week of finals, Julia was carrying her tray to a table by the window in the small room—the least popular room in the dining hall—when she saw a girl at one of the other tables. The girl had a broad face and sleepy eyelids. Julia almost passed by her, but when she got close, she realized who it was. Claudia Ortiz, the girl from Julia's orientation group whom she'd seen in the health center the day she found out she was pregnant.

Maybe part of the reason Julia hadn't recognized Claudia was that she was alone. In the first few months of classes, that had never happened. She'd always been surrounded by friends, at meals, at parties, on field trips. Everything was thrilling to Claudia, you could see it in her face. She looked like she was standing in line for a carnival ride. She'd been one of those people who just saw life as an exciting adventure.

But now she seemed completely different. She sat there, stabbing mechanically at her food, a flat expression on her face.

None of the articles had mentioned Claudia's name. But the second rape had happened that morning when Julia saw her in the health center, when the receptionist told Julia that the doctor was running a couple minutes late because something had come up. And Stradler was too small for people not to whisper, not to guess. Claudia, Julia understood, was the second victim.

On a whim, Julia asked if she could join her.

"Oh," Claudia said, looking surprised. "Sure."

Julia put her tray on the table, and already it felt awkward. She had no idea what to say to Claudia, how to start a conversation they wouldn't both hate, or even why she'd asked to sit down. What was she thinking? *How's it going? What have you been up to?* Every line that came to mind seemed ridiculous.

But it turned out Claudia started the conversation. "I'm sorry I didn't say hi to you that day in the health center. I guess you figured out why I was there."

It startled Julia, her directness. She wasn't sure how to respond. For a second she didn't know if Claudia was testing her, if she should pretend she didn't know anything, but then Julia realized all of

Claudia's friends must have figured it out, too. Julia was surprised Claudia would want to talk about it, but maybe when something like that happens to you, it feels silly to talk about anything else.

"I'm so sorry," Julia finally said.

It happened in an instant: Claudia's eyes filled with tears. She wasn't crying, at least not in the way you normally mean when you say someone is crying. Tears were just rolling out of her eyes, and she was hardly even moving.

Julia thought she needed to say something, so she asked, "How are you feeling?" She guessed Claudia would talk about how angry she was.

But instead, Claudia said, "I just keep thinking how stupid I was. How much of an idiot I was to walk back by myself. My uncle told me not to do that. He told me to call him if I needed a ride or someone to walk with. He gave me all these lectures about how I had to protect myself, and it wasn't safe for a young woman to be out by herself and all that. But I didn't think it would happen. Not here. Not to me. I thought I was safe. I'm so stupid you can't even believe it."

"No," Julia said, shaking her head. "You couldn't have known."

"It's my fault. Don't you see that?" Claudia's eyes kept spilling tears. "It's my fault for being so stupid."

Julia kept shaking her head, but she didn't know what else to say. She knew what it was like for an event to divide your life, so that the before and after seemed like two different lives. She could understand how you'd beat yourself up over a little mistake like that, a mistake anyone could have made, but it just happened to be you who made it. People could tell you a million times it was okay, it wasn't your fault, but you never believed it. And all you could do was keep going, eat your meals and do your homework and smile when you were supposed to smile, pretend it never happened, pretend you felt just fine, keep skimming over the surface of life and hope to God you didn't get sucked under.

"I just keep remembering it," Claudia said, shaking her head like a machine that wasn't working. Julia wanted to tell her it was going to be okay, tell her all the comforting and useless things people had told Julia, but she knew they wouldn't help.

"I keep hearing him," Claudia went on. "I never saw him. Just heard him whisper not to turn around or he'd hurt me. The sickest part was that while he was doing it, he sang to me. Do you believe that? He sang. I don't know if he was trying to calm me down or if he couldn't help it or what. But he was singing in this high voice. Like a kids' song. I can't get it out of my head."

"I'm sorry," Julia said again, but this time her voice was distant. She was somewhere else, in another room, and she was hearing that singing herself, that strained, high singing, drifting through her window as she slept.

CHAPTER 29
The Glove

❦

They were sitting around a table.

All of them were there, his ex-girlfriends: Claire and Marilyn and Patrice and Alyssa and Naomi. It was a round table, on a patio with smooth, brown tiles warmed by the sun. They passed food between them, talking and eating. They had wine and were using good plates and silverware. You could hear the clinking of glasses and the knocking of bowls being set down. It was late afternoon.

When Sam came onto the patio, they fell silent. They covered their mouths, as if he'd interrupted a private conversation. He could tell they were laughing at something. He asked what it was.

"Nothing," Claire told him.

"Really, you can tell me."

But they wouldn't. Sam noticed a large white platter in the middle of the table, covered by a metal dome like the food on a hotel tray. He asked what was under the dome.

That seemed to make them laugh harder. They were all so broken up that none of them could answer. Every time one of them opened her mouth, she was overtaken by a storm of giggling, her eyes filling with tears.

"If you don't tell me, I'm going to look myself."

They shook their heads, waving him off.

"Then *tell* me," he said.

Alyssa was laughing so hard she fell out of her chair. When her ass bumped the tiles, everyone else started cackling at her, even Claire, who rarely laughed. Soon Patrice had fallen out of her chair, too. Sam looked at her. She normally wore hiking boots and jeans, but tonight she was wearing a silver dress, and she'd had her hair curled.

"That's it," Sam said, and reached for the cover.

"No!" Marilyn screamed.

Naomi covered her eyes.

Alyssa let out a raucous belch.

Sam lifted the lid off the platter, and what he saw was so obvious and horrible he couldn't have put it into words.

"We told you," Marilyn said.

"You never listened," Claire said.

Sam's cell phone started ringing, waking him. It was early, before five. He saw that it was a private number and picked up, hoping for Julia.

But instead he heard that familiar strained whisper: "Things have been quiet," the caller said. "They've got the campus locked down. Nothing's going on. You're keeping to yourself."

"I always do," Sam said, at the edge of his patience.

The caller, whom Sam knew was Marcus, made a wheezy sound Sam took to be a laugh. "That's very funny. You're funny. But the thing is, I know you can't help yourself. You're losing control. You're going to do it again. And it's going to be your last time."

"I'm glad you know me so well." It seemed sarcasm was the best tack with the boy, who'd called Sam at least a half dozen times since the Thanksgiving weekend. He didn't respond to reason.

"Everyone knows you," the boy said. "Everyone's watching you. They're going to catch you very soon. Probably this week. Even the police are stopping by your apartment."

"Because you're telling them lies about me."

The boy laughed again, then hung up. Sam had thought the calls would stop after he'd talked to Marcus in the parking lot outside the boy's dorm. But strangely, they'd become more frequent, as if the boy were goading Sam. And another thing. Sam had started to receive text messages on his phone. The messages weren't explicit, but they were ambiguously threatening, saying things like, *You look anxious.* They came from a number Sam didn't recognize, though he suspected it was Marcus's. The one time he'd called it he'd gotten one of those machines that read the number back to you in a computer-ized voice, which didn't tell him anything.

Sam had spent most of his Thanksgiving night in the West-bury police station, answering questions about his encounter with Marcus, who'd called the police to report an assault. The officer, who looked bored and impatient and had taken an unnecessarily bullying tone with Sam, had let up once Sam explained that he'd had an ongoing conflict with Marcus, a spoiled Stradler student who tormented him at work, and who had possibly thrown a rock through Sam's window. Sam said the officer could call his landlord to verify he'd had to fix that. The police officer didn't seem to have very kind feelings toward the students, and shared a story with Sam about a kid who had puked on him the past weekend when he was removing the kid from someone's lawn. In the end, Marcus dropped his charges. It must have been clear to the police that Marcus had instigated the whole dispute.

Still, Sam had lost a night of sleep, which had affected the rest of his week. And the interview had caused him more than a little anxiety, being dragged into a police station like that.

Sometimes, when Sam woke up in the middle of the night, he thought of calling Julia. Of everyone, she was the one who would sympathize with him. She was the one who would trust in Sam's good intentions. But he was afraid to risk upsetting her, causing another unpleasant scene like the one they'd had in the courtyard.

Sam wasn't going to get back to sleep now, so he decided to get ready for work. He needed to make a good impression on Horacio anyway, since the manager had been on Sam's case after the joke he'd told about the girl baking bread. Sam felt horribly misunderstood.

"You look like my nuts after Megan's done with them," Lonnie told Sam in the stockroom. "What's going on?"

Sam let out a breath. "Rough week."

"You on a bender or something?"

Sam shook his head. "I don't drink."

Lonnie appeared disturbed by the news. He examined Sam with a puzzled look, as if Sam had revealed he suffered from a rare disease. "Maybe you should start."

Sam tried to smile, but thought it probably looked more like a grimace.

Behind the counter, he was slower than he'd ever been. The line piled up, extending out the door, down the hall, around the corner, and Sam felt as if he'd never be able to make all those sandwiches. He was mixing up orders, giving people cheese when they hadn't asked for any, making the same sandwich twice when he'd gotten a completely new order. He was sinking, nothing to grab on to. He didn't know how he'd make it through the day.

Finally, the lunchtime rush of students slowed, then stopped. It was two thirty, he could see by the clock over Megan's head. Sam had never been one to watch the clock. He'd always enjoyed work, the energy it required, the use it made of what he deemed to be his particular set of skills. But now he felt as if he were being driven into the ground by it.

It was almost three when Marcus walked in. Sam didn't understand why the boy would come here for lunch. It was a five-minute walk down the hill to the dining hall. He must have had a small break between his classes, or wasn't on a full meal plan. Or maybe he liked bothering Sam.

Before the boy could order, Sam started in on him: "You know the police came to my apartment over the holiday."

Marcus shrugged. "I didn't know what you were going to do. I guess I didn't have a choice. Should we call a truce?"

"I lost a night of sleep." Sam felt the pressure of eyes on him, and he thought Lonnie might have been watching him from the grill, but he didn't care anymore. He had things he needed to say. "Just leave me *alone*."

"That's what I want, man. You're the one who approached me."

What was the boy doing, messing with him this way? He called with disgusting allegations in the morning, then came to ask for a truce in the afternoon?

"You're making up lies," Sam said. "You're trying to turn people against me. But it's not working."

"Look," Marcus said, and Sam could see that hint of a smile on his lips, "I don't know what your deal is. But there's clearly something wrong. You should get some help."

Sam couldn't take it anymore. Where did this boy get the nerve to come into his workplace and tell him there was something wrong with him? Sam felt as if buckles were tightening over his chest, and before he knew it, he'd taken off his rubber glove. He threw it in frustration, as hard as he could, into Marcus's face. He knew the glove wouldn't hurt the boy, but still, he savored the release of anger. Marcus blinked when it hit him.

Before the glove fell to the floor, Sam heard the words behind him. "Oh, no," Horacio said. "Oh fucking no. I don't believe you."

Sam turned around and saw both Lonnie and Horacio staring at him, Lonnie in confusion, Horacio appearing on the verge of violence. The manager grabbed Sam by the upper part of his arm, hard, and said to him, "You're done. I don't want to hear a word out of you. That's it." He was speaking through his teeth. He shoved Sam toward the door with his oversized hand.

Marcus was shaking his head, that grin on his face. Even Megan was watching.

"Get the fuck out now," Horacio said. He started to turn, but something prevented him. "You yelled at a *student*. What the hell is in your mind?"

Sam took off his apron and walked out of the snack bar. He wanted Julia. He needed her. He'd lost everyone else. Julia was his only chance, the only one who could understand how badly he'd been treated. He had to find her before Marcus did.

Sam started down the hill toward Julia's dorm. It was the most likely place for her to be. He took the path through the woods, not wanting to be seen coming through town. The ground was frozen, and the air had a metallic smell. Sam's breath clouded as he strode along, not caring about turning an ankle or tripping on a rock. Above him, bare tree branches scraped in the wind.

It was as if he'd been carrying an armful of dishes, and now they were slipping from his grasp, one by one, falling and shattering on the floor. It was the way he'd felt just before things had ended with Naomi, in the woods at Backbone State Park. He remembered walking behind her, her feet rustling the plants, the sweat on the back of her neck, and feeling this way, like his whole life was gathering into one dark point.

Always, when things started to go badly in his life, he had this feeling. With Marilyn by the Charles. With Patrice on that empty beach. He'd known those times that everything was about to change, that they were going to leave him, that he'd end up packing his things and moving on once again, not being able to bear the loss. Even though he understood this was his life, that he was a wanderer, it was always hard to leave a place once he'd settled there. The truth was, he had never let go of things easily, moved on. A preservationist doesn't move on, Sam thought. A preservationist takes loss as a great betrayal.

He couldn't stay here, at Stradler, without a job. He'd have to move far away, probably across the country, to a place where Horacio wouldn't know anyone and they wouldn't check Sam's references. It would be tough, but not impossible. And of course Julia might be with him. That could still happen. It would make everything bearable.

He crossed the slatted bridge over the creek in three long strides. The mouth of the woods opened onto a lawn that appeared washed out by the cold. And just as Sam stepped onto the grass, into the clear winter light, an image came to him, struck him really, out of nowhere it seemed.

The image was of a girl lying on her back, her hair pooled behind her. Her face was hard to make out, blurry, but he could see she was sleeping. He didn't know where the image had come from, but it was so simple and sweet that it calmed him.

Then it was over. Darkness dropped on the image, and suddenly Sam saw the field again, the path to Julia's dorm. It was as if he'd been watching a play that felt so true he couldn't take his eyes off it, and the objects in front of him, the grass and trees and buildings, were like a curtain fallen over the action, separating him from the dream that was more real than life.

He stood in the field, breathing. The image of the girl had been so clear that it was almost like a memory. But when Sam reached for it again, there was a barrier, like a pane of glass he couldn't shatter. So he let it go.

Now he walked through the courtyard, past the cement bench, toward Julia's dorm. He took out his phone and dialed her number, heard it ring once, twice, three times, and then the machine picked up. He hung up. He walked around to the back where her window was, tried to look in, see if she was there, but the room was dark.

He walked back to the courtyard and waited there, his fingers and toes vibrating with cold. He didn't have the appropriate clothes on, and he shivered in the wind. For forty minutes he stood there, waiting.

At last, when his hands and feet were numb, Sam decided to leave. His thoughts were swirling, his lips dull as stones, and he wasn't sure he'd be able to speak to Julia even if he had the opportunity. He walked out of the courtyard, and just as he was about to turn up the path toward the parking lot where he'd left his van, he saw them.

Julia and Marcus were standing at the mouth of the woods, next to the slatted wooden bridge Sam had crossed a little while ago. They were talking in a way that appeared intimate, the way couples talk in restaurants. Sam couldn't believe it. He was too stunned to speak. He watched as Marcus nodded and talked, and then the boy reached out and took Julia's hand, squeezing it.

It felt to Sam as if it were his own heart the boy was squeezing.

He thought about running up to them, yelling, pulling them apart, explaining to Julia all that had happened. But he knew how that would look. It would look like he was the one who was crazy.

So he turned and walked away, keeping his jacket collar over his face so they wouldn't notice him. He was so angry he could have killed the boy.

But he walked back to his van.

CHAPTER 30
The Real Friend

J ulia was lying on a metal table at the end of a long white hallway. There was a nurse standing next to her who said, "Don't worry, honey," and looked toward the far end of the hallway. Julia guessed she was waiting for the doctor to come.

"What time does it start?" Julia asked her.

"Soon," the nurse said. She had wiry gray hair that curled out from under the elastic band of her nurse's cap. Her skin was so smooth, the smoothest Julia had ever seen, and her cheeks were red like a girl's.

"How long have you been doing this?" Julia asked. It was the way she'd thought of to figure out the woman's age.

"Since my daughter was born," the nurse said, which didn't help much.

Julia heard footsteps approaching from the other end of the hallway. There was a figure in scrubs coming toward her, his pants rustling as he walked. A faint beeping came from one of the rooms in the hallway. Julia already felt cold and a little sick from the medicine they'd given her.

"How long does it take?" she asked.

But the nurse didn't answer. She was facing away from Julia, getting something ready. Metal instruments scraped and clicked on a tray, hidden from Julia by the nurse's broad back. Julia was getting queasy, the way she always did sitting in a doctor's chair, waiting for whatever horrible thing they were about to stick in her.

"Does it hurt?" Julia said, a little frantic now.

Again, the nurse didn't answer. She was busy with whatever she was preparing, and Julia got the idea that maybe she wasn't speaking as loudly as she'd thought, maybe the drugs were affecting her speech. She felt close to passing out. The doctor was coming. Julia heard him talking to someone, but suddenly she realized she couldn't even lift her head to see what he looked like.

Finally, the nurse turned back to her. But now she looked different. She was older than Julia had remembered, probably in her sixties, and her skin wasn't smooth at all. Julia didn't know what she could have been thinking before.

The nurse held something up to Julia on a tray. Julia couldn't make out what it was. It looked like chicken pieces in a sauce, and she wasn't sure if it was supposed to be food or medicine.

So she said to the nurse, "What is it?"

The nurse laughed and said, "It's your baby. You're all done."

Julia woke up in her room. It was sunny. She couldn't tell how long she'd been sleeping, but she didn't think it was very long. She'd made the appointment at the abortion clinic in Milltown a few days before. She was supposed to go in the morning after her music final, December seventeenth. The dorms stayed open until the twenty-third, and Julia had told her parents she had a final on that last day, so she'd have six days to recover in her room if everything went as planned.

All week she'd been telling herself that it was just like getting a tooth pulled, a little pinch, over before she knew it. And while she could basically convince herself of that, a strange thing had started to happen. She began to feel like the little chores that filled her days—walking to class or taking an exam or eating lunch—weren't real. Like they were all part of a game she was playing. It seemed like everything she did was a distraction from her real life, a shadowy thing that tunneled deep below this game.

Leanette was leaving the next day on a flight to Drew's parents' house. She was going to spend Christmas there before heading to her parents' place for New Year's.

On her way out to Drew's room she said to Julia, "Please feel free to use the room for any amount of wild sex you'd like."

"I'll put down a tarp," Julia said.

Leanette laughed. "How do you always have an answer for everything?"

Julia looked at her, surprised. "It just seems like that. I'm pretty clueless about most things."

Leanette shrugged. "I guess everyone feels that way."

They hugged and said goodbye.

The music final tomorrow morning was Julia's last. She was ready for the written section, but needed to brush up on the listening section, where they had to identify some composers and pieces, so she decided to head to the music library where they kept the practice CDs.

On her way out, the phone started to ring. She debated letting the machine take it, but thought it might be the abortion clinic, so she picked up.

"Hello?"

"Hey, Julie. Your dad here."

"Hey. I'm on my way out."

"I'm sorry to bug ya, honey. I just wanted to give you a quick message that your mom and I are gonna be away for a few days. Since you're not going to be home, your mom planned a little hop over to the Caribbean. Antigua. She got us some last-minute tickets. We're headed out tomorrow, bright and early."

"How long are you going for?"

"Well, the only way we could get the deal was to fly back on New Year's Eve. It was a tough decision, missing Christmas with you, sweetie. But I hope we'll have a good celebration when we get back."

She assumed the tough decision had mostly been her mom's. "That's fine," Julia said. "Thanks for letting me know."

"We'll stick the key under the mat and some food in the fridge. Just get a cab home from the station. I'll leave a little cash for you to pay the driver."

"Okay, thanks."

"You okay, honey? You sound a little distracted."

For one moment, Julia had the wild idea that she could tell him everything, right then, about Sam and the pregnancy and the appointment. She wanted to share this with someone, to have someone tell her she wasn't ruining her whole life.

But she couldn't even imagine how to begin. Or what he could possibly say to help her.

"I'm fine," Julia said. "Just busy with finals. Have a good trip. Don't drink too many mai tais."

It was better he'd be far away. There wouldn't be a chance of him calling just after the operation, asking how she was doing and if there was anything special she wanted for Christmas. Julia didn't know how she was going to feel when it was over. She'd looked on the Internet, but of course people wrote about all the worst cases, the bleeding and the infections. People really loved to lay it on in the message boards. After about ten minutes of searching, Julia decided it was better not knowing, to just go ahead and not think about it.

She spent a couple hours in the music library, listening to the discs and making notes. She'd thought it would be hard to study, but it turned out to be easier than ever. With the headphones cupped over her ears, the music pouring in, Julia felt like a different person, cut off from her past. It was something she'd learned after the accident, to simply shut the door.

As she left the library, a little before three, she actually felt okay. She'd be able to pass the music final. She'd get through the operation. Someday she was going to look back on all this, and it would seem smaller in memory.

As she was coming down the steps of the music building, Julia saw Marcus coming up. He must have been on his way to study. His cheeks were flushed, probably from the wind, and he had one of those weird grins on his face, like he was thinking about something private. He was looking at the ground.

"Hey," Julia said to him.

"Oh, *hey*," he said with exaggerated surprise, looking up at her. "That's so weird. I was just thinking about you."

"Why? You need drugs or something?"

He smiled. "I just had a run-in with someone you know."

"Really? Who?"

He hesitated, looked around like he wanted to make sure he wasn't being followed. Then he said, "I wouldn't have said anything. I just think maybe you should know about it. Where are you headed?"

"My room."

"Mind if I walk with you?"

Something about his appearance seemed timed, like he knew he'd find Julia here. He sounded eager, and she had the sense he was gearing up for a serious talk that she wasn't sure she had the energy for. Julia wanted to tell him she was busy, she couldn't walk with him, but no excuses came to mind.

"Sure," she said, "but I have to hustle. I still have a lot of studying to do."

They took the path through the woods, out of habit. But as soon as they sank into the cool stillness of the trees, Julia realized that she'd probably made the wrong decision. It was more private here than in town, and she remembered the last time Marcus and she had had a "serious" talk, in the courtyard, when he'd gotten angry about Sam. There seemed to be some trouble, some worry or pain in him, and she couldn't say why, but it made her uncomfortable.

As they walked, Marcus talked to her, told her things about Sam. He said Sam had threatened him, put his hand on Marcus's throat before Thanksgiving break, and just a few minutes ago Sam had thrown a plastic glove into Marcus's face in the snack bar. Everyone had seen it, Marcus said. You could ask anyone. Sam had accused Marcus of calling him and harassing him, of telling lies about who Sam was and things he'd done.

"It was crazy," Marcus said. "The guy is weird. I never said anything about him."

It all seemed so distant and strange, the scene Marcus was describing. And Julia couldn't understand why he felt he needed to keep telling her these stories about Sam. If he thought she was making a bad decision, she didn't understand why he wouldn't just let her make it.

"I'm sorry to tell you all this," Marcus said. "I know it's awkward, and probably painful for you, but I thought they were things you needed to know."

"It is a little awkward," she said, not responding to his comment about pain.

He started telling her about how he'd pressed charges against Sam after Sam had assaulted him in the parking lot. He'd figured the police might find something in Sam's record, but nothing came of it. Marcus said he'd done an Internet search on Sam. It turned out he had such a common name that there was no way to track him, but he still had a bad feeling about him.

"I don't know what your relationship is like, but I would steer clear of him," Marcus said. "I'm not saying he's doing all these things, these rapes, on campus. But I wouldn't even test it."

Really? Julia thought. *You're really going to slip that in?* It seemed low to her, even cruel, to insert that last bit about the rapes.

They crossed the slatted bridge, the whispering creek. When they reached the other side, they stopped and faced each other.

"I'm just saying this because I'm worried about you," Marcus said now. "You seem so quiet. I don't know if it's because you don't believe me or because this is all hard to take or what, but I don't want you to think I had some other motive."

"Okay," Julia said, still troubled that Marcus had become so involved. Why would he care so much?

"Well," Marcus said, his neck pushing his head forward in that hunched posture, "I've probably bothered you enough. And I have to get back to studying. But I wanted to tell you I got a new cell phone. I wanted to give you my number." He took out a receipt from his wallet and wrote the number on it. He had a child's handwriting, large, shaky letters that couldn't stay on a straight line. "Anyway, if you ever need someone to walk with, or if you just feel nervous for some reason, you can call me. You know that, right?"

"Thanks."

He passed her the paper. When Julia took it from him, he gave her hand a squeeze. The gesture felt strange, too familiar. The whole discussion was weird, his accusations and his insistence about Sam.

"I mean it. Anytime, you can call me." Marcus let go of her hand.

At that moment Julia remembered a detail about him. "By the way, you said you're in Rackoff's class, right?"

He seemed puzzled by the question. "Yeah, I mean, like half the freshman and sophomore classes are. Why?"

"Someone was just talking about it the other day."

He looked away for a moment, like he was thinking about something, then turned back to Julia and said, "Anyway, if I don't see you, have a good break."

"You, too," she said, pushing the paper into her pocket and leaving him by the bridge.

That night in her room, as she was flipping through the music theory textbook, Julia kept thinking about what Marcus had told her during their walk. He hadn't accused Sam of being the rapist, but he'd gotten about as close as you could.

As she was thinking about it, she heard a tapping sound. It seemed at first like it was coming from far away. But then she heard it again, louder. Her shade was drawn, but she was sure something was tapping on the glass.

She thought of leaving her room. Dreams or not, there were so many odd things happening lately that Julia didn't even want to see who or what might be out there. Or worse, that she was imagining it.

But what was she going to do? Call the cops about a tapping sound? She needed to study, and it was too late to go to the library, too loud outside in the lounge. The dorm was full tonight, and if she screamed, lots of people would hear.

So she opened the shade. Standing outside, in the dim light from her room, was Sam. He had a bandage on his face, and what looked like scratches around his eyes. He had a scared, desperate look, and he motioned for Julia to open the window.

"Oh God, what happened to you?" Julia asked when she opened it.

"Can I come in for a minute?" he said. "I think it's important."

CHAPTER 31
The Truth

"What happened to you?" she asked him again when they were sitting on her bed. She could see now that he'd been badly hurt. His lip was swollen, and he had a dark bruise forming on his cheek. He looked vulnerable and sad, like a kid who'd been bullied. Julia guessed he'd been in some kind of fight, that someone had done this to him, but she wasn't sure.

"I just got back from the hospital," he said. "I got mugged. I guess that's not the right word. They didn't take my money. I got jumped. By three guys. They caught me in the parking lot. I was going to my van. They said I was the rapist. They were sure of it." He stopped to breathe, then swallowed hard like he had a sore throat.

"Why would they say that?" Julia asked.

"Marcus is telling people that. He's telling everyone. He's been harassing me, Julia. He calls. He threatens me. He won't leave me alone."

"Did you see who did this to you?"

He was shaking his head. "I didn't see anything. It was so dark. They were all wearing masks."

He just kept shaking his head, like he couldn't believe this was his life. What was happening? Why were they both approaching her with these stories about each other? Why did her opinion matter so much?

"What's happening between you two?" she asked. "Marcus told me you grabbed his throat."

"I know he talked to you. I saw you guys walking together earlier. I know he's trying to convince you I'm a bad person."

Julia didn't say anything to that.

"I did it to defend myself, Julia. He's trying to turn everyone against me. Telling these horrible lies. I know he's calling me at night, even though he won't admit it."

"Did anyone else see what happened when you grabbed him?"

"He called the police. They questioned me. When I explained what happened, they let me go. They know his story doesn't make any sense. He tried to tell them I was the rapist."

"Why would he say that?"

"I don't know. I told him I was having dinner with you on October twelfth, the night of the first rape. I've read all the articles. I know the facts. He knows it's impossible."

Just then she couldn't remember the date they'd eaten at the Italian restaurant, but she knew he wasn't lying. Why would Marcus keep tossing out that accusation about the rapes? He'd done it with Julia earlier in the woods. It seemed like he wanted to plant that suspicion in everyone's minds.

"This is all crazy to me," she said. "Everything you're both telling me. I don't understand what's going on between you two, but I don't want to be a part of it."

Sam closed his eyes and breathed from his nose. Then he opened them and said, "I'm sorry, Julia. I'm so sorry this is happening. That you're getting dragged into it. But the thing is, I don't think you can separate yourself from it. You're a part of it. It's about you, in a way. I think you're the reason he's doing this."

"What do you mean?"

"I'll show you something." He reached into his pocket, and the thought crossed Julia's mind that it could have been almost anything he was going to pull out of there. What did he mean to prove to her? That all of this was her fault?

He took out his cell phone. "Look," he said, holding it up so she could see the screen. He pressed some buttons. "These are the text messages I've gotten since Thanksgiving."

He scrolled through half a dozen texts, spread over the last two weeks:

You okay?
You look anxious.
Is anything wrong?
Can you breathe?
It seems like everybody's watching you.
Do you worry a lot?

Julia watched him, and could hardly believe what he was showing her. It was so amazing, it was almost funny. She had the familiar thought that maybe she was losing her grip on reality. She didn't know why, but in that moment, she imagined herself as a little black dot someone was seeing from outer space, the tiniest speck in a telescope lens.

"Do you recognize the number?" Sam said. "I'm not sure, but I think I figured it out."

It was Marcus's old cell phone. Julia had dialed the number a dozen times after the night Marcus had seen her kissing Sam, when she'd wanted to apologize. She'd felt so bad for Marcus then.

"It's Marcus," Julia said. "I can't believe it." Was that why he'd gotten a new phone? Because he didn't want Sam to call him back?

"It's a game to him. He just wants to hurt me, to make me suffer. He's jealous because you chose me. He came into my work and taunted me. He acts like nothing's happening, because he knows how frustrating that is. He's using all this stuff about the rapes to get me, to punish me for being with you. And that night we came back and found the broken window? I thought it was just a kid in the neighborhood, but I don't think so anymore."

"I don't know what to say. I really don't."

"You don't have to say anything. I just want you to know the truth, Julia. To know me. That's all I've ever wanted. For you to know I'm a good person and that I care about you."

CHAPTER 32
Sam at Home

⌐━━◆━━⌐

Back in his apartment, Sam started reading a new book, a novel called *The Sportswriter*, by a writer whose short stories Sam had enjoyed. It was a good novel, elegantly written, striking that perfect pitch between irony and earnestness. It reminded him of other books he'd loved, *The Moviegoer* in particular—something in the searching quality of the sentences, the respect for the mystery in everyday things.

In spite of losing his job, in spite of his bruised face, Sam felt more fresh and alert than he had in weeks. All of the drama had been helpful, in its way. It had cleared his mind, reminded him what was important. He'd be able to get another job. His face would heal. It wasn't even hurting much anymore. These were temporary annoyances, and it would be worth all this pain and more if Julia changed her mind about him.

And it seemed she might have. He could see the impact his story had made on her by the expression on her face. She was shocked to learn the tricks Marcus had played, the lengths he'd gone to to spoil the relationship Sam had worked so hard to build with Julia. Anyone would have been appalled by that.

Sitting there, in his mom's chair, Sam thought about the complicated connection between truth and fiction. He knew there was a way in which people could see the story he'd told Julia as a lie, and it would have been impossible to convince them otherwise, even though Sam believed wholeheartedly that there was a deeper truth in it.

He was aware of the point at which his story broke off from fact, which was different in his mind from truth. It was when he'd been walking back to his van, after he'd seen Marcus squeezing Julia's hand. In reality, he hadn't gotten jumped by three masked men who'd accused him of being the rapist.

What actually happened was that he'd gotten into his van and driven home. Back in his apartment, Sam had gone to the bathroom, stood in front of the mirror, and looked at himself. Normally he would have taken out the tweezers and moisturizers and whitening strips, hoping these familiar routines would calm him. But that afternoon he'd done something different. He'd opened his hand and smacked himself hard across the face.

For a moment, it seemed as if someone had turned the volume down in his right ear, then it was replaced by a ringing, a cleansing rush of pain. Sam stood there, watching the cheek turn red, the blood flowing beneath the skin. He breathed, relishing the clarity of his anger.

Then he made a fist and did it again.

Twenty minutes later, he was done with the beating, and he took out the bandages from his medicine cabinet. Some of the wounds were still bleeding, and his face had begun to swell, but even so, he washed the cuts, first with soap and water, then with alcohol. He began to bandage himself. He took time to make sure all of the tape was placed down evenly, smoothing it with his fingertips. He washed his mouth out with a mixture of water and hydrogen peroxide, spitting a liquid that was threaded with blood into the basin.

As he was finishing with the bandages, his cell phone had begun to ring. The phone showed a private number, and Sam had picked up.

"It's almost over," the caller whispered. "You lost your job, you don't have anything left."

"I have Julia."

"She knows all about you now. I told her everything. There's no chance she'd get within a mile of you."

"You're wrong. She trusts me and she's going to know the truth."

"The truth is you're a rapist."

"We've gone over this. It's impossible. I was having dinner with Julia when one of the rapes happened."

"What about that tear in your sweater? Where do you think you got that?"

"What tear?"

"The one in the sweater you were wearing that night at the restaurant. You got it from the girl in Harmonyville, the one who got away from you. She tore it with her nails and then ran away and you drove back to have your dinner. You had plenty of time to get back and make your reservation. You were fifteen minutes late. I figured it out. That's how it happened!"

"Don't gloat. You didn't figure anything out. And it's sick what you're doing to me. Everyone's going to find out the truth."

The boy laughed his wheezy laugh, then said, "The truth is that you're going to kill Julia. You knew it the whole time. You got further with her than most. But she still rejected you."

"She didn't reject me. You corrupted her. I saw you talking to her and grabbing her hand by the bridge."

"You must have known it would happen, though. Why did you take down that guy's schedule at the garbage dump, right when you started dating her? It wasn't because you enjoyed talking to him. It was because he didn't check the bags in your van. You knew you could sneak anything in there. You knew you'd have something to sneak one day soon."

"How did you know that?" Sam felt the buckles tightening around his chest.

"I told you, I'm watching everything. You're losing control. I can see it. You couldn't even wait for Julia. You had to go and rape those girls."

"I *didn't!*" Sam screamed. He wished he could have slammed the phone down, but instead he pressed the button to end the call.

He'd been about to dial the police when he decided to try something else. He called the operator.

When the man picked up, Sam said, "I need to find out who just called me. I know it's a private number, but the person is harassing me and I need to report the call to the police."

"I think it would be best to call the police directly, sir."

"Listen to me. I know you're not allowed to tell me, that you might lose your job, but you have to understand. I'm being stalked. My life is in danger. Please."

"I can't even—"

"Can you just look at the call record and tell me if the number is from the Stradler College campus?"

"I'm not—"

"Please just look at the record. I'm in danger."

"Hold on, please."

There was a long pause filled with static, and Sam thought the operator must have hung up on him. He was about to try again when the man came on the line and said, "Hello?"

"I'm here."

"Sir, our records show that you haven't received a call at this number in over a month. Is there anything else I can help you with?"

Now, as he read on in his book, the words played over again in his mind. *Our records show. Over a month.* It was an interesting phenomenon, the way he'd both known and not known all along. That was the way he felt, not bothered but intrigued, in a distant way, the way he could be intrigued by characters in a book.

Of course Sam knew that the rest of the story he'd told Julia was also a lie, at least in the usual sense. He was aware that he'd sent the text messages to himself, that he'd planned it since the day Marcus had dropped the cell phone in the parking lot during their scuffle. Sam knew that he'd noted the pouch in Marcus's backpack where the boy kept the phone, that he'd followed Marcus on six separate occasions until the boy had left his backpack unguarded—at the track, in a study carrel in the library, once late at night in the student coffee bar—and that Sam had taken the opportunities to send the texts and then erase them from Marcus's sent folder.

When he'd started sending the messages, Sam hadn't known what he'd do with them, only that they might prove useful in a situation like this. He was aware of all these details in the vague way he was aware there had never been a caller, that he'd created the whispery voice that had accused him of the rapes. Or that he'd thrown a rock through his own window that night before he'd met Julia for pizza, knowing that no one would believe he'd done that to his own apartment. Or that he'd killed the cat that used to hang around the dumpster behind the snack bar, then placed it in Julia's room. Or that before he'd followed the girls, he'd put thick insoles in his shoes to make himself tall like Marcus. Or that he'd overheard so many students complaining about the Rackoff exams that he'd made a lucky guess when he'd talked to that first girl on the campus. All of this was a knowledge he passed through from time to time, the way an airplane passes through a cloud.

None of that mattered, though. The story he'd told Julia was a lie in the way a good novel was a lie. What mattered in all these things, above any measure of factual truth, was emotional truth. That was the underlying lesson of great fiction, and a healthy lesson in life. The truth was that Marcus had tried to corrupt Julia, to turn her against Sam. Maybe he hadn't made the calls, but Sam was sure he'd said other things, leveled accusations. And he'd done it out of pettiness, smallness of character. Because he'd lost. Sam loved Julia, he'd be good to her, he'd care for her and look out for her, and that was all that mattered. It was the end of the discussion.

He was nearly fifty pages into the novel when his phone started ringing. It displayed a private number. Sam picked up.

"Hello?"

"Hi, Sam. It's Julia."

Her name like a breeze blown through the forest of his heart. "Julia. Thank you so much for calling."

"I wanted to apologize." She sounded tentative, but also practiced, like she'd been considering these words in the hours since he'd left her room. "I was wrong about a lot of things. I shouldn't have doubted you. I was going through a tough time, and I had a lot of issues to work out."

"You don't need to apologize, Julia. Everything's okay now. I know you've been going through so much. I feel for you, because of what I've been through with my mom. Why don't you come over and we'll talk about it? I want to be there for you."

"I can't. I have an exam tomorrow."

"How about tomorrow night?"

"I have an appointment the next morning."

"What's the appointment for?"

There was a pause. Sam listened to Julia breathe twice into the phone. Then she said, "That was the other thing I wanted to talk to you about. It's something I didn't want to tell you. I thought I could take care of it before anyone found out. But I think you should know."

"You can tell me anything."

CHAPTER 33
Waiting

Sam was leaning against a brick pillar outside Livingston Hall, Stradler's music building, waiting for Julia to finish her last final of the semester. It was sunny and cold. He was wearing a black wool pea coat, one he'd picked up a couple years ago at Value Village, but which looked like the ones the students got from Eddie Bauer or Banana Republic. He didn't use it much, not wanting to wear it out, but he thought this was a special enough occasion.

Julia was going to come with him. She'd agreed to let him help her with the abortion. He'd said it was his responsibility, he'd put her in this position, and he wanted to get her out of it. He wouldn't feel right about himself if he didn't.

"I already have the appointment set up," she'd told Sam on the phone. "There's a Planned Parenthood fifteen minutes from Stradler. In Milltown. I was going to take a cab. But maybe you could drive me."

"That sounds fine, Julia. I'd be happy to, of course. But let me ask you a question. I'm not sure this would have come up when you were making your appointment, but did you know that they're required to tell your parents that you're having the procedure done? It's a law. Anyone who's under twenty-one."

She hesitated, then said, "They didn't say anything about it."

"I only know because I've been through this once before. With another girl. My high school girlfriend actually. I'm not proud of it. But I'm telling you because I think you should know everything about me. I learned a few things from that experience. I learned that there are places you can go where they won't say anything, where it's all done very discreetly. My girlfriend, Rachel, she never told her parents about it and they never found out. She finished college and she's a doctor now. She was so thankful for what those doctors did for her."

Sam hadn't been sure if this last touch was too much, but it was hard to gauge when you were improvising.

"I don't know," Julia said.

"Think about it, Julia. Think about how much better your life will be. Why burden your parents with this now? And what if you run into other students from Stradler while you're at the clinic? It would be impossible to get over that. We can get it done at a good place and no one will ever know. You can go home for Christmas and it'll be just like normal. Just like it never happened."

"How much does it cost?"

"That doesn't matter. I want to do it for you. I know it's the right thing. It's my responsibility. I want to give you a life to lead. I wouldn't feel right about myself any other way."

They'd gone on like that for nearly an hour. Sam had assured her again and again that he knew this was the best thing, that the clinic where he'd take her was only a couple hours from Stradler, and he'd be happy to drive Julia and pay for everything. He said that if she didn't like the doctor, they could leave right away. He could sense that he was wearing down her defenses, whittling away to the core of fear and desperation she must have felt. It was too much to go through by herself, Sam knew. And at last she'd given in, had no strength left to resist.

Now he was waiting outside the music building because he'd told her they'd go today right after her final. He didn't want to take the chance that she'd change her mind, decide she wanted to do it on her own. And Sam worried about the possibility of Julia talking to Marcus, sharing some of the conversation she'd had with Sam in her room. He didn't think she'd do that, but he couldn't take the chance.

There wasn't any abortion clinic, of course. That was a fact he'd have to get around. He'd never had a girlfriend in high school, let alone gotten anyone pregnant. He had an idea about how to deal with these discrepancies, though. He knew that the purpose of this trip wasn't really to get an abortion for Julia. On one level of Sam's mind, a well-lit upper shelf, he saw this adventure as a romance. The outcome would be that Julia would fall in love with him, see how devoted and special he was. Perhaps she'd still have the abortion, or perhaps she'd decide to have the baby and let Sam help raise it. But either way, they'd be together, hold hands and whisper clever things to each other in dimly lit wine bars.

But there was another level of Sam's mind, a dusty lower shelf that the light rarely caught, a shelf he was so faintly aware of that he was able to ignore it for most of his waking life. On this shelf, the outcome of the story was different. There was no wedding, no baby, no jobs for him or classes for her. It was a story in which two people embarked on a trip they would never return from.

It was fifteen minutes before the end of the period, and students were starting to exit the building. They looked red-faced and harried, girls' hair coming loose from bands, boys chewing their fingernails. The sight of them touched Sam, this world that seemed so distant from his. He'd always wanted to go to college. It had been his dream, reading books and walking to classes and living in a dorm on a campus like this. Circumstances had intervened, a college counselor who seemed to have it out for Sam, but in his quiet way Sam had found a place in these schools, been able to participate in the students' hopes and fears. It was more than you could say for most of the people he'd grown up with.

Sam worried about what would happen if Marcus finished the test before Julia. If he came outside and noticed Sam here, he might say something, start a scene. He was the type of kid to make a fuss, a sore loser. Sam tried to angle himself next to the pillar in a way that would make it easy to duck behind if he saw Marcus coming.

But it turned out not to be necessary. The next person who pushed through the glass doors at the front of the building was Julia. She looked beautiful to Sam, with her large eyes, her skin clear and smooth. Breasts weren't a great interest of Sam's—he was more interested in a certain innocent look—but Julia's had a fullness now that Sam couldn't help noticing, and he knew that other men would find it appealing. He imagined walking down a street with her, arms linked, the heads of passersby turning toward her, toward them.

She waved to him, and he could see a look of anxiety flit across her face. He waved back, a little too excitedly, he realized. He had to check his enthusiasm, remember this was a sober occasion, and he should match his mood to hers.

"I guess we should go," he said.

"Okay."

As they walked across the quad he said to her, "There was just a small issue that came up, Julia. They couldn't give us the appointment for today. But I got one for first thing tomorrow morning. Do you think that'll be okay?"

"I guess so. I can go back to my room and sleep. I didn't get much last night." She'd lost all the brightness in her voice, and there was something flat and robotic about the way she talked.

They were emerging onto the path in front of Basking Hall when Sam said, "I think it's important for you to get a good night's sleep tonight. You have a big day tomorrow. I was thinking it might be better if we drive a little tonight. I found us a place we can stay not far from the clinic. I think you'd feel better knowing we were close by and wouldn't have to worry about traffic or getting up at some horrible hour. But what do you think?"

Only now could Sam see how exhausted she looked, her face pale, eyelids heavy. She couldn't have had much energy to think it over.

"That sounds fine," she said. "It's probably better to be away from here."

"That's the same thing I was thinking, Julia. It's like you read my mind."

She offered a weak smile.

"Let's go to my van. I'll drive you back to your dorm, you can pack a few things, and we'll head off."

She nodded, like a child receiving instructions from a parent. Sam noticed she was staring at the sky.

He put his arm around her. "It's going to be okay," he said. On other days, he would have been more cautious about showing affection. He would have waited until they were away from the campus, alone. But now he didn't care if the students knew they were a couple. In fact, he welcomed it.

As he squeezed her shoulder, thinking of what a wonderful time he and Julia had ahead of them, an image came into Sam's mind. It puzzled him, being so out of place, so discordant with the generally bright and positive mood of the day. The image he saw was of himself, holding Julia by the hair, and beating her head against the side of a bathtub. He saw himself do it over and over again, heard the crack of her teeth on the porcelain, until her head was nothing more than a bloody sponge in his hand.

He shook himself free of this distasteful image. Why would such a sight appear before him now?

He had no idea. The mind held an infinite store of images, and who could say why one rose to the surface at any given moment? It was one of the great mysteries of life, part of its bizarre poetry, the alluring magic of this star-sprinkled universe, and he preferred not to examine the topic closely.

He kissed Julia on the scalp and told her in all sincerity, "I love you. We're going to be just fine."

Part Three

THE CABIN

CHAPTER 34
Too Late

All day long Marcus had been thinking about Tree. His conversation with Julia yesterday had plunged him into those memories, and now he was drowning in them.

He had only one final to go, the one in chemistry tomorrow, and he was about as ready as he was going to be for that. So he decided to head over to the music building, get some practicing in. Other than running, it was the only thing he knew that would clear his head. He hadn't played all week because of exams.

Since everyone was studying, the music building was empty. He took the stairs to the fourth floor, where the practice rooms were. He knew the room he wanted, the one with the Bösendorfer grand. They always kept it well tuned, even with all the students who came in to play it. On a regular weekday afternoon, it never would have been available. But today Marcus had it to himself. He shut the door to the room, opened the top of the piano to the long stick, sat down, and played some two-five-one progressions, thick chords with sevenths and ninths and thirteenths packed in, relishing the vibrations in the small room.

After playing a couple progressions, he began his scales and arpeggios. As soon as he let his hands free to perform their mechanical tasks, he started thinking about Tree again, remembering.

Theresa, her real name was, even though no one ever called her that. She was Marcus's first cousin, and they'd been best friends growing up. Tree's dad had left when she was young, and her mom, Aunt Penny, dropped Tree off at Marcus's house when Penny had to work late, or when she had a date.

Marcus and Tree used to wander by themselves in the farmland around Marcus's house. You could do that out there, let kids go off by themselves and not worry. He and Tree would make up missions for themselves, hiding in pastures, sitting on their skateboards and riding down hills until they spun out of control, tumbled into the grass. Sometimes, when they were very young, they pretended they were husband and wife, asking each other, *How was your day, dear?* and serving each other imaginary dinners, even doing a pantomime of sex, which mostly involved Marcus lying on Tree and saying, *Hey baby*.

They always said they were going to marry each other. Once, they conducted a ceremony where they exchanged Native American bracelets made from braided yarn to symbolize their commitment to each other. Marcus had gotten a purple and orange one for Tree, and Tree had bought him a blue and yellow one with a pattern of birds in the sky.

After Marcus had gotten through his two-handed arpeggios, he started in on the Bach fugue he was learning, the one in C-major with four voices. He'd worked through all the three-voice Inventions, and now he wanted to try something more challenging. He was naturally drawn to the Romantic composers, because of the harmonies and the expressive quality in the music, but he knew that Bach would give him the technique he lacked, especially the independence of his fingers, which was his weakest point when it came to jazz.

As he played through the familiar opening bars, Marcus enter-tained the idea that Tree was more like a Bach fugue than a Chopin étude. She was complex, layered—giving and loyal and flexible, but at the same time strong-willed and competitive and capable of long grudges—and all of those voices were confined in a calm exterior. Tree never told you when she was mad at you, or why, and when you pleased her—like when Marcus had gone to Spain with his parents and brought her back the knitted hat with her name on it—she didn't make a show of hugging you and telling you how great you were. Like Julia, Tree had the most expressive eyes, and Marcus always looked there to find her true reactions to things.

Marcus had been close to Tree until high school, when he changed to the school for the arts that was a forty-minute drive from his house. Tree was old enough to stay home alone at that point, and Marcus was so busy with his commuting and his school work that he didn't have time to stop by and see her the way he used to.

He was already getting serious about music. He had a band with some friends called Stone Age Computer, and when he wasn't prac-ticing piano or doing homework, he was rehearsing with the band or composing the electronic rock that had interested him at the time. He loved Radiohead, kept posters of Thom Yorke on his walls, and often spent time staring at them. In order to look the part, Marcus left his hair messy and started wearing dark clothes and collared shirts under his sweaters. He even spent a couple weeks attempting to tweak his accent toward a more British-sounding one, but it came off as affected. His yearning, not so much to meet this man, but to actually become him, sing his songs in that same reedy voice, was overwhelming, a kind of pure ache. It seemed a miracle that a feeling like that could actually be contained, not destroy you.

He didn't know when he'd first heard Tree was sick. It was the kind of news his parents shared at the dinner table or that his mom would have told him when she was driving him home from school, but he couldn't remember a specific instance when he'd found out. The information floated through his world, like the news of the war in Iraq or the slowly warming climate; they were developments he felt bad about in a vague way, but never paused to focus on. He had the sense that he would stop by to visit Tree at some point—was she still in the hospital?—but he kept putting it off.

Months went by. He thought of calling her, just to say hi, but didn't know how sick she was, wasn't sure if the call would be a nuisance, or if they'd have anything to say. Stone Age Computer was starting to perform then, to get gigs. Mostly they were student parties, or local talent shows, but people seemed to appreciate what they were doing. They had ten or twelve kids who came to all their shows. Marcus figured Tree would be fine. Everyone else he'd known who'd been sick had turned out fine—it was a rule of his childhood, along with the fact that illness was a load you bore in private—and he knew the same would be true of his cousin. He planned to invite her to a show when she was feeling better, maybe bring her up on stage.

That was the worst part of how he'd acted, Marcus thought now, as he pushed on in the fugue, the way he'd imagined her thrill at his music, how he'd fantasized that the misery of those months would evaporate in the glare of his success. He'd been afraid to call Tree, he knew, because it might entail some obligation for him, something that would get in the way of a band rehearsal or composition time. He might have had to hold Tree's arm and walk through a shopping mall with her. Or he might have had to push her in a wheelchair, if she was that sick.

At last he visited her, during the summer before his junior year. She was at home. Aunt Penny had pulled her out of school in the spring, and it didn't look like she'd be going back in the fall. Penny brought Marcus into the room where Tree was lying, and told him to make himself comfortable, that she'd be in the other room if they wanted anything to eat.

Tree was lying on a couch under the window, wrapped in a blanket even though it must have been eighty degrees in the room. She was bald, her head a snowy hill above the blanket, and her face was bone thin, shadowed under the eyes. Those eyes. Marcus leaned over and kissed her. Her skin was cool when he touched her. He'd expected her to brighten when he came in, but he saw now that she was occupied with other thoughts, that his presence was not the balm he'd imagined it to be.

He sat on the cushioned chair across from the couch. He didn't ask how she was doing. He had that grin on his face, he could feel it, the one he always got when he was nervous or stressed or scared. He knew how it looked, sarcastic, arrogant. But somehow he could never stop it. If he'd seen his own face, he knew he'd have wanted to punch it.

Marcus couldn't recall all they'd talked about during that visit, but he knew it wasn't anything important. He'd told her about his band, his school, his thoughts about college. She gave him a brief and sanitized summary of her medical hardships, which was all the news she had to offer. It was a perfectly nice conversation, but he'd left that day with the feeling that he'd already lost her.

Marcus had gone over the part of the Bach fugue he'd learned several times now. This was how he always mastered a classical piece, repeating the bars he knew again and again, as if tracing lines, darkening them in memory. He'd worked through four new bars today, which was a lot for him, and he took down the music so he could move on to the next part of his rehearsal.

This was when he started working on jazz. He began with a few choruses of "'Round Midnight," savoring the deep minor chords, the shifts of harmony. It was his greatest strength as a musician, the way he poured one chord into the next, the notes rearranging themselves like water finding its level.

He liked the sad, low songs the best, ballads by Monk and Mingus and Bill Evans. It was where he felt at home, where he felt closest to Tree. He'd never gotten back to see her. One afternoon, about a month after Marcus had visited, the phone had rung while he was practicing piano at home, and he'd kept going, figuring his mom would pick up. An hour later, when he'd left the den where the piano was, his mom was waiting outside the door.

"I wanted you to know Tree died. Early this morning. She was back in the hospital. Penny was there."

Marcus touched the top of his head when she said that. He didn't know why. It was like he was feeling for something, the way you do when you think you've lost your hat.

"Are you sure?" he'd said. He felt foolish every time he remembered that. *Always the wrong thing. You always say the wrong thing.*

At the funeral, Marcus expected Penny to be angry at him for not visiting more. He forced his mom to sit several rows back, saying he didn't feel comfortable sitting in the front, he wanted to leave those rows for family.

But when they went up to Penny at the end of the service, she smiled at Marcus. Thanked him for coming to visit that time. Said it meant a lot to Tree. Marcus felt his face getting hot. *You don't have to do this, Penny. I know I fucked up.*

Since that day, he'd carried the feeling inside himself that he'd ruined everything, because of his selfishness. And then he'd met Julia, who'd looked like Tree, and even acted a bit like her, and Marcus had wanted her, wanted to lie on her and say, *Hey baby* the way he'd said it to Tree all those years ago.

Marcus left the music building around four, his messenger bag, packed with the music he'd been practicing, weighing on his shoulder. He walked through the quad, up the path toward his dorm. As he was coming down the path, Marcus passed by the place behind the snack bar where the dumpsters were. And that was when he remembered it, what he'd seen that night, the night he'd been running, shortly after Julia had broken things off with him. Sam and the cat. He should have told Julia about it. It might have convinced her about Sam. But as always, Marcus had fucked up. And now it was too late.

CHAPTER 35
The Cabin

"So this is the cabin, folks," the man said when they were in front. He tried the knob, but when it didn't work, he had to lunge at the door with his shoulder. The door parted from the frame with a loud pop, so loud that Julia jumped a little, and she noticed the walls of the place vibrating with the sound.

The man showing them around was named Rex, and he was a short, jaunty guy probably in his late fifties or early sixties. He had a gray beard and gray hair that looked matted like steel wool. His belly stretched the Christmas sweater he was wearing, which showed a picture of two reindeer touching noses in a snowstorm. The fabric was worn in a way that made it look like something he'd gotten a long time ago.

Rex flipped on the light and held his arm out for Julia and Sam, signaling them to go in.

They walked inside. Following them was Dena, Rex's wife, who owned the Squirrel Ridge Cabins with him. Julia and Sam had gotten here only ten minutes ago, after a long drive from Stradler during which Julia was dozing on and off, all the way until the tires of Sam's van started crunching the gravel on the driveway up to this place. They were in the woods somewhere. Julia thought it was the northwest part of the state, since they'd been driving on I-80 West for a while, and then on I-79 North. She hadn't seen many road signs after that. It was the off-season here, Rex had told them when they arrived, and they were the only guests he'd scheduled the whole week.

Part of the reason Julia was foggy on all the details was that she was so tired. She'd gotten hardly an hour of sleep the night before, after all the talking with Sam, and then her dad had called early to say bye before his trip and give Julia his hotel information. She hadn't mentioned anything about her own trip, of course.

Now she felt like the details of this trip were simply washing over her. The cabin in the woods, the abortion clinic in the far northwestern edge of the state—Julia didn't want to trouble herself with it on an hour of sleep. That night when she'd called Sam to tell him she was pregnant, she'd been so exhausted that she'd simply let go. To doubt him would have been to doubt herself. And now Sam had reassured her so many times that everything was going to be all right that she'd finally believed him. She'd be able to get home just before Christmas, the slate wiped clean. All her life in front of her.

Inside the cabin, Julia was struck by the smell of mildew, and then a fainter smell that might have been fish. This must have been a place people used for hunting and fishing during the summer. It was deep in the trees, and you couldn't see any other buildings from here. The walls were covered in faux-wood paneling, and the only decorations were some knitted doilies with little sayings sewn into them like *A fish on the line is worth two in the brook* and *There's no place like Rome (Ohio)*. Against the wall was a faded striped couch, and across from it a mismatched chair and ottoman. A mini refrigerator buzzed in the corner, and there was a small counter with a stovetop and two pans hanging from hooks above it. The floor was covered by a red rug that was probably the source of the mildew smell. Only a small window above the couch and one by the front door let any light into the room.

"It's a simple place, but good for a quiet retreat," Rex said. "You got two rooms. This is the living room. Your bedroom's over there." He pointed toward a door to their left. "Bathroom's attached to the bedroom. One towel each per day. I'd give you more, but those are the general's orders." He hooked a thumb in the direction of his wife.

Dena looked at the floor and shook her head. It wasn't clear to Julia whether she was disagreeing with the towel policy, or the title of "general," or to some larger pattern in her husband's thoughts. She was a big woman with bowed shoulders, and it looked like she was wearing several heavy layers of clothing: a gray sweatshirt pulled over a thick flannel shirt, a beige skirt over jeans, and what must have been a pair of leggings underneath.

"My wife loves online shopping," Rex said. "Spends her whole day hunting deals. Women love their shopping." He nudged Sam. "Wouldn't you agree, snakeskin?"

"What?" Sam said.

"He calls everyone that," Dena said in her flat voice, still looking at the floor.

"Okay, couple rules," Rex said. "No smoking in here. The general won't tolerate it. You get one key to share, which means even if you quarrel, you better come home together." He handed Sam the silver key. "Me and the general are in the management office from ten till five. Not a tick later. Want to get to the office, go about five hundred feet back down the driveway, take the first path on your left. She'll be shopping, I'll be working."

Dena shook her head, watching the floor.

"There's a landline, and an emergency number posted over the phone in the bedroom. That's only for real emergencies. Like, grizzly in the shower emergencies."

"Do you have Internet access?" Sam asked. "My girlfriend might want to check her email." In the van, Sam had said he thought it would be best to refer to Julia that way, and she hadn't seen why it would matter one way or the other.

"No wireless," Rex said. "Cabins are too spread out. We have a computer in the management office you're free to use during business hours. So long as my wife isn't making a purchase. I'm sorry about the hassle, but if it's a problem, you'll have to take it up with my commanding officer." He saluted in the direction of his wife.

Dena made a soft wheezing sound, almost like she was growling, in the back of her throat.

"Let me show you the bedroom," Rex said. He walked across the room, opened the door. They all followed him in. Julia was expecting a large room with two beds, but instead she was greeted with only a double bed and a small, high window. There was maybe a foot or two of space to walk on both sides of the bed, and a bureau in one corner. Julia couldn't tell if there was even enough room to open the drawers.

"One other funny thing I'll tell you, snakeskin," Rex said to Sam— and it occurred to Julia that he addressed all his comments to Sam— "we've heard the cell phone reception isn't too great over here. But our guests tell us the best place to get a signal is in the bathroom, strangely enough."

"Sometimes I lock myself in there," Dena muttered.

"What's that, General?"

Dena shook her head, growling softly.

"So we'll help you get your bags in and then you can come over to the office and settle up for your two nights."

"One," Julia said. She assumed they'd head back after the operation.

Rex looked at her with a startled expression, like he'd just realized she was in the room.

"It's okay," Sam said to Julia. "I want you to be comfortable. We don't have to rush back."

Before Julia could say anything else, Rex said, "All right, snake-skin, I can see you take good care of her."

They all walked outside, where the cold struck Julia with the force of a body. The wind was fierce, and the trees leaned under its pressure.

"Snow's comin'," Rex said. "Can smell it. I've got the nose of a wolf. This is the month when it really starts to dump."

"How bad?" Julia asked.

"Might be here longer than you think."

"Hope not," Sam said.

"By the way," Rex said to Sam, "what happened to your face there? Get in a little scuffle, snakeskin?" He laughed and slapped Sam on the shoulder.

Sam smiled. "Just some bad luck. Coupla guys took my wallet. Not a big deal."

Julia was surprised by how easily he came up with the story about his wallet, how comfortably he slipped into the rhythms of Rex's speech.

"Nothing like that out here," Rex said. "No need to worry."

That evening Sam and Julia went to a supermarket to get food. Sam insisted on buying enough for several days, just in case they got snowed in. He bought a package of sliced deli meat and one of sliced cheese, mustard, a loaf of bread, cans of string beans and mixed veg-etables, bags of chips and popcorn, bottles of water, beef jerky, three vacuum-sealed packages of different meats to cook on the stove.

Back at the cabin, he made steaks and skillet potatoes for dinner. Julia was so tired she could only pick at the heavy food, but she told him it was good, thinking about the weight-loss shakes in his refrig-erator. He must have learned how to cook at work, since he didn't seem to keep much food at home.

After dinner, she could hardly hold her head up, and she told him she needed to get some sleep. She went to bed right away, hoping to avoid the question of affection between them. When Sam got into bed, she felt the mattress shake, and for a moment Julia thought he might reach out and put his arm around her, but he didn't do that. She wondered if she should ask him about setting the alarm for their appointment, but assumed he'd take care of it.

Some time later, she woke up in darkness, hearing the wind and Sam's slow breathing. The air seemed heavy. Julia felt like her head was clear for the first time in days.

Suddenly, a feeling of intense fear dropped on her like a net. What was she doing here, next to a man she really didn't know very well, carrying what could become his child inside of her?

She started to panic. A bunch of strange and frightening thoughts bounced in her mind. *I'm trapped. There's no way I can escape.*

But why would she need to escape?

She took some deep breaths, telling herself this was silly, she was acting like a child. There was nothing to be afraid of. Maybe it was just the fact that she'd woken up in the middle of the night in a foreign place. *Sam's only been kind to me,* Julia told herself. *It's just that when you're in a new place, you realize how vulnerable you are all the time.*

She got out of bed, trying not to disturb Sam. Her eyes had adjusted to the dark, and since the window was uncovered, Julia could see the room by the moonlight. She noticed Sam's suitcase pushed against the wall. He'd packed too much for an overnight trip, probably a week's worth of clothing. Maybe he was going somewhere else after this trip, for the Christmas vacation. The zipper of his suitcase wasn't fully closed, so Julia pulled open the lid of the bag with her finger to peek inside.

Inside the bag, there was actually only a couple days' worth of clothing. Shirts, underwear, socks, pants, and sweaters. There was a large plastic bag of what looked like toiletry items, creams and washes. But there were other things that seemed out of place. A small box that looked like an old cassette tape. A few scarves that might have been meant for women. A shoebox with a striped pattern.

At first she wasn't sure why the shoebox looked familiar, why it gave her an uneasy feeling. Julia thought maybe she'd seen something like it in a movie one time. But then she remembered that first night she'd slept at Sam's place. This was the shoebox she'd seen on the table.

Sam stirred in the bed. He sniffed and cleared his throat. Julia dropped the lid of the suitcase, hoping he hadn't seen her looking in there.

She went into the bathroom and turned on the light. She didn't really have to pee, but thought she should wait there for a minute until he fell asleep again. She didn't want him to know she was awake. Maybe she'd have a chance to peek in the shoebox when she went back out, if she could do it without him noticing.

She sat on the toilet lid, which had one of those fuzzy covers on it. While Julia was sitting there, she counted to a hundred, slowly, trying to keep down the nervous feeling that rose in her like murky water.

Then she walked back into the bedroom. Sam had changed positions. Julia knew he might have been awake, so she didn't look in the suitcase again. She got in bed beside him and pulled the covers over herself.

When she laid her head on the pillow again, he put his arm over her. "It's just us," he whispered. "Just us."

CHAPTER 36
Complications

⊶——⊷

"Some bad news," Sam said when he came back inside the bedroom, waking Julia. It was almost nine thirty. "I talked to the people at the clinic, and it seems there was a mix-up with your appointment. They had you on the books for tomorrow."

She sat up in the bed, blinking and looking around like she didn't know where she was. Sam noticed that the cabin appeared dingier in the daylight, and when he came in from outdoors he'd detected a dusty smell, like it hadn't been used in a long time.

"I tried to get them to slip you in," Sam continued. "In fact, I gave the man hell. I told him we'd made a special trip for this. I did everything I could, Julia. But they couldn't do anything for us. They're booked solid."

"So I have an appointment tomorrow?" she asked, her voice craggy from sleep. Her hair was pressed down on one side of her head. There was an intimacy to seeing her this way, a sweetness Sam wished he could draw out like taffy. To him, this closeness, this private conference in their shared bedroom, it was better than sex, which he'd never cared much about, and which he'd known enough not to ask Julia for the night before.

"Of course you still have your appointment tomorrow. I wouldn't cancel it without asking you. I just didn't know how you'd feel about delaying everything a day."

She opened her mouth to say something, then hesitated.

"Tell me your honest opinion, Julia. I want to know whatever you're thinking. If you think it's best to drive back to Stradler now, I'm happy to do that. I was only thinking that even if you called the Planned Parenthood, it would still be at least a day before you could get an appointment there, probably more. And there'd be all the same problems we talked about."

"Do I definitely have the appointment tomorrow? I mean, is it confirmed?"

"Set in stone. If you want to keep it. I confirmed three times with them. I knew there was a chance you might still want to keep it. Do you think that's a good idea, Julia? To keep the appointment?"

Again, the hesitation. She was looking at him in a curious way, as if she hadn't quite understood what he'd said. He wasn't sure why she'd doubt him, after all they'd been through together. In fact, he found himself getting impatient, and had to remind himself that it wouldn't do any good to rush her.

"I guess we should keep it," Julia finally said. She chewed on her lower lip for a second. "I mean, you booked the cabin for two nights anyway. But maybe we can go straight back to Stradler tomorrow, after the appointment. I'll lie down in the back seat."

"Anything you want, Julia. Let's just see how you feel. I want to make sure to do the best thing for you."

"I think I'd like to go back after."

"Whatever you want."

She nodded, still looking uneasy. He had the impulse to grab her shoulders, shake her, tell her not to worry; he hated this distance between them so much. He couldn't believe she'd fuss this way, after all he'd done for her, all he'd arranged. Most men would have headed out of town as quickly as their cars would drive if they'd found out they'd gotten a girl pregnant. But he'd stuck around, looked out for her, called to check on her. And now she was repaying him with these accusing glances.

Sam took another breath. He recognized his thinking was heading in a bad direction. He had to pull himself out of it.

"Okay, good, we'll stay," he said. "I was thinking that, too, but I just wanted to see what you thought." He breathed. "I'm considering taking a walk, Julia, if that's okay with you. Just to get outside and clear my head."

"Do you think I'm doing a bad thing?" she asked him. "I mean, I don't want to look back and feel like I made a huge mistake."

"I don't think so at all. I think you're doing a very brave thing, and a good thing for yourself and your parents. They don't have to worry about you, because you're taking that worry on yourself."

She chewed her lip again. "I'll be okay," she said at last. "Sometimes I just get a little dark. Go ahead on your walk. There's plenty of food around here. I'll make myself something."

He went to the bed and hugged her, thinking it was the right thing to do. "That's perfect, Julia. I think that's a perfect idea. I'll see you later."

Outside, clouds like wet cement spread over the sky, and Sam felt the prick of a snowflake on his face. His cheek throbbed where he'd hit himself a couple days before. Rex must have been right: it looked like they were in for a real storm. It would be a good excuse for the appointment getting canceled again tomorrow. Though the truth was already descending on Sam that there wouldn't be a need for that kind of excuse. He couldn't draw this out indefinitely. She was going to realize there wasn't a clinic. She was going to ask to go home, insist on it. He couldn't put that off much longer.

He needed to walk. His head wasn't right. He felt as if he were a radio with a bad signal, turned to the highest volume. The static filled his ears. He'd sensed his temper rising with Julia in the cabin, and he didn't want that. He didn't know what was wrong. He was with her, in a private cabin in the middle of the woods, the way he'd always imagined it. And yet he couldn't seem to get his thoughts in a row.

He walked down the gravel drive they'd driven up the day before, only vaguely conscious of the fact that he was counting his steps, measuring the distance to the management office and the county road they'd turned off to get here. On one level, Sam was telling himself that he was out for a walk on a brisk day, enjoying the scenery just before snow began to fall. But he also knew—couldn't help knowing—that on another level he was preparing for something. Below the decks, other forces were working. They always were. He did his best not to think about that, but if he was honest with himself, he had to acknowledge those motivations were there, too.

It was a position he often found himself in, performing some pleasant and mindless task, while aware that in a shadowy back room, calculations were being made. He'd searched the Internet to find this isolated cabin for just that reason. The same was true when he'd taken down the man's schedule at the dump. Or when, years ago in Cambridge, he'd spent weeks walking along the Charles, noting which boat houses were in use and at what times, so that he knew where he could find an empty one when he needed it. Or in Long Island, when he'd hiked all the way down the oceanside beach on Dune Road, trying to find a stretch of sand long and wide enough and concealed by dunes in a way that made it impossible to see from any of the houses on a winter afternoon. It was meticulous, this part of himself. He couldn't help it. He knew that stopping the process would be like ceasing to breathe.

After Sam walked the length of the driveway down to the county road, he veered off the path, into the woods, crunching twigs and dead leaves underfoot. Old, knuckled trees reached from the earth around him. In the wind, their frozen branches clicked against one other. To his left Sam spotted a lone deer, still as ice, eyeing him like he was an intruder. He took another few steps, and the deer fled into the woods. Sam loved this season, when it felt as if everything in the forest was stripped down to a raw core of survival.

Julia was pulling away. There was no question about it. He could see it in her face when he told her about the mix-up with the appointment. She didn't trust Sam anymore, didn't care about him. If there'd been a clinic, she would have dropped Sam as soon as she got back home. It was the same way Marilyn had begun to treat him when he'd come up to her table and asked her for book suggestions, like he was a burden, an inconvenience. Or the way Patrice had started to pack her lunches so she wouldn't have to see Sam in the campus cafe. Or the way Naomi had told him she had openings for friends' gallery shows every night, that time he'd asked her to the movie.

But with the other girls, he'd always stopped there, just as the coldness was setting in. He'd known better than to press further, to make a stronger impression. That lonely accountant in the dark office in his mind had told Sam to stop, to cut his losses, or else he'd find himself in much deeper trouble. Even asking Naomi out on the date had been too much. The police had questioned him because of that, asked him how well he knew her, where he'd been on certain nights. But they hadn't found anything. Hadn't even taken fingerprints. Sam had simply told the truth, that he'd thought Naomi was a sweet girl, that he'd liked her and asked her out, and that she'd rejected him. That was all he knew. He could have passed a lie detector if they'd given it to him.

This relationship, though, the one with Julia, had gone so much further than any of the others, so far past the casual conversations you'd strike up with a girl when you were taking her tray or she was waiting in line for a sandwich. Which was really all that had happened with the others. To even call them relationships was a stretch of the word, Sam had to admit. But to him, they had all felt real. He'd embarked upon those journeys with the hopefulness he'd brought to the one with Julia, the feeling that at last he'd found a person who would appreciate the love he was able to give.

But why had he taken it so far with Julia? He'd asked himself that question a hundred times, never getting close to an answer. Was it just that she'd accepted him, that she'd seemed willing? Was that why he'd kissed her that night in front of the party? Was it that he'd sensed her loneliness, her need for him, her desperation? Or was his desperation part of it, too, the fact that he felt youth slipping through his fingers like sand? All he'd ever wanted was to be one of them, to walk among them and be treated like a member of their team. But the invitations would stop soon, he knew that. A middle-aged man couldn't show up at a student party. A girl in a lunch line wouldn't be interested in an old man's conversation.

He'd kissed Julia because he could. Because he wanted to and she wanted to. And in the moment he'd done it, he'd believed they would love each other forever. But he'd also known that he was backing himself into a corner, and that if the relationship didn't turn out as he'd hoped, if it ended the way the others had, there wouldn't be another one. There wouldn't be any more chances. The accountant had made all the calculations, and Sam wasn't walking away this time. He wasn't packing up and moving on. He was roped to the mast of this ship.

He'd traced a wide arc through the woods, impressed by the amount of undeveloped land, most of it forest, that the cabins sat on. He'd seen only three other cabins as he'd been walking. None of them were occupied. And there were no houses or stores anywhere in the immediate area. Now he was a few hundred feet behind the management office, where he could see the lights on, Rex and Dena's truck parked out front, snow chains on their tires. Dena had the hood up, and looked to be doing some work.

Sam didn't want to hurt Julia. He loved her. She was a kind person, regardless of the mistake she'd made with her brother. He saw that in her, along with her vulnerability, and he hated the idea of damaging such a fragile and lovely creature. He could drive off, leave her here. She'd find her way back to Stradler somehow. He could forget about this whole adventure. Because if he stayed, he knew what would happen. It was unavoidable.

But he also knew, with the same certainty, that he couldn't leave, that the idea of leaving was as much a fantasy as the idea of building a life with Julia. He didn't have it in him to go. There was something stronger than his own will that would keep him here.

When he got back to the cabin, he was feeling better. His face didn't hurt, and he had the sense that the swelling in his lip and cheek had gone down. The snow was coming harder now. He hadn't noticed it because most of it was caught in the net of branches above his head. But now he felt the flakes on his cheeks, melting into his collar. The sky looked darker, and the snow in the tree branches dimmed what light there was. There might have been a half inch of powder on the gravel.

Sam took the key from his pocket and opened the front door. To his surprise, the knob turned freely. He must have forgotten to lock it on his way out, he was in such a rush. Inside, it was dark. He guessed that Julia had gone back to sleep. He hadn't brought a watch with him, and didn't know what time it was.

But when he turned on the lights, she wasn't on the couch, or on the bed. He knocked on the bathroom door, didn't get an answer, and when he looked she wasn't in there either.

Worry sounded an alarm in Sam's mind. He walked back into the living room, got on his hands and knees, and pulled the shoebox from under the couch, where he'd stashed it. He couldn't bear to leave it at his apartment, knowing there was a good chance he wouldn't be going back there. He'd packed only the things that had mattered most to him. This morning he'd hidden the shoebox while Julia was sleeping.

Now he opened the top. Everything was there. He put it all back in the box and closed it, pushing it deep under the couch where Julia wouldn't see it.

Then he felt for the lump in the rug, near where he'd placed the shoebox under the couch. When he found the lump, he reached his hand between the rug and its liner and pulled out the other item he'd stashed there, the knife in its leather sheath. It was a six-inch hunting blade. Sam couldn't remember when he'd packed it, but the knowledge that it was there, between the rug and the liner, had been floating in his mind all day.

He put it back in its hiding place. Then he went out to find Julia.

CHAPTER 37
The Office

＝—＝

The shoebox hadn't been there when she'd woken up. It was the first thing Julia noticed, after Sam had come in and told her about the mix-up with the appointment, after he'd gone out for his walk, saying he needed to clear his head.

He'd been acting so strangely since they'd gotten to the cabin. Julia didn't understand what had happened. He seemed like he was wrestling with some hidden dilemma, and every time she asked him if everything was okay, he'd say, "Sure," like he was annoyed she was asking. Julia had been close to telling him she wanted to go back to Stradler when he'd asked that morning, and she might have done it if she hadn't gotten the sense he would have been really disappointed, maybe even angry. And anyway, there would have been problems if she'd gone back to Stradler for the operation.

As soon as he'd shut the door, she'd gotten up from the bed and looked out the window, watching him walk away. Then she looked in his suitcase. When she saw the shoebox was missing, Julia knew there was something important in it, something he didn't want her to see. Why else would he move it? He'd taken it away that first night she was in his apartment, too, when it had been sitting on the kitchen table.

What could possibly matter that much? she kept thinking. What could be so important that you'd need to keep it hidden even from the person sharing your bed?

She started opening all the drawers of the bureau, finding nothing but dead spiders and mouse droppings, and a yellowed issue of *Playboy* from about five years ago that she didn't want to touch. She looked in the bathroom medicine cabinet, under the bed, behind the headboard.

Sam probably didn't know that Julia had seen the box the night before, since she thought he'd been asleep, so he might not have even made a big effort to hide it. She walked into the living room, took all the cushions off the couch and then put them back, looked in the refrigerator, the closet. Then she got down on her hands and knees and searched the floor.

That was when she saw it: under the couch, back by the wall, a dark shadow.

She crawled over to the couch, pulled out the box, and opened the lid, making a mental note to herself to remember how everything was arranged so she could put it back in the same order.

At first, it didn't seem like there was anything that unusual in the box, and Julia was a little relieved. It just looked like some keepsakes. An old ticket to get into some kind of public park. A piece of fabric from a coat or a pair of pants. A shiny pebble. The only confusing thing was how each object had been sealed so carefully in a plastic bag. Julia couldn't tell why these objects were so important to Sam, but she knew they were, just by the effort he'd put into preserving them, which seemed like the way archaeologists would keep the findings of their digs.

Then she saw the labels. Names, cities, dates. He'd taped a strip of paper onto each bag and written this information in black pen, tracing over the lines a few times like he wanted to make sure they'd never be erased. She counted that there were five bags in total, and they were ordered chronologically:

Alyssa, Cal's Mountain, San Diego, California, February 1996
Claire, Oregon Ridge Park, Cockeysville, Maryland, April 2001
Marilyn, Charles River, Cambridge, Massachusetts, August 2004
Naomi, Backbone State Park, Strawberry Point, Iowa, June 2005
Patrice, Roger's Beach, Westhampton Beach, New York,
November 2007

Reading the labels, Julia thought of the conversation they'd had the night they'd eaten in the Italian restaurant, when he'd told her about living in Pittsburgh with his mom, how he'd never left Pennsylvania in his life. So why would he have items from all these women in different states?

Maybe he'd never been to these places. He might have had pen pals all over the country, for all she knew, or maybe these were people who'd donated to a charity he'd set up for his mom. There could have been a hundred reasons.

But Julia knew that none of these explanations would turn out to be true. In that moment her worry, which had been a soft and jellylike thing, became a solid and heavy certainty. She'd let herself be tricked. She'd been half asleep, following along because she was scared and it was easier than protesting. Sam had lied to her, and there was something wrong, and possibly dangerous, here. She needed to wake up and do something.

Julia took a pen and a scrap of paper out of her bag and wrote down the information on the labels. Then she put everything back, the keepsakes, the shoebox, pushing it under the couch just as it had been.

It was only when she'd shoved the box back in place that she felt the lump under the rug. She thought it might be something gross—an old chicken bone or a dead rodent—so she left it there.

Her mind was flipping through possibilities like pages in a book. She couldn't ask him to go home now. He'd wonder why she'd changed her mind, and he might suspect she'd found something. Julia thought of asking Rex and Dena to give her a ride to the nearest town. But how was she going to explain why she was leaving Sam? She couldn't tell them it was because he had a box of keepsakes. And even if she got away, it wouldn't have been hard for him to follow her to the nearest gas station or drugstore.

And what if there was another explanation for the items in the box? What if there was something completely normal Julia hadn't even thought of? There was a good chance she was just worked up because of the appointment tomorrow, and maybe all that worrying had gotten her imagination running. She decided she needed to check on some facts before she made any decisions.

She got dressed and walked out of the cabin, leaving the door unlocked, hoping she'd get back before Sam knew she was gone. The snow was already coming down, flakes settling on the driveway, frosting the top of the van and the roof of the cabin. Julia turned down the path toward the management office, glancing behind her to make sure Sam wasn't there.

Outside the office, Dena was putting snow chains on their truck tires.

"Is it okay if I use the computer for a minute?" Julia asked.

"Fine with me."

Julia went inside. The office had a similar look to the cabin Julia shared with Sam: two rooms and a bath. Next to the door, a bunch of coats and fleeces and vests hung from a coat rack, and there were a few pairs of shoes and hiking boots and galoshes beside the mat. The furniture seemed nicer here, more modern, than in the cabin Sam had rented. There was a large wooden desk, and a small computer table with a rolling chair where Rex was sitting, clicking through websites. Julia noticed the words *Giant Christmas Sale Extravaganza!* across the top of the screen.

"Hey," Julia said, and Rex spun around in his chair, looking startled.

"Oh, hi there," he said. "I'm just clicking out of these web pages the general left open."

"I was just wondering if it would be okay if I used the Internet for a minute."

"I'm not using it myself," Rex said quickly. "It's all yours, snakeskin."

He got up from the chair, and Julia sat down in it. It was warm, which meant he must have been sitting there for a while. He shuffled some papers on the large desk, banged them twice on the tabletop, then went into the other room.

From her pocket she took out the piece of paper on which she'd written the information. There was another slip of paper in there, some other note Julia must have written, but she couldn't remember what it was and didn't have time to think about it. She did a search using the information written on one of the labels: *Alyssa, Cal's Mountain, San Diego, California*, and then the date, *February 1996*.

The results that came up didn't seem promising at first. There was an article by a local columnist named Alyssa Martin about nature conservation. A list of people who'd participated in a 5K run for a lupus charity.

Then there were some articles about a girl who'd gone missing. The articles didn't say much, and didn't mention Cal's Mountain, which was probably why they didn't appear first in Julia's search. But all the articles talked about how the girl, a UCSD student, had disappeared. They weren't sure if she'd run away, or if it was a possible kidnapping, but the police were asking for information. They gave a description of her, and mentioned she enjoyed hiking and biking on local trails.

Julia tried the next name. She had to weed through some articles, but then she got to a piece about a missing girl, never found, an unsolved case that had been a local story, then a national one for a day or two, before it faded away.

Again and again, the same results. It seemed that girls by these names, in these cities, had disappeared around the dates Sam had written on the labels in the plastic pouches in the shoebox.

For a few minutes, Julia didn't really understand what all this meant. Or she understood, but her mind was holding it off. It was like seeing a film about a person in danger. For those few moments Julia felt like she was at a safe distance from tragedy, and this news about Sam was more interesting than frightening.

Then it hit her, the meaning of what she'd been reading. Julia stopped typing, stopped clicking, staring at the screen. She was cold, and her body felt strangely light, like she was floating up from under water.

She was about to get up from the chair and go find Rex when the door to the office opened. Julia thought Dena would walk in, stamping snow off her boots, but instead Sam came through the door. The swelling had gone down in his face, but he looked tired. He'd taken off the bandages, and Julia could see the damage wasn't too bad, mostly just bruising on the one side of his jaw.

She clicked out of the article she'd been reading, then said, "Hey."

"What were you reading?"

"Just checking emails. Wasting time."

"That didn't look like email. Were you reading an article or something?"

"Just some junk. Hollywood gossip. It's embarrassing how entertaining all that stuff is for me."

Sam smiled. "Should we have some lunch?"

"Sure. It's just, there's one thing I wanted to ask Rex and Dena about."

"What is it?"

Rex came out of the other room as Sam was asking the question. "Hey there, snakeskin. What's on the agenda?"

"I think we're going to have a little lunch."

"Sounds good to me. I think we'll have ours at home, on account of the snow. The general wants to leave early today, so we're planning to head out in a few minutes."

"Is there going to be a lot?" Sam asked.

"Shouldn't be too bad. The general heard we're not supposed to get the worst of it. But you never know around the snow belt. She wants to play it safe so we don't end up camping out here with you, no offense. But you two should be fine on your own. Wouldn't mind the privacy, I'm guessing."

Julia felt her breath coming more quickly as he talked. She didn't want them to leave, to be alone with Sam. Her hands were trembling, and she had to keep them clasped in her lap so no one would notice.

"Would you be able to run me over to a drugstore really quickly on your way out?" Julia tried asking Rex. Then she looked at Sam, forcing a smile. "I can get a cab back."

"Couple issues with that plan," Rex said. "First, there isn't a drugstore the way we're headed. I wouldn't mind taking you in the opposite direction, but I think the general might have my head. Also, it's not so easy getting a cab around here. You usually have to book a day in advance."

"I'll take you, Julia," Sam said. "Don't even worry about it," he told Rex.

Julia saw she was running toward a dead end. She tried to think of another direction.

"I was just wondering," she said to Sam, "if you think maybe we should stay somewhere else tonight? What if the power goes out or something? It seems kind of isolated."

"You don't have to worry about that," Rex said. "You've got a generator. If you need to use it, which you won't, just give us a call at that emergency number and we'll tell you how to switch it on. Phones work even if the power's out."

"What if we get snowed in tomorrow before our appointment?" Julia asked Sam.

But Rex jumped in to answer. "If there's any accumulation, we'll have Ewing come in with the plow by four thirty. You'll be able to get wherever you're going." He cleared his throat, looking back and forth between Julia and Sam. "And I'm sorry to mention this, but the general doesn't give refunds on prepaid nights."

"That's fine," Sam said. "I think this is a good place, Julia. We're so close to where we need to be."

Julia figured she needed to get to a public place, either with or without Sam, it was the only way. If Rex and Dena left, she knew Sam might not end up taking her. Julia could tell Rex she needed to go home now, demand that he take her with him, but she didn't know how Sam would react, or even if Rex would be willing to do it. If Sam was really crazy, he might kill them all right then. Or at least Rex and Dena.

Julia had to pretend everything was fine, just get Sam to drive her to a store as soon as he could, before the snow piled up.

"If we do need to get to that store," Julia said to Rex, "where's the closest one?"

"You go all the way down the driveway to the county road, then take a right. About four miles down, you've got a gas station on your left. They've got a convenience store. If you need a full drugstore, you have to go another six miles into Croughton."

"Okay," Julia said, trying not to sound upset. "Thanks for your help."

"Always want to do everything I can," Rex said. He opened the front door and called to Dena, "Hi-ho, General! Ready to march?"

"Let's go," Dena said.

Sam and Julia waved to them as they pulled out of the driveway. It was just past one in the afternoon, and the snow was streaming down.

"What was it you needed at the store?" Sam asked as they were walking back to the cabin.

Julia looked down. "A bottle of Advil." She was about to lie and say she needed tampons, but realized Sam probably knew enough about the female anatomy to see through that.

"I've got Advil in my suitcase." He looked more serious now, more focused. The cheerfulness he'd shown with Rex was wiped clean from his face. And Julia noticed he was hardly looking at her, almost like she wasn't there with him. Like he was concentrating again on that internal problem he'd been grappling with since they'd left campus. "I'm glad we won't have to go out."

"Me too," Julia said, forcing the words out of her throat. "The snow looks pretty bad."

CHAPTER 38
A Call for Help

———◆———

S he took the Advil, even though she didn't need it. Sam stood there, watching her swallow the pills. It was dim in the cabin, since they only had the two windows, and the sunlight was already fading outside. Neither of them had turned on the lights.

When she was done taking the pills, he said, "I think I need to take a shower. After all that hiking."

"Did you want to have lunch?"

"That's fine."

"I can get it started while you're in the shower."

"That's fine."

She could tell he was hardly listening.

While Sam was in the bathroom, Julia started the lunch. Snow was piling on the window frame, and she knew there wasn't much time before they'd be snowed in for the night. She laid out four slices of bread on the cutting board, then took out a couple plastic packages of lunch meat and sliced cheese from the refrigerator. She couldn't get the packages open, her hands were shaking so badly, and after several seconds of pulling on them, she heard the water turn on for Sam's shower.

That was when Julia had the idea she could run. She could open the front door, start down the driveway. He'd be at least fifteen minutes in the shower, and Julia could probably get a mile away in that time. She'd need a good head start, since he'd be able to follow her tracks in the snow. If she stayed off the main road, he wouldn't find her in his car, and she could probably zigzag her way to the gas station. Then Julia would call the police. Or get a ride out of town from someone. Anyone. Charles Manson would have been a fine companion if he was headed in the right direction.

But she had to leave now. In a few hours, the snow would pile up and it would be getting dark, the temperature dropping, and she'd never make it. There'd be no cars on the road, and the pavement might not even be plowed.

Julia walked to the door, unlocked the knob, twisted it, and began to pull. But the door wouldn't come open. She pulled harder, and still nothing. For a second she thought Sam had sealed it shut somehow, then remembered how it stuck and the sound it made whenever you yanked it open. If she opened the door now, the whole cabin would shake, and there was a good chance Sam would hear it, even in the shower. If he came out and saw Julia running down the road, that would be the end.

She locked the knob and went back to the sandwiches.

The plastic packages wouldn't tear. Julia opened the kitchen drawer, looking for something to help her slit the bags. In the drawer she found a can opener, and, more surprisingly, a wood-handled kitchen knife. The blade was speckled with rust, and the serrated edge must not have been very sharp, but it was better than nothing.

She took it out of the drawer. Instead of using it to open the lunch meat, though, Julia tried to think of a place to stash the knife, in case she needed it later. She thought of the sofa cushions, the cabinets, the refrigerator, but all those places seemed hard to get to if she needed the knife quickly. If he was going to do something, it would probably be in the bedroom. Though she stopped herself from imagining any more than that.

She listened to make sure the water was still running, and when she heard the whistling pipes, she opened the bedroom door. The bureau was a possibility, but Sam might want to use that for his clothes. Julia lifted the corner of the mattress, near where her head had been the night before, and slipped the knife under there, between the mattress and the box spring. It would be easy to reach if anything happened while she was lying there.

As she turned to go back to the kitchen, she saw the phone. It was an old, jellybean-shaped phone, placed on the night table between the bed and the bathroom door. Above it the emergency number for Rex and Dena was posted. It was the only phone in the cabin.

She thought of picking up, dialing 9-1-1, but Sam would hear her talking, and the cord wasn't long enough to stretch into the other room. She could dial the number, then hang up, but they'd definitely call back.

She was about to give up on the idea of making a call when she noticed something else. Sam's jeans were laid on the bed, where he must have left them before going into the shower. The room was dusky, and she couldn't be sure, but Julia thought she saw, peeking from the top of his pocket, the edge of his cell phone.

She reached into the pocket and pulled it out. It was a flip phone that he must have bought at a drugstore, probably so he could prepay his plan and not have his number listed. Julia opened the phone.

Her parents were too far away to call. She thought about the police. She could take the phone to the far end of the cabin and whisper. But when she walked out of the bedroom, Julia could already see that the phone said *Searching for signal . . .* and she knew she wouldn't be able to make the call. If she went outside, he'd definitely hear her leave. The best she could hope for was to send a text. But how do you send a text to the police?

Then she remembered the other slip of paper in her pocket, the one she'd brushed with her fingers earlier in the office when she'd taken out the note with the girls' names on it. Julia knew what that other paper was, Marcus's cell phone number, which he'd given to her when he tried to warn her about Sam. *I would steer clear of him*, Marcus had said.

The memory rushed back to Julia with all the force of her regret. She didn't think Marcus could have said anything to convince her in that moment. It was something more than stubbornness that made her resist him, made her assume he was just getting revenge on Sam. Was it that the idea of him looking out for Julia seemed too implausible? Since the accident, the thought of someone caring for her always made that person suspect in her eyes.

It didn't matter now. Maybe Marcus had meant well, maybe Julia had sided with Sam only because she didn't want to admit how wrong she'd been about him; whatever it was, she'd made the mistake. And whatever Marcus's motivations were, Julia knew he must have been right about Sam, that he was dangerous, even that he'd raped those girls.

And something else slipped into place in her mind now. Marcus's new cell phone. Those messages Sam had shown her, the taunts from Marcus—they must have had something to do with Marcus needing a new phone. It was obvious that Sam had sent the messages to himself somehow, using Marcus's phone.

And then Julia remembered the other part of what Marcus had said. *Anytime, you can call me. You know that, right?* And he'd meant it. He must have meant it. Why else would he say it?

She went back into the bedroom. Sam's cell phone seemed to get a very faint signal here, a single bar. The shower was still running. Sam had probably been in there for six or eight minutes already.

Julia typed out a quick text to Marcus: *This is Julia Stilwell. Writing from Sam's phone. I'm in trouble. At Squirrel Ridge Cabins in NW PA. Don't know address. DON'T WRITE OR CALL BACK, but please help if possible.*

Then she dialed the number Marcus had written on the paper and sent the message.

The screen of the phone said *Message sending . . .* Julia watched as a little graphic of a letter bounced back and forth between a picture of a phone and one of a mailbox. The water was still running in the shower, but she didn't know how much longer she had.

At last, a notice came up on the phone: *Message failed.* Then it took Julia back to the text she'd written, which hadn't been sent. The signal wasn't strong enough. Julia thought of what Rex had said, how the best signal was in the bathroom, and she knew it was the only place she'd be able to send the message. But Sam was in there. She couldn't just walk in and send a text.

Julia thought for a minute. She was almost ready to erase the message. But then an idea came to her.

She put the phone back in the front pocket of her sweatshirt, just above her waist, and held her finger against the send button, not pressing it, but ready to press it as soon as she had the chance. She knocked on the bathroom door with her free hand, then opened it, saying to Sam, "Sorry, I have to pee."

"It's okay, Julia," he said from the shower. He was blocked by the curtain, and Julia could see him only in silhouette. "You should feel free to come and go. It's your place, too."

"Thanks," she said. Her finger was still on the send button. She opened the toilet lid with her free hand, then pressed the button before pulling down her pants. She sat and peed a little, listening to Sam scrub himself in the shower. Steam billowed over the shower curtain. He'd been in here almost ten minutes. Julia thought of the bag of creams and washes in his suitcase, the precision he used to perform even the smallest tasks. There was a fierceness to it, a ruthlessness, an inability to let go of even the tiniest details, and maybe that was what scared her more than anything about him.

She sat for as long as she could, hoping to give the message plenty of time to send, and when she didn't think it was plausible for her to be sitting on the toilet any longer, she finished up and flushed, then left the room.

Back in the bedroom, Julia took the phone out and opened it. The screen said *Message sent*. She let go of a breath, which she realized she'd been holding since she'd left the bathroom. Julia was about to put the phone back in Sam's pocket, when it occurred to her that there'd be a copy of the message in Sam's *Sent* folder. She didn't know how often he sent texts, but as soon as he checked his messages, he'd see the one she'd sent.

Julia pressed some buttons, trying to figure out how to erase the message. Her thoughts kept leaping to what Sam would do if he saw that she'd written Marcus. She knew he'd kill her. He hated Marcus. Why else would he have told her all those stories about Marcus calling him and harassing him?

As she was thinking all this, fumbling with the phone, Julia heard the water shut off. The curtain slide on the rod.

There was no time. She shut the phone and put it back in Sam's pants, then went back to the kitchen to make the sandwiches. Her heart was pounding, her body filling with a strange energy, a force so wild she couldn't possibly contain it. Her hands were weak, and she had to use her teeth to open the lunch meat.

CHAPTER 39
Message Received

⟡——✦——⟡

Marcus had the afternoon free. His train wasn't scheduled to leave until six, and he'd finished the final in chemistry that morning around eleven. He'd gone to the dining hall after the exam, figuring there wouldn't be many people eating at that hour, and he'd had a long lunch by himself, listening to a Brad Mehldau album on his headphones. After lunch, he walked out of the dining hall and was surprised by how empty the campus was. At least half the students had finished their exams and left for winter break. The quiet was anticlimactic. Even though Marcus didn't want to go to any parties, it seemed odd that no one was here to celebrate. All semester, the work at Stradler had made Marcus feel like he was roped to a truck, jogging along to keep from getting dragged in the dirt, and finally he was free and there was nothing to do but pack up and go home.

At loose ends, he decided to go for a walk in the woods behind the train station, wrapping his scarf around his face for warmth. He had a good memory of the walk he'd taken with Julia here, at the beginning of the school year, that time they'd kissed. It wasn't a moment Marcus remembered with lust or even disappointment; it was as if the memory gave off a warm radiance in his mind, like afternoons he'd spent with Tree, before she'd passed away. The whole relationship with Julia had gone in such an unexpected direction that Marcus didn't know which basket to place his memories in: Hope? Regret? Fondness? How could you be sure?

Now he took the path slowly. The woods appeared so much thinner since the trees had shed their leaves. Earlier in the year, this place had seemed a wilderness, and Marcus had thought you could walk on and on without glimpsing any sign of people. But now he could see how close he was to Sacramento Pike, where cars sped past. He noticed one of the school parking lots, and the side of a house. He looked up at the sky, silvered by clouds and webbed by tree branches, like a cracked mirror.

He knew he hadn't said the right things to convince Julia when they'd had their conversation about Sam. It kept coming back to him, that conversation, plaguing him really, the wary look on Julia's face as he'd talked. Over the last day, Marcus kept thinking he wanted to call her to see if she was still planning to hang out with Sam, but he knew it would hurt his case if he became too insistent. He'd had his chance. Talking to her again about Sam would have made him seem jealous and competitive, which wasn't exactly how he felt. He was concerned for her, didn't want to let her put herself in a bad situation. *You can't let her get hurt.*

He'd told her about the scene in the parking lot when Sam had choked him, and the one in the snack bar, when Sam had thrown his glove at Marcus's face. He thought that would have been enough. But there was one more incident he hadn't told her about, since he hadn't found the right time to bring it up. It was the thing he'd remembered yesterday when he'd been coming back from the music building, what he'd seen the night he was returning from his run and the snack bar had been closed. Marcus had looked behind Slade Hall, back where the dumpsters were, and he'd seen Sam, by himself, kicking the stray cat. The one he was always feeding.

It was hard to describe why it bothered Marcus so much. If Sam had simply been shooing it away, or even if he'd tossed something at it to make it run, that would have been one thing. But it wasn't like that. Sam had taken a step back and aimed like he was kicking a soccer ball, and Marcus had heard the cat screech. There was something premeditated and sadistic about the way Sam did it. And it was so strange after seeing him feeding and petting the same animal. Marcus had thought of yelling at Sam that night, but for a few seconds he'd been afraid. He got the sense that it was best to keep his distance. Marcus had hustled up the path, out of sight.

The intense fear had passed, and once again Marcus had felt ashamed of himself, like he hadn't stepped in and helped when he should have. Who knew what had happened to that cat? And what was Sam really going to do to Marcus? The worst was when he'd put his hand on Marcus's throat, but in a funny way, that had been less frightening because it was so straightforward and Marcus knew it wasn't going anywhere. Marcus had thought about when to tell Julia about the cat, but he'd seen how defensive she was about Sam, and he knew she'd think Marcus was blowing the incident out of proportion.

He'd almost told her about the cat when he was describing Sam's assault, but he'd held back because at that point it seemed minor, in comparison to choking and threatening someone. And Marcus wasn't sure if Julia would have seen the significance in the way Sam had treated the cat, what it said about his character. It was the reason Marcus had gone into the snack bar that day and told Sam he was watching him. He'd hoped it would be enough to prevent Sam from doing anything cruel to Julia, but it had just drawn Marcus in and made the situation worse. *Typical. Never the right thing.*

After an hour in the woods, Marcus's face was numb, the air like steel wool in his lungs, so he decided to go in. He got back to his dorm room a little after one, and took his keys out of his pocket. Onto the key ring he'd tied the bracelet Tree had given him all those years ago, the blue and yellow one with the pattern that looked like birds. It was faded now, the colors hardly distinguishable. One of the birds had a wing missing where a thread had pulled loose. Someone had told him once that Navajo tribes intentionally make at least one error in their crafts, as a way to pay tribute to the fact that only gods are perfect. Marcus wasn't sure if it was true, but he liked the idea, wished he could blame his imperfections on a belief like that.

He went inside. His roommate, Doug, had already gone home, and half the room was stripped bare. Doug had left nothing on his desk, hadn't even left the sheets on his bed. He might have been the only person at Stradler more antisocial than Marcus.

Marcus started packing his own things. He didn't need much, just some clothes and a copy of *The Well-Tempered Clavier*, which he'd promised himself he'd practice while he was at home. It was funny, the way Julia and Tree seemed to be with Marcus all day, almost like they were walking with him. They'd been weaving through his thoughts, and everything he did—the walk in the woods, taking out his keys and thinking about the old bracelet—seemed to remind him of them. That was why it didn't even feel like a surprise when Marcus's phone beeped. Aside from his parents, Julia was the only person who had the new number, which Marcus had gotten after the phone company charged him for half a dozen texts he was sure he hadn't sent. Now, when Marcus saw the message from Julia, it seemed like he'd finally arrived at the purpose of his day.

His breath caught. *I'm in trouble*, the message said. But what did she mean by that? Was she locked in a car? Was she lost in the woods? He knew the trouble must have something to do with Sam. Why else would Julia tell him not to write or call back? She must not have wanted Sam to know she'd written Marcus.

Marcus didn't understand why she'd write him, if she was way off in Northwestern Pennsylvania. Why wouldn't she call the police there? Wouldn't they be able to get to her sooner? Marcus flipped open his laptop and did a search for the place she'd mentioned, the Squirrel Ridge Cabins. He found the place she was talking about.

Even the website looked bleak, spelling words incorrectly and offering a dim and unflattering view of the cabins. The main attraction seemed to be the "piece and quiet" the website kept mentioning, which must have been a code for saying it was in the middle of nowhere's armpit.

As he scanned the site, trying to get an idea of the situation, Marcus cursed himself again for not telling Julia about the cat. What if it had made the difference? What if it had been the grain that tipped the scale? Maybe she wouldn't have started out on this trip, the purpose of which Marcus couldn't fathom. Though he felt as if the result—Julia in danger—was clearly his fault.

He did a couple more searches and found the number for the local police in the town of Croughton, which wasn't far from where the cabins were located. He dialed and listened to the phone trill once, twice, three, four times in the wire.

Then someone picked up.

"Croughton Police," said the cheerful female voice on the other end of the line.

"Hi," Marcus said, "I was hoping I could speak to an officer."

"You're speaking to one right now," the voice said, less cheerfully. "Chief Williams here."

Marcus swallowed, feeling his face get warm. Luckily, the officer couldn't see him.

"I'm sorry," he said. "I wasn't thinking. I'm calling because a friend of mine is in trouble. She's in the Squirrel Ridge Cabins, which look to be off North Road. I think she might be stuck there."

"Where are you calling from?"

"Stradler, Pennsylvania."

"That's a good couple hours from here."

"I guess so."

"I know the cabins you're talking about," Chief Williams said. "I pass by them on my way to Laser Tag every Thursday. Dena's on my team, actually. She owns the cabins with her good-for-nothing husband. Spends all his time shopping on the Internet."

"Well, do you think you could go up there and see what's going on?"

"You know, there's a landline in every one of those cabins. Why didn't your friend just give us a call herself?"

"I can't answer that."

"Also, Dena and Rex are there all day. She could talk to them."

"Maybe she's stuck in her cabin. I think she's with a man who might be dangerous."

"How'd she get in touch with you?"

"She sent me a text."

"And did she do that with the use of a phone?"

"I'm assuming. Yeah."

"And is this the type of phone that's equipped to make calls?"

"Okay, I get what you're saying." Marcus felt as if he were trying to squeeze a quarter into a slot intended for a penny. He didn't know why he couldn't do a simple job correctly. "I don't know why she didn't call you. I don't know the whole situation. All I can say is that I got a text from her, saying she's in trouble, and she needs help. I know the man she's with could be violent."

"Look, kid," Chief Williams said, her voice stripped of any patience she'd previously shown, "do you hear what you're asking? I don't know what the weather's doing over there in Stradler, but it's snowing like a bitch here. You're asking me to risk my life on those roads in the middle of what's probably going to be the worst blizzard of the year, just to look for a girl who never called us, who might not even exist, who you claim is your friend, just because you got a text from her that I can't verify."

"I know it sounds weird."

"I got other words for it."

"Is there any chance you can help?"

"I can do two things. I can give a call up to the office and see if Dena can go check it out for me. She's usually out working and Rex can't always take a break from his shopping. So if I don't reach her, I can take a drive up there tomorrow, after they've cleared the roads."

"My friend might not make it that long."

"I've had enough prank calls this week, kid. Don't try me. I've heard it all—houses caving in, asses on fire. You're lucky I'm not going to come out to Stradler and bust *you*. Tell your friend to text you if anything else happens." Then Officer Williams hung up.

Marcus sat in his desk chair. He could hardly believe the conversation that had just taken place. Only he could bungle something so easy. *Never right.* Now there was no chance of getting the police to go up there. Even if he called 9-1-1, they would almost definitely contact Chief Williams, the closest law enforcement to the cabins, and she'd be quick to tell them how legitimate the emergency was.

Marcus thought for a minute. He didn't know anyone in that area of the state, and he couldn't just call random people or businesses and ask them to check it out. They'd all think it was a prank and report him to his friend Chief Williams. It would be a waste of time to make those calls.

He'd have to go himself. It was only a couple hours away. It wouldn't be such a big deal to miss his train that afternoon. He could rent a car, call his mom, and tell her something had come up. She'd understand. He had nearly five weeks to spend at home. What would one night matter? He'd find Julia, get her back to campus, tell the police what had happened. And that would be the end of it.

CHAPTER 40
In the Bedroom

They hadn't talked much during lunch. The conversation had been the real purpose of the meal—without it, Sam would have been happy drinking a protein shake—but striking up a discussion that afternoon was like trying to light a pile of damp twigs. Julia looked pale and tired, in spite of having slept ten hours. Maybe it was the pregnancy wearing her out—Sam wasn't sure what that could do to you—but he didn't think so. He got the sense that something else was going on.

There was a good three or four inches of snow piled on the window frame, which meant there was at least half a foot on the ground. By three o'clock, the light felt like evening. No one was getting out of here tonight, whether they wanted to or not. Sam could sense the darkness closing in, the beautiful isolation. It was all he'd ever wished for, these moments alone with someone who loved and understood him, and his mind should have been as calm as a lake on a windless day. But for some reason it kept getting disturbed, panic rippling out to the edges. Why couldn't he just be happy?

"What do you feel like doing?" he asked Julia after they'd wiped up the crumbs from lunch. He could hear that he was speaking more curtly than he had in the past, but he didn't know how to change that. He would have liked to be tender with her, but it seemed everything was coming out wrong, almost like he didn't have control over his own voice.

"Anything you want. We could watch some TV?"

"That's fine."

They sat on the sofa together, and Julia turned on the set, a small color one that was hooked to a pair of rabbit ears with foil on the ends. It turned out the TV got only one channel, a local station playing a courtroom program with a judge who kept stopping to lecture the people involved in the case about "getting their acts together." Snow warnings scrolled across the bottom of the screen. Sam didn't have the energy to follow what was happening in the case—something about a car getting borrowed and returned with a smell in it—but he decided to put his arm around Julia.

He noticed her flinch when he touched her—an awful moment— but then she settled into him. She seemed tense. He expected her to ask again about their appointment tomorrow, but she'd stopped doing that, which was a relief. He didn't like lying to her. She seemed to be sweating as they sat there, and again Sam wondered about the effects of pregnancy. As they watched the show, images kept flashing in front of Sam, images he would have preferred not to see. In one, he had his hands around Julia's throat, and he was shaking her head, squeezing the air from her till her face was blue. In another, she was on the floor and he was kicking her in the stomach, and she was making a sound like she was going to throw up. He knew the images weren't real, that they were like a movie in his mind, but still, they troubled him. He tried to resist, but they kept coming.

After ten minutes, Sam had a splitting headache, and he said to Julia, "I think I need to lie down."

She nodded, appearing to think it over. "I guess I'll take a walk."

"I don't think that's a good idea now. It's snowing pretty hard. I wouldn't want you out there by yourself."

"I'll stay close. I just want a little air."

"I'll go with you then. I'll feel safer that way."

She hesitated as the idea seemed to play through her mind. "No," she finally said, "you should lie down. You're tired. You already had a walk."

"I'm happy to do it, Julia. Anytime you want to go outside, just let me know. You can get me up from my nap. I just won't feel safe if you do it by yourself."

"Okay, I'll wait. We can go later."

"Promise me you won't go outside while I'm lying down in there. I'll be really upset if you do. I don't want to worry."

"I promise."

Sam left her then, went into the bedroom, laid down on the bed with his shoes still on, looking at the ceiling. He kept seeing those violent images, so he picked up his copy of *The Sportswriter* and read a few pages. But his headache got worse, and he had to put down the book. He closed his eyes.

Lying there, Sam thought of his parents. The memory of his dad's death was clouded by the time that had passed, but there was a part of that night he thought of now, a part he always skipped over like a song he didn't like on an otherwise pleasant album. It had been when his dad and mom went into the bedroom that Thanksgiving, when he'd gone for a walk with that glass of water. He knew what the water was for. He'd been doing a lot of reading about cars, about what caused problems. He'd told himself it was just out of interest, but the truth was that he was preparing, just as he'd been preparing a few hours ago when he was counting his footsteps in the woods.

That night, at his mom's house, he'd taken a funnel over to Herbert's car, put it inside the gas tank, and poured the cup of water into the funnel. Then he'd sealed the tank back up, and returned the funnel to the cabinet in the garage. He'd known that neither a drunk Herbert nor the road down the mountain would accommodate a misfire very well. He'd also known that no one would have a clue about a cup of water poured into the gas tank.

But why had he thought of this now? It seemed that so many unfortunate feelings and memories were visiting him today. Maybe it was the TV playing in the next room. After Sam's dad had died, his mom had taken to staying up nights, watching reruns and old movies and infomercials, whatever was on, and Sam could always hear it through the wall as he tried to go to sleep. She'd brought the TV into her bedroom, and she'd lie there, watching and eating. She liked all the sticky cakes and pies with glutinous fillings that Herbert used to bring over. It was as if she were summoning him back through the junk food he ate. She started to get heavy, then plainly fat.

It wasn't at all the way Sam had thought it would be. He'd expected Herbert's death to affect his mom the way it had him, that she'd feel the same invigorating lightness. But it seemed the opposite was true for his mom, who looked draggy and burdened. She'd always had Thursdays to pull her out of the glums, but now she seemed to just sink deeper into that swampy territory, further away from Sam.

He did his best not to let himself get dragged in. He knew she'd come around, once she saw how much better their life together was without Herbert in it. Sam focused on school, not so much on the work, but on the social aspect of it. He'd never been popular. It seemed the other students could always pick him out of a line as being a little odd, a good target for teasing and any pent-up aggressions they might have had. But Sam was adamant about winning them over.

There was one girl in particular, Haley Winters, whom Sam would have liked to spend more time with. She was a senior, a year older than he, and far from the most popular or desired girl in school. She wore prim sweaters, earth-colored headbands, and had a plain, moon-shaped face, but to Sam she seemed sweet. She had one friend, Megan Klug, and Sam had never seen her around with any guys. He had the idea Haley might be lonely.

But when he'd asked her to a movie, she'd looked at him and said, "Are you serious?" Not even *yes* or *no* or *I have to think about it* or *I have something else that day*. She thought he was joking.

But since Sam always answered people's questions directly, he said, "Yes."

It seemed to catch her by surprise. Later, Sam would hear about rhetorical questions, but at the time he didn't take note of those subtleties. There was a flicker of something that could have been sympathy on her face, but it was quickly replaced by what seemed to be repulsion, as if his asking her out had contaminated her with whatever strangeness afflicted him.

"Sam, I'm going to college next year," she informed him.

When she said that—*college*—an image came into his mind, of a blank-faced girl, wearing a sweater and jeans, a heavy book clutched to her chest. He didn't know why, but the girl seemed like someone who would treat Sam well, who would appreciate the unique way his mind worked, the particular gifts he had to offer.

"So am I," Sam said to Haley, and he watched her stifle a laugh.

He'd gone to the college counselor, Mr. Frank, later that week, and Mr. Frank pointed out a number of obstacles to Sam, including his grades, the fact that he hadn't taken the SATs, and the absence of compelling extracurricular interests. This was a high school from which only a minority went on to college, and Mr. Frank was suggesting that Sam didn't necessarily belong to that group. He said that junior college could be an option, but he also tried to open Sam's mind to the possibility of "the trades," as a brochure on Mr. Frank's desk called them. He asked Sam if he knew how expensive college was.

The next day, when Sam came into school, it seemed everyone knew about his conversation with Haley, and his trip to Mr. Frank's office. Reese started calling him "simple Sam," the name that stuck with him through the remainder of high school, and told him he wouldn't get into a college even if he fucked the dean. Sam didn't come back with anything. He was too hurt by it. He knew Haley had been the one to tell them, and he felt betrayed.

And there was something else Sam saw. He'd always been attracted to innocent girls, sweet girls, and he would continue to be; but he also realized that many, if not most, of the girls who appeared this way were in fact quite the opposite. They had a fearful, mean, and selfish aspect to their personalities, and could be skittery as rats. Whenever that was revealed to Sam, it made him bitter and hateful toward the girl, and toward himself for being fooled.

His mom's health had been getting worse, as she ate and watched TV and didn't go outside. They still had enough money to keep the house—from some kind of inheritance, Sam guessed, as well as from the money he started to earn—but not enough for much else. Especially with the medical bills. Sam's mom was getting into her late fifties, and she'd already had a small heart attack. The doctors said her heart muscle was failing.

Whenever Sam took her to appointments, his mom smiled and nodded, like she understood and agreed with everything the doctor said. She promised to eat the recommended diet, without the salt and cholesterol, and she said she understood the medications. But when they got home, it was clear to Sam she hadn't listened to a word the woman had said. Sam had to organize her pills and read the labels and tell her when to take them, or else she'd forget. She didn't have a head for that kind of thing.

After high school, Sam got a job at UCSD, working in one of the cafeterias. He didn't have the confidence to take the SATs and try for college—Mr. Frank had slammed the lid on that—but he thought he could at least be close to it this way, and maybe one day someone in a position to help would take notice of him. Sam didn't have friends, and he went straight from work back home to tend to his mom, who'd ask him where he'd been if he was ten minutes late.

He'd been at the job at UCSD more than five years by the time he met Alyssa, who was the president of her sorority. He always took her tray when she handed it in at the conveyor belt, and sometimes when he was changing the trash or sweeping, he'd see her walk by and she'd say hi in a friendly way.

The relationship didn't work out, but afterward, for some reason Sam kept seeing Alyssa around, even though he knew it wasn't really her. It couldn't have been. She was gone. He was vague in his mind about where she was, but he knew for certain she wouldn't be coming back. All the sightings were making him nervous.

"I think it would be good for us to leave San Diego," he said to his mom one night, when she must have been in her early sixties, and she said she'd think about it.

But when he brought it up again, she seemed agitated, and she said to Sam, "There's no way, bucko. I'm not going anywhere. And I need you. You're the best I have."

This last comment hurt him more than anything she'd ever said to him.

She seemed to revel in the burden she created for Sam, eating more and more junk food, not even getting up to fetch it from the kitchen, but asking Sam to do it for her when he was around. She started to smell like cheese from being in bed all day.

Once, when she'd gotten very sick, she said to him, "I know why you want to leave. You're scared, Sam. I can see it."

He'd thought about that comment many times afterward. He never asked her what she meant by it, too afraid to hear the truth, but he was convinced she was talking about Alyssa. He didn't know how she knew about her, or why she'd be suggesting Sam had anything to be afraid of, but he was sure of it. And he knew what that meant.

In the end, it had been easy to do, switch her pills. She hardly knew what she was taking, swallowing it all down with chugs of soda. And the pills were so tiny, the Provenum. Even the name sounded poisonous. He'd stopped giving her the drug for a month, then gave her twelve times the normal dose, substituting it for other pills, for three days running. He took the days off work, so he could watch her, be with her, as her heart slowed. Sam had pretended to call the doctor and listen to her suggestions, then he disconnected the phone. On the mountain, they were too far from other houses for neighbors to know what was going on. By the time she realized she was dying, his mom was too weak to scream, or to get up from the bed. She looked at him with fear in her eyes.

Sam watched the life drain from her. Sometimes she spoke to him, sometimes to people who weren't in the room, to Herbert or her sister or friends she hadn't seen since high school. For three days Sam waited. At times he cried. He fed her crushed ice with a spoon, watching it spill from her cracked lips. Twice a day he washed her body with a cloth and changed her nightgown. Her head leaned to the right, and her mouth began to droop on that side. By the end, she was breathing once a minute and her pulse was so faint he couldn't feel it.

But he could do nothing to stop the process he'd set in motion. He was powerless to help her, to correct the dosage, to call the hospital. It was as if his arms and legs were attached to strings that someone else was pulling.

The medical examiner performed a few tests, but never suspected anything. Her health had been deteriorating, her heart had stopped. It was as simple as that.

Now Sam felt something nudge his foot. He realized he'd been sleeping, or not sleeping exactly, but in one of those half sleeps where your mind ranges over a thousand subjects. He heard the TV in the next room, which Julia must have left on. Then he felt it again. It was a hand, shaking his foot, shaking him awake. He opened his eyes.

When he saw what was in front of him, he shook his head, thinking it was a dream. But it didn't change. Sitting on the edge of the bed, hardly a foot from him, was his mom. Not the fat mom with the wheezy breathing, but the young and pretty one, the one who'd attracted Herbert, with the long neck and defined collarbone and thick hair and small, shapely breasts. She was watching Sam with a grin on her face, like she knew something he didn't.

"Wake up, bucko," she said to him, the way she used to on the days she remembered to get him out of bed for school. "It's time."

"How long have I been lying here?"

"Oh, I don't know. But you're late."

"For what?"

"You have to finish your work." She had a look like she couldn't believe he didn't know what she was talking about.

"I'm really tired."

"No complaining. It's getting late. We don't have time."

Behind him, Sam heard rustling, then a sound like stifled laughter. It was the giggling of girls, a back-of-the-classroom, flashlight-under-the-sheets type of laughter. He turned to look.

There they were, all of them, huddled in the corner by the bed. Patrice and Alyssa and Marilyn and Naomi and Claire. He couldn't imagine how they'd gotten there, or how they fit in the space beside the bed. But they were exactly as he'd remembered them, just as fresh and pretty and excited.

"Julia's really cute, Sam," Patrice said.

"She's hot," Alyssa added.

"She seems nice," Claire said.

They all giggled more, covering their mouths with their hands, like there was something they were hiding from him.

"Tell her to come in," Naomi said. "We want to meet her."

"I'd love to get some book suggestions from her," Marilyn said, in a tone that sounded pretentious to Sam.

"I don't think she—"

"Don't waffle, Sam," his mom said. "No one likes a waffler."

Alyssa was cackling.

"You better do it soon," Claire said. "Or else she's going to leave you. You know she doesn't care about you."

"She loves me," Sam said, though he heard how weak his voice sounded.

The girls burst out laughing.

"You're such a cute little fool," his mom said, laughing with them.

"She loves you?" Naomi said. "Is that why she wants to drive back the second she's done with the operation?"

"Oooohhhh," Alyssa said, as if Naomi had challenged him to a fight.

"You think you can trust her?" Claire asked.

"You better be sure!" Patrice shrieked.

"I can trust her," Sam said, but even as he spoke, his mind ranged over the events of the day, the possibilities, the holes Julia could have discovered in the wall he'd built around her.

"Are you getting nervous?" Marilyn said.

He didn't answer. He was looking in his suitcase to make sure everything was there, which it was. When he finished searching, he pulled his phone from his pocket. Julia could have called someone while he was in the shower. She knew he'd brought his cell.

He pressed the green button. No calls placed today. He was feeling pretty good about that, and was about to put the phone back in his pocket and tell everyone to lay off when he thought of something else.

The text message folder. He opened it, and when he saw that a message had been sent today, he knew. It was a number Sam didn't recognize, but he had his suspicions. He opened the message.

They were right. She was a liar and a traitor. She wanted to get rid of Sam, to hurt him. She always had.

"It's important for both adults and children to see the world as it is," Sam's mom said. "Fantasies and illusions never help anyone."

Sam stuffed the phone in his pocket. He felt as if his entire body were expanding with rage.

"Just give me a few minutes," he said.

"You don't have much time, Sam," his mom said. "You're already late."

"Okay, stop *nagging* me!"

She shrank back, a trickle of blood rolling from her ear.

Sam got up from the bed. The girls weren't laughing any longer. He wasn't even sure they were in the room.

"I'm going," he told his mom.

"That's right," she said. "That's exactly right." Then she got on the floor and rolled under the bed.

Sam took a breath and released it. His skin was buzzing, like he was hooked to an electrical current. He took a step toward the door to the living room, and just as he was about to put his hand on the knob, the shrill cry of an alarm stabbed at his ears.

CHAPTER 41
On the Road

———◆———

The man at the rental counter told Marcus they didn't have any cars left.

"What do you mean?" Marcus said.

"We rented them all." His nametag read *Clive*. He was wearing a red short-sleeved shirt with yellow palm trees on it, the top three buttons undone, revealing an expanse of pale, hairless chest beneath the silver chain fastened around his neck. He had a beard that was styled into a sharp point at the chin.

"How's that possible? I really need a car." Marcus had spent twenty-four dollars on the cab ride here, and if he had to take a cab to another rental place, he wasn't sure he'd have enough to rent the car and buy his train ticket home. He hadn't thought to call ahead to see if they had cars; he'd never heard of a rental agency running out of cars.

"How do you think it feels for *me*?" Clive said.

Marcus shook his head. How did he get stuck with these people?

"Is there anything? I don't care what kind of car it is. I'll drive a Hummer."

"We don't have any of those left."

"I'm not asking for that. I'd be happy with anything. You could give me a horse and buggy."

"We don't have that either."

"Can you just check if you have anything?"

Clive shrugged and tapped his computer keyboard, making a series of faces—raised eyebrows, grimaces, cheeks puffed out—that didn't seem to have any relation to what was appearing on the screen. Then he asked Marcus to wait a minute, and walked into a back room of the rental agency, closing the door behind him.

Marcus was the only one in the office, which was what made it hard to believe they didn't have any cars left. He looked at his watch. It was ten minutes to two, and even if he left now, he'd be hard-pressed to get to the cabins by four. Then it would be getting dark, and the police chief had mentioned snow in the area. The weather looked clear through the windows at the front of the agency, but that didn't mean it wouldn't change up by Lake Erie.

After five minutes, Clive returned.

"You're in luck." He tapped the computer keys twice.

"How so?"

"We've got a car for you."

"Where is it?"

Clive made a clicking sound with his teeth, but didn't say anything. Marcus was about to ask him what was going on when Clive raised his chin at the long window behind Marcus. "The guy's bringing it around for you."

Marcus settled up with Clive, electing not to purchase the insurance, since he wasn't sure he could afford it. In a few minutes, a small Hyundai (Clive called it a "subcompact") pulled up outside the window and braked to a stop. The car would do nothing if it got stuck in the snow, but it would be fine on a clear highway.

"I hope you're not planning on driving a lot of folks around," Clive said.

"It's great. I'll take it."

Marcus took the keys from Clive, went outside, and got into the car, which had a smell like garlic inside, probably because they hadn't had time to clean it. Marcus had rented a GPS, in case the need arose, but he had a pretty good idea where he was headed and didn't want to waste time setting it up. He adjusted his mirrors and pulled out of the lot. His last thought, as he was leaving the rental agency, was that he could have been eating a bag of chips and listening to a Wayne Shorter album at that moment, if he were just a little better at talking.

But once Marcus had gotten on the road, it wasn't that bad. There was hardly any traffic on I-80, and Marcus sailed through the first ninety miles. He found a jazz station he liked, and when that got fuzzy, he switched to some alternative rock. He still liked that music, but it brought back memories of Tree and the way he'd ignored her in favor of his band rehearsals. *I'm such a fool.* It was the overwhelming impression he had of himself, as someone who was selfish and incompetent, who did much better when he was shut in a room by himself with a piano. If it were possible to live your whole life that way, Marcus would have been the first to sign up.

He got onto I-79 with no problems. Traffic was thin, and Marcus couldn't imagine many people would be heading this direction in December. He thought there might have been a metaphor in the fact that he was driving the opposite direction from the one any reasonable person would go. Who visited Lake Erie in December? Either Julia must have been kidnapped, or else she was on some good drugs when she'd agreed to make this trip.

By four it was getting dark, or at least the clouds made it feel that way. The sun cast only a weak gray light over the road. Marcus was driving the Hyundai over eighty, close to eighty-five when he was sure there weren't cops around. He was riding atop a rare wave of well-being, feeling confident in his ability to handle this situation.

Snow started to fall. Marcus looked to both sides as it began to sift over the fields and pastures to his left and right. Soon, large flakes dashed against the windshield, crumbling into a pile over his wipers, which he had to turn on to clear the glass. The clouds were thick as velvet, blocking out the sun, and Marcus flipped on his headlights.

By four fifteen, his was one of the only cars on the road. Once in a while, a pair of headlights rushed by, but mainly, he was alone. He looked at the houses he passed, the caramel light in their windows, and longed to be sitting in a warm room, drinking coffee and listening to his music. He turned off the radio so it wouldn't distract him. Ghosts swirled and drifted above the pavement. Because of the darkness and the empty road, Marcus had the feeling that, besides the hurtling snow, his car was the only thing moving for miles around, like a traveler passing through an abandoned city.

The sky had that odd glow of snowstorms, the sun like a bulb held beneath the thick fabric of the clouds. Houses and the tips of trees cut silhouettes in the sky, like shadows on a screen. Marcus heard the wind whistle through the car, and once in a while a gust shoved the Hyundai into another lane or onto the shoulder, leaving it rocking on its axles. Marcus had to reduce his speed. He'd kill himself if he kept on like this. He let the needle of the speedometer fall to seventy, sixty, fifty, where it rested for a while.

Marcus was just starting to feel comfortable in these new conditions when he saw the shadow in front of him, the pair of yellow eyes in his widening headlights. A raccoon or possum, it looked like. Marcus hardly did anything, maybe touched the brake, maybe nudged the wheel to the right. But the suddenness of the movements started him skidding, and when he tried to adjust the wheel, he realized the car wasn't in his control any longer, that it had snapped its reins. It began spinning, a blur of snow and sky and trees across the windshield, and Marcus could do nothing to stop it.

CHAPTER 42
The Alarm

◦═━◆━═◦

S am opened the door to the kitchen area, and the alarm got louder.
A smell of smoke in his nostrils. He looked for the source of it,
but couldn't see any flames. Everything looked the way it had
before he'd gone into the bedroom to take his nap. Scanning the
room, he didn't spot Julia, and panic swept over him. She'd left. She'd
abandoned him.

Then he looked down. There she was, curled on the floor, knees
to her chest. She was coughing, hacking so hard she barely made a
sound, or at least not a loud enough sound to be heard over the alarm.
Her face was a deep red, almost purple color, as if the air had been
squeezed from her. Her body convulsed each time she expelled more
air, and then she would gasp for breath.

It was impossible for Sam to think, with the alarm blaring and
the smell of smoke filling the room. He couldn't understand what had
happened. Had she been cooking and set something on fire? Did the
TV blow out? He'd come into the room with a clear idea of what he

was going to do, what he needed to do, but now it was like everything had been jostled in his head, and he needed to set his thoughts back in place. His anger at Julia, which had been pure, now felt muddied. The sight of her on the floor was enough to stir his pity.

He felt stuck, caught between the urge to help her and the urge to do her enormous harm, for betraying him, rejecting him. For her part, it seemed Julia hadn't noticed Sam was in the room, she was so absorbed in her coughing. What if he saved her? What if he helped her into the fresh air? Would it be enough, then, to lay claim to her affections? Would she at last appreciate how much he cared about her, accept the love he'd wanted to offer all along? Either way, he had to stop the alarm, stop Julia from coughing, and get her off the floor. Then he'd be able to think.

Now, at last, she looked up at him, eyes wide with pain and fear, and she gestured at the door, waving her arm and pointing. At first, Sam wasn't sure what she meant for him to do, but soon it became clear she wanted him to open the door, to air out the smoke. He didn't know why he hadn't thought of it. His head was so jumbled, and the alarm was so loud, and he'd been so focused on what he'd promised his mom he would do, the act he didn't want to name; he was so occupied with all of that that he hadn't done the most obvious thing.

He walked to the front door, turned the knob, and pulled. The door burst open with its bracing pop, the walls of the cabin shaking, and the smoke began to clear. He swung the door on its hinge, open and closed, fanning the smoke from the room.

It was when the door was open at its widest, the cold and snow streaming in, that Sam felt it, the hands on his back. He knew right away what was happening, but it was too sudden to stop it. Both her hands were pressed against the base of his spine, and he sensed the entire force of her body, charging, shoving him out the door. His foot caught the jamb, and he tripped, stumbling into the snow, throwing out his hands to catch himself but having nothing to grasp. The snow bit his palms as he landed.

There he lay, stunned by what had happened to him, how he'd been tricked, as the cabin door slammed behind him. He had on his sweater and shoes, no coat. He heard Julia lock the bolt, and only as the snow began to melt inside his clothes did he get up, shaking his head and telling himself there was no more room for sympathy.

"See where it gets you," he heard his mother's voice say faintly, as if from inside the cabin. "She doesn't love you, bucko. She never did. All she'll do is take advantage of you. And then where will you be? She already got you fired from your job, and she's going to get you arrested, if not killed."

Julia was thankless. She'd never learn, never appreciate him, and it was time for her to pay the price for her dishonesty. She would pay for every bit of it.

CHAPTER 43
Inside the Cabin

⌇⚬

Locking the bolt on the door, Julia wondered again where the police could be. What could be taking this long? If Marcus had gotten her text within a half hour of when she'd sent it, the police would have been here by now. Maybe Marcus never got the text. Maybe he was in a final. Maybe he had his phone off. Maybe he was just sick of her, felt he'd tried his hardest and Julia hadn't listened, and thought it was time for her to clean up her own mess.

The reason she'd made the plan to push Sam out of the cabin—lighting the doily on fire with the gas burner, then holding it up to the smoke detector, pretending to have a coughing fit when the alarm went off—was that she figured she didn't have much time. She didn't know what Sam had done with the other girls' bodies, but she guessed he'd want as much time as possible to make Julia's disappear. Unless someone got here soon, he'd have the rest of the night. It seemed like he definitely wasn't going to let her out of the cabin. And Julia couldn't wait for Marcus to call the police, since she had no idea when that would happen.

The smoke alarm stopped. She could hear Sam pounding on the front door, saying, "Julia, it's not funny. I don't like these kinds of jokes. Please let me in now." It was strange, how calm his voice was, like she was just playing a prank on him, and Julia felt almost like she could open the door and they'd both laugh and call the whole thing off.

But she didn't say anything back to him. The thought had already crossed her mind that he might have a gun, and in that case, the locked door wouldn't help very much. But she didn't think he'd have one. It would be too loud, draw too much attention, and be too messy to cover up afterward. A gun wasn't likely.

"Julia, if you let me in now, we can forget all about it."

She went into the bedroom, where she'd seen the landline earlier. There it was, between the bed and the bathroom door, with Rex and Dena's phone number posted above it. Her plan was to call the police, and all she'd have to do was keep Sam out of the cabin until they arrived. It shouldn't be that hard, especially since she had the knife.

She picked up the phone, but even as she brought it to her ear, Julia knew something was wrong. Silence. That's what greeted her when she put her head against the plastic receiver. Julia looked down, following the cord from the phone to the wall with her eyes. The cord was sliced in half. Sam must have done it while he'd been in the bedroom, supposedly napping, since it wasn't like that earlier when she'd used his cell phone.

It was at that moment that fear seized Julia, wrapped her in its arms, squeezing so hard she had to sit on the bed to catch her breath. She was trapped, and she'd done it to herself. She had no other thoughts or plans or places to hide.

The banging on the front door was getting louder. "Julia, I'm not kidding with you!" Sam said. "It's cold out here. I want you to open that door right now!"

He sounded like a father disciplining a child, as if he had a certain amount of patience for her mistakes, but not an infinite amount. Julia wondered why she hadn't seen this in him before, this aggression. Was it just that she needed him so much, needed to believe there was someone she could love and who could understand her? Was her judgment so bad that she could ignore all the signs?

Julia got up from the bed. She lifted the corner of the mattress, and felt underneath for the knife. When she found it, she let out a sigh, so sure was she that he'd taken that from her, too. Julia pulled the knife out and tried holding it in a couple of different grips, not certain what was the best way to use it. She knew it was likely these would be some of her last thoughts. Maybe it wasn't worth the struggle. He would win in the end, because he was stronger and he'd done this before and he'd thought it all through. But still, she couldn't let go.

As she was adjusting the knife in her hand, listening to Sam pound the door, Julia saw something on the bureau by the bed. She walked over to it. It was Sam's keys, the ones he'd used to drive the van here. There were a number of different keys on the ring, at least a dozen, and Julia couldn't imagine what they were all for. He must have taken them out of his pocket when he'd lain down for his nap. He hadn't expected to be going outside.

She put the keys in her pocket. Maybe they'd come in handy if she got a chance to make a break for the van later. Then she walked back into the living room, where the sound of Sam's knocking was louder. "Julia, I'd hate to have to force my way in there," he said through the door.

She got on her knees, still gripping the knife, and with her free hand found the place by the wall where Sam had stashed the shoebox. It was still there. The sickening thought passed through her mind that she could soon be a name on one of those plastic bags. It seemed especially unfair because of the unnamed person—that's how Julia was starting to think—she was carrying inside herself.

Then she remembered something. She felt around the carpet, where the lump had been, just next to the box. It wasn't there anymore. The rug was flat. Sam must have taken whatever he'd been hiding there. Julia thought of the phone line slit in half. A knife. It had to be. And one that could do a lot more damage than hers. She was sure of it.

The pounding stopped. Julia backed up and stood in the middle of the room, facing the door, wondering what Sam would do. Was he going to lunge at the door with his shoulder? Would he kick through it or stab through it with his knife? The silence was more frightening than all the pounding and shouting and threats.

Julia gripped the knife more tightly, ready to lunge at him the moment he opened the door. It was all she had left, the chance of a lucky stab. She couldn't keep him out until morning. She was too weak, and he was too steady and strong. He'd find a way in.

She'd been so focused on the door that the sound of the window breaking took her by surprise. Julia sucked in a breath. It was the living room window, and she saw the stone he'd used to break it—one about the size of a tennis ball—lying on the rug. She didn't know whether to move closer to the window, to stop him, or whether she should keep her distance, in case he was going to throw another stone.

But then she saw his arm come in the window, his hand groping for the latch. She didn't have time to think. An animal instinct took over, and Julia leaped at his hand, bringing the blade of the knife down on it.

As soon as she made contact, feeling the blade tear the meat of his hand, she heard him scream. It wasn't even as much a scream as a howl, a wordless cry. He drew his hand back through the window. Before she backed up, Julia saw his eyes through the glass. She'd expected rage, but it wasn't just anger in his face. There was something like terror there, as if he were as scared as she was of what was happening. That was when she realized they were in the grip of something larger than either of them, and any ideas of talking to him or coaxing him or reasoning with him were useless.

She stepped back from the window, in case he got hold of more rocks. But that image of him, gripping his bloody hand, his eyes full of that enraged horror—it had been burned in her mind. Julia didn't know how badly she'd cut him, but she knew it was only enough to put him off for a short time.

She waited in silence for what must have been five minutes. Then, as if picking up on a conversation they'd only just dropped, Sam said through the shattered window, "You're not getting out of here, Julia. I'm waiting for you. I'll come in there and get you if I have to. You can let me in now and apologize, and I'll be nice to you. Or you can do it later, and I'll be mean."

He was walking around the cabin as he spoke, and Julia couldn't tell exactly where he was. His words echoed, and each time she thought she'd located him, his voice seemed to come from somewhere else. She couldn't get close to that window again. So she listened and watched the broken window, and the door, and the window in the bedroom, knowing she'd have to do this all night, guard these entrances, shifting her eyes every few seconds from one to the other. Maybe, if she could figure out where he was, she could make a dash for the van. But how would she know, if he kept moving?

His voice fell silent. She could hear nothing but the sound of the wind, shaking the snow from the trees.

CHAPTER 44
Stuck

⟨━◆━⟩

By some miracle, the Hyundai hadn't flipped. The front tires were still on the pavement, which was carpeted with an inch of powder, but the rear tires were sunk in the lip of snow left by the plows that must have passed sometime in the last hour. When Marcus pressed the accelerator the engine growled and the tires whined. The car didn't move, though. He'd tried backing up and lurching forward, but each time the tires caught and began spinning in the snow.

He reversed and drove forward several more times. The sulfur smell of the laboring engine poured through the heater's vents. It wasn't going to give.

Marcus got out of the car, stepped into the snow. On the side of the highway where the car was stuck, snow-draped fields spread into the distance, and on the other, a wall of forest shielded Marcus's view. Ahead the road snaked toward Lake Erie. The snow streamed down, brightened by the car's headlights. The air scratched Marcus's throat.

Outside the path his headlights burned, everything was dark. Marcus felt the gigantic emptiness like a weight on his chest, the burden of his own poor planning, another bungled effort. He shouted—no words, just sound—but only the echo of his own voice answered. There was no one for miles around, and he'd have to wait until the plow came through again before he had a chance of getting someone to tow him. If he called AAA, they'd be over an hour, probably more.

What a fucking waste, Marcus said to himself, with a hopelessness that fell on him sometimes, and which he usually hid from the people around him. *I'm such a goddamn waste.*

A gust of wind shook the Hyundai, leaving its metal body quivering from the impact. Marcus's thoughts whirled. When he was a kid, Marcus used to watch snowstorms with his parents through their bedroom window, a large glass pane overlooking the countryside behind their house. He remembered the security of being tucked in that private dark, listening to his parents talk. Even the sight of his father's face, the flattened nose, and high pale forehead, had given him a feeling of protection, shelter, and there was a part of Marcus that believed he'd never outgrown that. He'd never experienced the world, had to make decisions for himself, and face their consequences. He'd been spoiled and ill-prepared, and whenever it fell to him to do something meaningful, he found a way to botch it.

Marcus got back in the car. It wouldn't do Julia any good if he froze to death. He shut the door, then blew into his hands, which ached from the cold. He looked around in the back seat of the car, to see if there was anything he might be able to use to help him out of this situation, but couldn't find even an ice scraper, let alone a shovel. He got back into the front seat, sweating, and that was when he thought of the floor mats.

Marcus took all four of the mats from the front and back seats, then got out of the car and wedged one mat under each of the Hyundai's tires. He knew he'd have to move quickly, or else the snow would cover the mats, too. There wasn't much chance this idea would work, but it was the best he could think of, and he couldn't bear the idea of Julia having to wait while he called to get the rental towed.

When he was done with the mats, Marcus got back inside the car. He put it in drive, then stepped on the accelerator, hearing the engine roar and the tires shriek. The car drifted forward, then sank back. In the mirror his taillights splashed the snow. The car rocked forward and back, the rear wheels bobbing on the edge of the road. The burning scent flowed through the vents.

It was almost there, he could feel it. He didn't want to let up and have the car sink back into its divots, so he revved the engine harder, wondering what kind of damage he was doing to the car. But he didn't care. He didn't have time to consider it, because soon he heard a thud, and with a sudden pull, the car lunged forward onto the road. It was so fast Marcus nearly drove over the divider, across the other lanes and into the trees on the far side of the highway. But he managed to ease the car to a stop on the pavement, the front wheels nudged against the divider.

He backed up and then started forward again, slowly now. He didn't stop to pick the floor mats off the snow. He'd already lost twenty minutes, and he wasn't sure how much longer Julia could wait.

CHAPTER 45
Outside

➤—✦—➥

t wasn't a deep cut, but it hurt. He wasn't sure why it hurt so much, the gash she'd made in the web between his thumb and index finger, but Sam couldn't shake it off. Maybe it had something to do with the cold air. He tried putting his hand in his pocket, but that didn't help, and when the fabric of his pants brushed the cut, it felt like fingernails in his flesh. Sam wasn't someone who normally felt pain intensely, but this was excruciating. He would have screamed if he hadn't needed to keep his composure for Julia.

He couldn't believe she'd stabbed him. That was the thing he kept working over, saying it to himself as if he were talking to her. I can't believe you stabbed me. After all I've done, all I've given up for you. Perhaps that was why the cut hurt so much, because the attack was such a betrayal. She'd locked him out of the cabin, in the cold, and all he'd wanted was to come back inside and be with her. And she'd stuck a rusty blade in his flesh. He was lucky he hadn't taken his shoes off while he was napping, or else he'd have frostbite by now, probably need to have his foot amputated. She deserved to be punished. He wasn't going to let himself feel bad about it.

But for the time being, he had other problems. For one thing, the cut on his hand needed bandaging. It was oozing blood, and his whole hand felt stiff, like he was getting an infection. He had to find something to sterilize it. And he was cold. His shivering had turned to tremors that racked his whole body. He sensed his toes only as a dull throbbing in his shoes. He'd called to Julia through the window so many times his throat was raw.

The van keys were still inside the cabin, so he couldn't get in the van for warmth. He had worries about what Julia would do if he left her alone for too long, but her options were limited. He'd cut the phone line, and he didn't think she'd risk leaving the cabin. That was the real reason he'd yelled to her for so long after she'd locked him out. He wasn't foolish enough to believe she'd change her mind and let him in; he just wanted her scared enough that she wouldn't run away the second he took his eyes off the door.

Sam had a way of knowing these things, of predicting the way people would move and behave. He'd always been an observer, even as a small child, and when he cared about a girl, it was natural for him to watch her, to find her patterns. With the other girls, he'd always taken his time. He could observe a girl for months, even a year, before so much as speaking to her. He knew their schedules, their routines, when they left their rooms and when they returned, the times when they were with other people, and the times when they were alone. He'd known about the walk Marilyn took home from her improv group on Thursday nights, where, for a space of half a mile, her path skirted the Charles and no one could see if a man who'd been sitting on one of the benches by the river happened to approach her. He'd known about the sections of isolated beach where Patrice took her water samples, and the boardwalk that he could lie under for hours, unnoticed, during the winter season.

Julia was the girl he'd taken the least time with. Odd because Sam also believed she was the one he cared most about, if someone had pressed him to choose, the one he truly loved. Still did love, in spite of the position she'd put him in. He'd always love her, no matter what.

Sam knew what he needed to do now, while Julia was hesitating inside the cabin. He started down the driveway, stepping quietly so she wouldn't hear him leaving. A funny thing was going on inside him, a feeling that was both familiar and strange. On one level, he felt focused, unwavering. But on another level, Sam felt untethered, dreamy, as if the objects around him were part of an elaborate fantasy, beautiful but not quite real. He'd never been drunk—it was something he'd promised himself after Herbert had driven off the cliff—but he imagined this must be the way drunk people felt, this sense of losing a grip on the world.

This feeling was the one that always descended on him at the very end of a relationship, just before the part that became vague to him, the part he couldn't seem to remember, or possibly chose not to. At these moments, it seemed to Sam like there were two worlds, like two strips of film, one laid on top of the other. Most of the time the worlds were so similar, pressed together so tightly, they appeared to be one. Then there were these rare occasions when one film peeled back, parted from the other enough that you could make out the difference between the two, a blurring at the edges. It would have been nearly impossible to describe to someone who hadn't experienced it, this cellophane of distance between yourself and the objects around you.

Sam took the turn toward the management office. Ahead of him, the trees presented a series of archways, like entries into a dim cathedral. Because of the roof of snow, it was so dark now that Sam couldn't see the turns and rises in the road until he was only steps away from them. He couldn't make out the border of the road, and sometimes he wandered off it, stepping onto branches and rocks and leaves left over from the fall. When the wind blew, snow fell from the trees. There were storms of it, when the limbs shook, and the rush of powder was like the sound of trucks passing on a highway. And there were smaller events, shooting stars falling to earth around him, trailing their dust behind.

What was it he couldn't get a handle on? What was the slippery thing at the back of that dark pantry in his mind, the darting thing that brushed against the hand of memory? He'd never forced himself to look. It had always been easier to close the door, tell himself he'd investigate another day. But he wasn't sure how many other days there would be. He didn't know how much time was left, or if he'd gone too far down a path he'd never be able to retrace.

As he walked toward the management office, Sam felt as if he were walking deeper into some unlit space in his own mind. There were images, flashes, like when lightning strikes, illuminating a darkened room for a moment. He'd told Naomi to be quiet. He'd told Patrice to wait with him under the boardwalk until night fell, and then he wouldn't hurt her. He'd shown Claire something, a shiny object. *If you're good and no one hears you, I'll let you go.* He'd taken Alyssa to his van. He'd told her he was going to drop her off in a place where people wouldn't see him. She was crying. When he opened the van doors, the rear was covered in plastic tarps.

The rhythm of Sam's heart beat a dull pain into his hand. He had the knife in his waistband, pressed against his leg, assuring him it was still there. Black shadows stretched across his path. It was like being out of time, transported to another world.

He was always meticulous. Nothing got on the seats or the walls. He wrapped it carefully, in layers of plastic. He didn't think of the bundle as a girl any longer, as someone he'd loved. It was like the meat he'd butchered in kitchens, there was a science to it, an order, a specialized knowledge that helped you perform the tasks you needed to accomplish. He wore rubber gloves while he worked. There were always garbage dumps where bags weren't inspected. He took his time, spread out what he needed to dispose of, distributing it among balled-up paper and yard waste and plastic wrappers and empty bottles of moisturizer. Calmness and steadiness were the keys. Hurrying was what could get you in trouble, taking a step before you'd thought of every result. That was what had caused problems here, with Julia, the fact that he'd rushed in and kissed her, not even caring that he was probably signing his life away.

As he approached the management office, which was dark, without a single light to brighten the path to the door, Sam was sweating, in spite of the cold. His face was wet with a salty residue that could have been tears. When he lined up the images in his mind, he could see the story they told. His mom had always warned him against deception, even of oneself. It wasn't healthy, and it didn't help anyone, least of all the deceiver.

The only thing Sam could say in his own defense, if he were ever called on to make such a defense (an event he knew was unlikely, since only the people in books ever got to explain themselves), the only justification he could offer was that none of these acts was controllable. Telling him to stop would have been as good as asking him to make the rain stop falling. We're all in the grips of forces we can't understand, he thought, and there are things we do, feelings we have, that we wish weren't ours. We wish we could pick certain traits and pass over others like items in a salad bar, but the truth is that we don't have a choice. We're handed a tray, and we do the best we can with what's on it. Life is about dealing with your tray. If you don't want to, there's only one other choice.

Sam picked up a rock and shattered the window of the management office, found the latch, and pulled it open, crawling inside. He flipped on the lights and saw the collection of coats and shoes by the front door, where he remembered them from earlier when he'd found Julia working on the computer. He took a heavy-looking hooded coat off the tree, and pulled it on over his sweater. Then he went to the bathroom and found Rex's first-aid kit. He was about to use the ointment in the kit when he noticed a small bottle of whiskey behind the toilet.

He picked up the bottle and unscrewed the cap. It smelled like the cleaning solution he used to wipe down the counters at work. Sam put his injured hand over the sink basin, took a breath, then poured the entire bottle onto the cut. He couldn't help screaming as he did it, though he kept his teeth clenched and the scream came out as a strained grunting.

When he was done cleaning the cut, he dried it and bandaged the hand. The cut was still bleeding, but not enough to soak through the bandage, and he felt good about the possibility of using his hands later on. As long as Julia hadn't left, everything would be okay. It didn't matter that this was the ending. There was always an ending. There'd been a time when he'd loved her and she'd loved him, and that was the part that mattered, the part he would preserve.

Outside the bathroom, his mom was waiting for him. She didn't look as young as she had before, and her eyes were tired as she said to him, "You'd better hurry, Sam. It's getting late." Her voice didn't have the patience or kindness he'd hoped for.

"I know. I had to do this. I was freezing and my hand was bleeding. It could have gotten infected. I couldn't help it."

"She'll leave if you wait longer."

"She's not going to leave."

"You don't know everything, bucko. Sometimes people are smarter than you give them credit for."

He shook his head. He didn't know why she was being so tough on him now, of all times, when what he needed was affection, a little support and encouragement. Hadn't he suffered enough? Did he need this nagging and abuse on top of it?

He left his mom in the management office, closing the door behind him but not bothering to lock it. He'd changed his shoes to another pair he'd found by the door, which fit well and seemed more water-proof than his own. He started up the path, confident again, ready to handle whatever awaited him.

It was only when he made the turn onto the main driveway that he noticed the lights in the cabin he'd shared with Julia were out, as if she'd gone home, abandoned him here, and he wondered if he knew her as well as he'd thought.

CHAPTER 46
Arrival

 ⌾━◆━⌾

F ive miles back, it hadn't seemed possible that snow could fall any more quickly, but now Marcus saw that it could. He had his windshield wipers on high, splashing snow left and right, but he still had trouble finding the road. It was four thirty, and, shielded by the clouds, the sky was black. All Marcus could make out was the tunnel of light his headlights carved in the snow. He'd taken the exit off I-79, and he was driving under thirty miles per hour, walled in by the darkness on both sides of him.

A lot of the street signs were covered in snow, and Marcus couldn't read the names clearly. He had to stop and turn on the GPS, but when he put in the address, the computer couldn't find it, so he had to choose an address up the street from where he wanted to go. He turned onto North Road, which seemed to be the main county road. There were some houses here, and Marcus caught glimpses of TV screens, silhouettes of lamps and bed frames, but he didn't see any people, which made this expedition feel more like a strange dream. He wondered if anyone would be there when he arrived, or if maybe this was some kind of hoax. The cabins would be empty. Everything would be quiet. Marcus would be stuck out here, having made the trip for nothing. *Sucker.*

He passed a gas station, the prices mounted on a long pole in the dark mouth of the sky. How could she take a risk like this? Marcus thought. How could she believe anything Sam said? It was beyond obvious that he was a liar, and dangerous. From across campus you could see he was crazy. At least Marcus could.

At the same time he knew Julia wasn't tricking him, that she didn't have it in her to do something like that. She's not that kind of person, he thought. She wouldn't lie. So what's the end of this going to be? What if she gets in the car and we drive back to campus? Or if Sam won't let her? Where's it all headed?

He stopped there. He was getting ahead of himself. He needed to focus on what he was doing, finding the turn off the road, and not get lost in his thoughts. The GPS said the turn was a mile ahead, but Marcus remembered now that the address he'd entered wasn't exact. The address for the cabins was on North Road, but Marcus knew from the website that there was a long driveway. This part of the road wasn't populated the way it had been by the gas station. He couldn't make out the lights of any houses, and only once in a while a street light pierced the veil of falling snow. He was in the woods, and he could see the frosted limbs of trees in his headlights. He could only make out the border of the road by a small indentation in the snow.

When he got to the address he'd entered in the GPS, Marcus knew he'd gone too far. He stopped and did a U-turn. The road was blanketed by a couple inches of powder, so Marcus made sure not to drive over the edge. When he got turned around, he started back more slowly, under ten miles an hour, scanning the right side of the road, where he expected the turn to be. He had his brights on, and he was leaning over the steering wheel.

Then he saw it, on his right, a wooden sign growing in his head-lights. He couldn't fully make out the words in the blustering snow, but he could tell they pointed the way to the Squirrel Ridge Cabins. It was hard to know exactly where the driveway was, but as Marcus inched up, he thought he saw a groove in the snow that probably corresponded to the turnoff.

He took the turn to his right and started up the driveway. But when he got about ten feet onto the road, the Hyundai's tires began to spin. He pressed the accelerator, and the rear tires spat snow into his taillights, but the car didn't move forward. The road sloped upward, and Marcus knew the Hyundai wouldn't make it any farther. He got out and closed the door, telling himself he was an idiot for not bringing a flashlight.

Marcus walked up the driveway. He didn't know which cabin Julia was in and he had trouble making out the turns in the driveway. He assumed he'd see lights at some point, or some indication of where they were. How big could this place be?

The slope became steeper as Marcus walked. He couldn't hear anything aside from the wind. The road was covered in a good six inches of snow, a foot where it had drifted. He wasn't following the road any longer, it was too difficult, and Marcus had to grip branches of trees to pull himself up the hill. He held onto the smallest trunks, the young, smooth ones and the broken ones that bit through the snow. He hadn't worn gloves—another dumb decision—and the bark scraped his hand. His palm got chafed and his fingers rang with cold.

Marcus had thought his shoes were waterproof, but was finding out they weren't. His feet were soaked. He could hardly feel his toes. Beneath his sweater, his T-shirt was damp with sweat and melted snow, and it adhered to his back. The wind breathed snow at him, and the tree branches chattered like teeth. Marcus heard some light-footed animal darting around, and once or twice he thought he saw the shadow of something dashing into the trees, but he couldn't be sure. It might have been his imagination. He ducked under a branch as big around as his thigh, then came up against another one that would have hit him in the eyes if he hadn't stopped. He slipped and caught himself on the branch that had almost hit him, hung on, shaking his head.

He found several darkened cabins on his walk, but none of them seemed to be inhabited, so he continued on. He didn't want to knock or make a lot of noise, because he wasn't sure if Sam was hiding somewhere, waiting to attack him. He thought of the rustling in the trees again, and wondered if he was being followed. He had that feeling, like he wasn't alone. Who knew what a man like Sam could do? Marcus had known he was crazy, he could see it in Sam's face, and he didn't understand why no one else did.

At last, Marcus came up the path to a cabin that looked more promising. His eyes had adjusted to the dark, and he could see the outlines of a car—a van, it looked like—parked in front. He knew it was Sam's van, even though he'd never seen him driving it. It looked old, boxy, and probably a muddy shade of orange or brown.

He kept walking up the path, past the van, toward the front door. He didn't understand why there weren't any lights on. Were they sleeping? Maybe they'd had a fight, Julia had sent Marcus a text in desperation, and now everything was fine. She would open the door, laughing, shaking her head, saying she'd forgotten all about the message she'd sent. She couldn't believe he'd driven all the way here.

Marcus got to the front door. He wasn't sure if he should knock. He lifted his hand, deliberating, but before he had a chance to do anything, he heard something lunge at him from his right side. He didn't have time to look, it was so fast. He jumped to his left, an instinctual reaction. And then he felt a sharp pain in his leg.

CHAPTER 47
The Van

Julia heard the scream. She knew it wasn't Sam, that it had to be Marcus, and suddenly she understood why the police hadn't come: Marcus had driven here himself. Maybe he hadn't thought her message was urgent enough to call the police, or maybe they just didn't respond to his call, but whatever the reason, he'd come for her.

She'd been standing in the living room of the cabin, in her coat and shoes, holding the rock Sam had thrown in the window in one hand, the rusty kitchen knife in the other. She'd turned out the lights because she figured it was easier for her to see outside without the glare, and she didn't want Sam to be looking in at her. The van keys were in her pocket, but she'd been too afraid to run. She'd had no idea where Sam was.

Now she dropped the knife so she could open the front door. There was a good chance she was sacrificing herself, she knew that. But she couldn't abandon Marcus. When she yanked open the door, it popped, and she saw Sam pulling the knife from Marcus's leg, just above his knee, where he'd cut him. It all must have happened in no time, and the light was so dim, but somehow it felt like everything was moving slowly, and she could take in all the details, the blood on Marcus's pants, the flash of the knife blade, the fear on Marcus's face, the blankness in Sam's eyes.

Taking advantage of the pause after she'd opened the door, before Sam had the chance to thrust the knife at Marcus again, Julia put her free arm in front of Marcus. She must have thought Sam would stop attacking Marcus now that she'd come outside—wasn't Julia the one he wanted?—so it was a surprise when she felt the hot slash of the blade in her forearm, just below her elbow.

She stopped thinking after that. She lifted the rock and brought it down on Sam's head. He must have seen it coming, because he shifted, and the rock didn't hit him as solidly as she'd thought it would, but it was enough to knock him down. He made a whimpering sound as he fell to the snow, and the rock slipped from Julia's hand.

"I have his keys," Julia said to Marcus, and took his hand, pulling him toward the van. She could feel her sweater was sticky from the wound on her arm, but it didn't seem to be hurting, and she couldn't stop to look at it. Marcus was following her, not talking, and Julia couldn't tell how bad his injuries were. She was too busy pulling the keys out of her pocket.

Julia dropped Marcus's hand and riffled through Sam's keys, trying to find the one that opened the van door. Julia was jogging, Marcus hobbling behind. The snow squeaked under their shoes. It felt to Julia as if she were in one of those dreams where a shadow was chasing her, and for some reason she couldn't run, couldn't get away.

When they got to the van, Julia tried one key, but it didn't fit the door.

"Shit," she said.

She looked back. Sam was rolling in the snow. Julia was hoping she'd knocked him out, but it looked like she'd given him a glancing blow at best. Now she'd dropped the knife and lost the rock, and she and Marcus had nothing but the keys. Julia tried another key, which also didn't work. It was hard to see without any lights, and Sam had so many keys on his ring she could barely keep track of which ones she'd tried. Her hands were shaking, and her arm started to throb.

Sam was up on one knee. Julia noticed he was wearing a winter coat, and new boots. He looked unsteady, but also like he was getting his balance back. When Julia glanced back at him this time, she noticed something else, a dark trail leading from where Marcus had been standing by the front door right up to where he stood now, by the van.

"You're bleeding," she said to Marcus.

"I'll be fine," he said.

She tried another key. This time it slipped into the lock, she turned it, and when she pulled the handle, the door popped open.

Julia loaded Marcus into the van first, then got in behind him, slamming the door and locking it. The driver's-side window was open a crack, and she tried to roll it shut, but it was stuck. She wasn't sure how well the van would make it down the path in all this snow, but since it was downhill, she figured they needed only a little momentum and they'd be able to do it.

She put the key in the ignition and turned it.

Silence.

She tried again.

Nothing.

"What's the problem?" Marcus asked.

"It's not starting—" And even as the words came out of her mouth, she knew what was happening. Sam wouldn't have let her go that easily. If he'd thought of the phone in the bedroom, if he'd found himself a coat and boots, he wasn't about to let her drive off in his van. He'd done something to it, disconnected the starter or drained the gas, because it didn't make a sound now when Julia turned the key.

"Do you know anything about cars?" she asked Marcus, who was settled in the passenger seat, leaning back against the headrest. He was taking slow breaths, and Julia got the sense he was feeling sick. She couldn't see how bad his injury was, it was so dark, but she imagined Sam must have cut him deeply.

"I don't. Do you?"

"No." She took a long breath, then let it go. She didn't want to examine her own arm. Julia could still use it, and that was enough for now. They were safe for the moment in the van, the doors locked, and Sam was still on his knees in the snow.

"I want to see your cut," Julia said to Marcus. "How bad is it?"

She reached up and turned on the dome light. But before she even looked down at Marcus's leg, Julia noticed something. The back of the van was covered in plastic tarps. Even the walls were draped in it. It wasn't anything so amazing in itself, but the sight of it was like a blow to her chest. She knew what it meant, the plastic. It came to her as clearly as a voice whispering in her ear. This was the place where Sam intended to kill her.

She looked down at Marcus's leg, not saying anything about the tarps. It was too horrible to mention. Julia saw that Marcus was cut badly. The blood had soaked through his pant leg in the area above the knee, and it was running down his leg, into his sock.

"Do you have any ideas?" she asked Marcus.

"I don't right now. I'm trying to think."

They wouldn't be safe for long. It was cold in the van, and wind whistled through the slit where the window wouldn't close. Marcus was losing what looked like a lot of blood. Julia probably was, too, judging by how faint she felt. But she couldn't look at what had happened to her. She flipped off the dome light, and looked back toward Sam. He was on his feet now, staring at the ground. He had the knife in his left hand. He might not have even been injured. He was searching the ground for some reason, or maybe just gathering his thoughts, making a plan.

"I have my phone," Marcus said. "You want to try calling someone?"

He took it out of his pocket and put it in Julia's hand. He looked like he was too nauseated even to dial himself. The phone was sticky from his blood. She dialed 9-1-1, hit *Send*, and watched the screen.

The call wouldn't connect. When Julia put the phone to her ear, all she heard was a rustling static.

"No reception," she said to Marcus.

Sam had kneeled again, and this time when he got up, Julia could see why he'd been looking at the ground. He had the rock she'd hit him with in his right hand. He turned toward the van, and even though he couldn't have seen through the window, Julia felt like he was looking right into her eyes. She remembered then what it was like having sex with him, the way he'd watched her, the intensity of it, that unwavering focus. It was the way he was looking at her now, like she was the only light in a big, dark room.

Sam started toward the van. Julia pressed the lock down again, to make sure. She didn't know where they would go, or what they'd do, but she wanted more than anything to keep Sam outside, away from her.

When Sam got closer, she heard something. At first, it sounded like beeping, or something mechanical related to the van, or maybe even the whistling of the breeze in the window. Then Julia began to make out a melody, sung in a high, strained voice. The music was so gentle, so achingly gentle, she almost couldn't believe it was coming from Sam. As he approached, she saw his lips were moving.

> *One day you'll find me waiting*
> *As the light is slowly fading . . .*

"What is that?" Marcus asked.

Julia thought of the voice drifting through her window late at night. She thought of Claudia telling her, *I keep hearing him. I can't get it out of my head.*

In a house that's built for two . . .

She knew now that this was where Sam had wanted her all along.

And one is me and one is you.

"It's him," Julia said. "He's singing to me."

CHAPTER 48
A Plan

After she said that, Marcus leaned back against the headrest, and he seemed to fall asleep for a second, then come awake. Julia knew he couldn't last like this much longer. He was slipping away.

When he opened his eyes, she said to him, "I'm sorry." Just like that. It sounded so cheap. "I'm so sorry for pulling you into this. I never—"

"I wanted to." His speech was slurred, like he was drunk. Julia wasn't sure if he knew what he was saying. But he kept on, "I wanted to help. I was watching out for you."

"I should have believed you about Sam. I don't know why I didn't. It's like I didn't want to admit the mistake I'd made. And the more you tried to convince me, the more I resisted. I've always been stubborn. I didn't want to admit how bad my judgment was with him. I felt like I didn't have anyone else. I just wish you'd never got involved. It was my selfishness that made all this happen."

"Don't think that way. You don't deserve any of this." He sat up, like he was coming out of a dream. He looked at her. "It was my choice to get involved."

Julia wanted to tell him he was wrong, that she did deserve it, but she knew it wasn't the time to argue. However much she blamed herself, the truth was that he cared enough about her to help, that he didn't want to see her hurt. She couldn't understand it.

Her thoughts were interrupted by a tapping on the window glass. Sam had been approaching the car, and now he was touching the rock to the window. He'd stopped singing. He seemed tentative, like a lost person who wanted to ask directions. That was the mystery of him, how he could seem like a helpless child one minute, and then ruthlessly violent the next. There didn't seem to be any order to it. Or maybe it seemed so calculated it was hard to believe he was human.

"Julia," Sam said. "Will you please let me in?"

His face was hardly a foot from hers. She could see the bruising along his jaw, and for the first time she wondered how he'd really gotten hurt. She had the feeling that if she stayed still, somehow he wouldn't see her. But if she moved, he would attack. Like a wild animal, he'd respond to fear.

He tapped the glass again with the rock. "Please, Julia, if you let me in now, I'll be nice." As he said the words, his face seemed to brighten. "Please, Julia, please," he kept on, like a chant. "I don't want to get all worked up. I don't want to get angry, Julia."

She kept staring at the wheel. Her arm throbbed, but she didn't want to reveal she was in pain. Marcus didn't say anything. He must have had the feeling, too, that it was best to keep quiet.

"Julia, please don't make me angry." He loved saying her name, she knew that, repeating it like the refrain of a song, or the way children will say a word again and again until it loses its meaning. "It'll be your fault if I do something bad."

She could see his face out of the corner of her eye, and she noticed a funny thing. Where he'd seemed about to break out laughing a moment ago, now he appeared on the verge of tears. The change was so fast, and so subtle, Julia almost thought she'd imagined it. But she could see the pain in him. And again she had the feeling he was in the grip of something he couldn't control.

"Do you think he can get in?" Marcus asked.

Before she could answer, the rock slammed against the window. Julia screamed, ducking toward Marcus, and he put his arm over her. They stayed like that, crouching in the space between the front seats of the van.

Sam disappeared from the window for a moment, then reappeared with the rock, which he hurled again at the window. Julia could see the glass beginning to crack. It would cave in soon, and then there would be nothing but air separating him from them.

"We have to run," Marcus whispered. "It's the only way."

"He'll catch us."

"I have the key to the rental car. It's at the entrance to the cabins. If we can get there, we'll be able to drive away."

"You can't make it. Your leg. It's probably a quarter mile down the driveway."

"I don't think he wants me, Julia. He could have killed me in front of the house, but he waited until you came outside. He knew you would."

She heard the rock smack against the window, and saw the web of cracks spread.

"There's no other way," Marcus said. "He's going to come in the front window. If we get out the back doors right when he tries to come in, we'll have a head start. He'll try to follow us out the back. I can hold the doors to stall him."

"No, you can't."

The rock slammed the glass again, and the cracks widened to a net across the whole window.

"Just promise me if I'm not behind you, you'll still drive away."

Julia felt his breath against her ear. They were whispering to each other like a couple would. It felt intimate, his lips so close to her, but at the same time like a joke, a parody of the closeness she'd always imagined with someone.

"No," she said again, but they were already crawling into the back, over the seats, onto the plastic tarps. Julia felt like she couldn't control any of this anymore, like she was floating somewhere above it, watching it happen. She heard the rock knocking the glass. The window wouldn't hold much longer.

"You have to promise me," Marcus was saying. Julia didn't know where this new energy of his was coming from. "If you start heading down the hill, he'll follow you. He's not interested in chasing me. After he gets out of the van, I'll run in a different direction from you. If you get the car started, I'll cut through the woods and meet you a quarter mile up the road. Just turn right out of the driveway. He won't know where I am, because he'll be following you."

"I can't."

"It's the only way. You have to." He reached into his pocket and handed her the key, which was sticky like the phone. It was so dark in the back of the van she couldn't see what Marcus was doing, but she felt the key in her palm, and Marcus's fingers brushing hers.

"Wait until he gets in the front, and then we'll go."

"Please," Julia said again. She wasn't even sure what she wanted. She just couldn't think of anything else.

"We have to. Just promise me you'll keep driving if I'm not there. I've got my phone. I'll find reception and call someone. He won't come after me."

Julia couldn't answer him this last time, because the rock broke the window. She heard it fall into the passenger seat, and then Sam's hand groping for the lock.

"Okay," Marcus whispered. He had his hand on the back door, and when she heard Sam climb into the van, Marcus flung the back doors open.

Julia jumped into the snow, then started running as quickly as she could, tripping down the path. She heard the van doors slam, the way Marcus had promised, and she knew he was doing what he'd said, holding Sam in the van while Julia got a head start to the rental car. She looked over her shoulder, and saw Marcus holding the doors closed.

Julia took the turn onto the main driveway, and started down toward the car. She thought she could see it, a shadow at the edge of the driveway, and beyond it the lone streetlamp on this section of the county road. As she ran, the blood beat in her temples, and also in the part of her arm where Sam had cut her. She was breathing heavily, and the wind burned her face. But she wouldn't let up. She knew Sam could be behind her at any second, and if he caught up to her, she wasn't the only one who would die.

Julia caught her foot on a stick and fell face-first, splashing snow, then got up and kept running. She'd had those dreams of being chased, started having them not long after the accident. Different things would chase her—sometimes they were people she knew, or sometimes a shadowy presence she never saw. And she always woke with a feeling of dread, an anxiety she couldn't name, like the residue of some horrid event. It seemed as if now she was enacting that scene, like she'd finally arrived at the place she'd always been destined for.

The slope was flattening. She could make out the streetlight, snowflakes whirling in its glare. It wasn't snowing as hard anymore; maybe the storm was ending. The trees were spaced farther apart here, and the light poured through them.

Julia saw the car ahead. The wind picked up, no longer blocked by the trees, and she felt it on her ears and her face. It was like the trees were parting for her, welcoming her into the brightness ahead. Her arm didn't hurt anymore.

As she approached the car, Julia checked behind her, and no one was within sight. The plan had worked. She looked at the county road, which had been plowed, and there was a dusting on it of only a couple inches of snow at the most. They could drive through that. She heard the wind, and the sound of her own breathing. Her heart worked like a raging clock in her chest. Galaxies of snow swirled and trailed across the road, vanishing in the darkness around her.

Julia unlocked the car and got inside. She put the key in and turned it. The engine started right away. She put the car into reverse, lifted her foot from the brake, and pressed down on the accelerator. The tires spun, but didn't catch.

She pressed again, and the same thing happened, the tires squealing.

Julia was hesitant to turn on the headlights, but she wanted to see what kind of situation she was in, so she flipped them on. And that was when she saw him, Sam, coming down the driveway, toward the car.

He was walking. That was the first thing that surprised her. It was like he had all the time in the world. Julia was stuck and she couldn't do anything. It would be useless to get out of the car and run. He'd catch her in five seconds. And anyway, there wasn't anywhere to run.

She stamped on the accelerator, felt the car drift. Then it stopped. The tires spun and squealed. Sam was getting close. Julia could see his head bobbing in an odd way, almost like he was laughing.

She threw the car into drive, and stepped on the pedal. The car jerked forward, then got stuck again. The light shined into Sam's face, which looked wet, and she saw now what was happening, why his head was bobbing and his shoulders were shaking. He was crying.

It was such a strange sight, Julia didn't even know what she felt about it. Or maybe she didn't want to know, didn't want to feel. Because if she did, if she reached down to her heart and pulled out the answer, she'd have to admit the truth, that it was beautiful to her, his pain, that cleansing agony, the way he'd lost himself to it. If she was being honest with herself, she'd have to admit it was the most moving sight she'd ever seen.

He held up his arms. They were darkened with something. He was still shaking, and now she wasn't even sure if it was laughter or sobbing. Maybe it was neither, or both. Maybe it was something clearer, deeper, a pure expression of all the misery of living in this world. He had the knife in his hand. And he was calling out something she couldn't hear.

He called again. And again. And there was a part of her that wanted to get out of the car, rush over to him, help absorb some of his pain into herself.

He was getting closer. Julia pressed down again on the accelerator, and she heard the whining of the tires in the snow. Sam had dropped his hands by his sides. He was close enough that she could hear the noise he was making, that sobbing laughter.

She pushed down all the way on the pedal, and this time something happened. The wheels bit the road with a screech. She knew what she was doing, hated what she was doing, but she had to do it. Sam's eyes widened. And just before the car slammed into his body, Julia thought she saw him lean into it, give himself over to it. To me, she thought.

She felt the impact in her hands. He went down, hard, in a way he should never have gotten up from.

Julia shifted into reverse, and when she pressed the pedal, the car started backward, following the tracks she'd made. She knew how it was supposed to go. She was supposed to throw the car into drive, run over him one more time, finish it all.

But she couldn't. Later she'd wonder why she held back, why she still felt pity for him after all he'd done. What did it say about her? What did it mean that she felt sympathy for a monster?

She didn't want to know.

Julia backed onto the road. Then she started toward the place where she was supposed to meet Marcus, where she still hoped he would be.

Part Four

THE WORLD AHEAD

CHAPTER 49
Birthday Dinner

꞊꞊꞊✦꞊꞊꞊

Julia has plans for tonight.

She got out of work early, since it's summer and there's not much to do, and it's so suffocatingly hot in Philadelphia that it would have been impossible to be productive anyway. Julia works as the assistant to the events coordinator at a small music venue in Center City, a job she enjoys and feels lucky to have gotten, considering she never finished college. Her boss, a woman named Peyton who's under five feet tall, is a more forceful presence than her height suggests and can be demanding sometimes—asking Julia to work late most nights during the busy fall season, expecting Julia to know what she wants for lunch and where to put her mail and which calls to forward to her and which to send to voice mail—but Peyton likes Julia. She picked her out of the group of interns for the assistant job, and hasn't had any major complaints in the two years Julia has held the position.

Julia's happy to leave early today, because it's Marcus's birthday and she's planning a dinner for him, a meal she's actually going to cook, even though she sometimes refers to herself as the "O.K.D." (Official Kitchen Disaster). She's thinking of a pasta dish, since she wouldn't have to watch the sauce too carefully, and it would be pretty inexpensive. Or maybe a slow-cooked meat. The main thing is to avoid burning whatever she makes, since her biggest pitfall as a cook is getting distracted and forgetting whatever she has in the oven. She sometimes jokes that she uses the smoke alarm as a timer.

Heading up the street to the market, Julia glances over her shoulder, a habit of hers. It's something she's done half a dozen times each day in the five years since that night in the cabin when she was nearly killed, when Marcus came to save her. She's looking for Sam, of course, imagining that one time she'll look and he'll be right there behind her. She'll never forget the words the policeman said to her that night, after she'd explained what had happened, and they'd gone to the place at the foot of the driveway where she'd told them Sam would be. *Not there. Disappeared.*

Now, even though she's walking in a crowd on a sunny street, she has the feeling of being watched, a feeling she gets a lot. She's not sure if it's just how she's learned to express her anxiety, focusing on this one fear. Maybe she's nervous about messing up the dinner, or about whether she'll ever be able to move forward in her career without a degree, but whatever it is, it always comes back to Sam.

She walks into the co-op where she likes to shop, taking a couple minutes to check out the fresh vegetables. She tries to buy the organic ones, even though the price is ridiculous, since she knows it's healthier for her and Marcus, and she has every hope they'll both live a long time. It's funny to worry about which broccolini to buy when a minute ago she was afraid of being stalked and killed, but she guesses that most people aren't very rational about the future. The world is so unpredictable, and you can spend your whole life piling your blocks into a neat little tower, only for the wind to strike up and topple the whole thing in a second.

Seeing all the fresh food, she realizes that pasta would look a little frugal for Marcus's birthday dinner ("You guys doing okay?" her dad might ask), and she knows she shouldn't fall back on the easy option just because she's scared of cooking anything else. So she picks out some vegetables for a salad, and then a few steaks and some baby red potatoes. What the hell. On her way out, she picks up a chocolate cake with raspberry filling, Marcus's favorite.

As she starts up the street with her two grocery bags, she remembers she has to call her parents. They're coming for the birthday dinner, too, driving up from Maryland, and they'll already be on their way. Julia's relationship with them has gotten closer in the last couple years, since she settled in Philadelphia. During the year after the events at the cabin, Julia had kept her distance from her parents, partly out of embarrassment over what she'd done, and partly because of the media attention she was getting, which would have been uncomfortable for them. Their daughter getting lured into the woods by a serial killer—"But other than that, she's great," Julia imagined them telling friends. She'd assured them in emails and phone messages that she was fine, but they hadn't seen each other often. Julia kept telling them she was overwhelmed.

Once the frenzy died down, Julia let them back into her life, slowly. Her mom called to apologize to Julia, saying she wished she'd been less harsh, that maybe none of this would have happened if Julia had been able to rely on her. Julia thanked her mom, told her she wasn't angry. Which was the truth. Anything her mom said to her that night wasn't half as bad as things she'd already said to herself. And she can't see what happened in the cabin as her mom's fault, or as anyone's but Sam's and her own.

She doesn't want to hurt her parents anymore. That's what it comes down to. She wants to make her relationship with them as easy and pleasant as possible. After the articles started coming out and Julia told them not to read the papers or listen to the reports about that night, they've never talked about the details of what happened. It's nothing noble. Julia simply can't deal with the guilt of making them suffer anymore.

Because of all Julia had to deal with in the years following that night at the cabin, she couldn't continue with school. That was a disappointment, both for her and, she knows, for her parents. They haven't said anything to her about it, but she's aware they'd like her to go back sometime. It's just not possible right now, and she couldn't ask her parents for money. Maybe it's a way of punishing herself (she knows they'd be happy to help her and Marcus out), but if she thinks of it that way, it feels petty. She knows she's not making up for anything by denying herself.

One thing she has done for herself is to start playing trumpet again, two afternoons a week in the orchestra at Gibbons College in Chester. They let her use the practice rooms whenever she wants, so she tries to stick around for an hour or two after rehearsal to play a little and stay in shape. She'll never get back to where she was—a truth she's had to accept—but she can hold a high-D without much pain, and is doing a half-decent job with a Haydn concerto. No one knows she's practicing, not even Marcus. She doesn't know where it'll lead, but thinks maybe there's a local orchestra that could use her one day, or she could teach at one of the colleges. It wouldn't be a bad life. If she focuses on the present, and forgets about what could have been, she can get by.

Walking into Chinatown, Julia passes the restaurants and massage parlors and the shops with ads showing alabaster-skinned Asian women eating snack food and talking on cell phones and taking laxatives. All the things you want to look beautiful for. The smells of fish and cooking oil and fresh flowers and incense greet her. They're smells that would have seemed foreign a few years ago, but now there's a comfort to them, because of their association with home and with Marcus.

Leanette said she might come by later, too, maybe for dessert, if she can get off work early. Most nights she eats dinner after ten. She works in consulting, traveling most weeks, and she and Julia have stayed in touch pretty well, mostly because Leanette calls Julia at work whenever she has a layover. "Stilwell Entertainment," Julia says when she picks up, and Leanette launches into whatever gossip she'd been planning to discuss.

For a while, after that night, Julia had avoided Leanette, too. She felt foolish, especially since Leanette had seen the relationship with Sam unfold. Julia assumed Leanette would think she was a moron for getting involved with someone like him.

But around six months after Julia dropped out of Stradler, Leanette called Julia and Marcus's apartment in Shady Grove. Julia was working as a cashier in a bagel shop, and most of her conversations at that time involved the words "sesame" or "cinnamon-raisin." When Julia picked up, Leanette said, "So now that you're famous you think you're too good for me?"

Julia laughed. She told Leanette to call her agent next time.

Leanette married Drew the summer after they finished college. He works in banking, probably longer hours than Leanette. Amazingly, Leanette asked Julia to be a bridesmaid at the wedding, and Julia agreed and was soon stuffed into a pink dress that looked suspiciously like a cake decoration. Even so, she was grateful. She doesn't have many other friends.

Julia turns down the street—an alley, really—that leads to her apartment. She's suddenly alone, walled off from the noise and traffic of Chinatown. She can hear her own footsteps. And something else. The soft tread of a person behind her. She glances over her shoulder. Doesn't see anyone. There's a dumpster, and she knows he could be hiding behind that. She can sense someone is with her, that another person is sharing this space.

She keeps walking, hurrying now. Looking back again, she still doesn't see him, but she notices a shadow in the doorway, an easy place to hide. He can watch her from there, see the building she goes into, follow her up the stairs. Or wait until nighttime. Break the lock and come inside. There are a hundred ways he could do it.

At night, every creak in the hallway is him. Every raindrop tapping the window is his finger on the glass. Every time Marcus shifts in his sleep, Julia knows it's because he's heard something, someone.

She knows Sam is there, on crowded streets, behind her in movie theaters, in dark alleys, behind doors, in closets, waiting, waiting for the lights to go out. It's the power he holds over her, the way he intrudes on every moment of peace.

That night, when the police reported to her that they couldn't find Sam, Julia was struck with the feeling that the whole trip had been a bad dream. It couldn't have been real, she told herself, it was too horrible, too strange. Was she crazy? No one else knew Sam the way she did. It was as if she'd invented him, and for a moment she wondered if she was delusional, if the police were going to tell her that no one named Sam Blount had ever worked at the Stradler snack bar.

Glancing back again, Julia is certain he's there, a shadow in the doorway of her building, waiting. She stops in the alley. Her breath quickens, like she's just run up a flight of stairs. He's here. He's come back.

But it couldn't be. She has to tell herself to calm down, that it's just her imagination, that it couldn't be Sam. After the police initially reported to Julia that they couldn't find him, they followed up and told her that they'd pursued his tracks through the snow. He'd tried to sweep over them with some branches, hoping the falling snow would cover up the remaining marks and any blood, but it hadn't worked. He didn't have time to get back to his van and reconnect the starter, so he hid in one of the unused cabins. When the police knocked on the door, he stabbed himself in the stomach, and then in the heart. He was dead by the time they got inside.

Still, because she never saw him dead, there's a way in which Sam lives on in Julia's mind, a way in which she's preserved him. She knows it's irrational, but she can't shake the belief. It doesn't seem like a line as thin as the one between death and life would be enough to keep him away from her, he wanted her so badly. And she knows it's wrong, maybe even insane, but there's a part of her that wants him, too, that can't let go, a part of her that needs him for something.

Now she walks up the stairs to her third-floor apartment (the shadow in the doorway was just a shadow) and lets herself in. She starts putting away the groceries, organizing them for her cooking, washing the vegetables, excited because she knows Marcus will be home soon. It's going to be a good night, she tells herself, no matter what.

At five thirty there's a knock on the door, and Julia knows it's Marcus. She feels a pulse of anticipation. It's the same every day, after all these years.

She walks to the door and opens it.

The boy, a little taller than Julia's waist, runs inside, hugging Julia's legs, saying, "Mom, I'm *hungry*!"

"Where's Carla?"

"She dropped me off. She watched me go up the steps. She said I could come in by myself."

Carla also has a kid in the extended day program where Julia leaves Marcus on most weekdays. The school offers the program cheaply, and it's the only way Julia can afford daycare for him now.

Marcus lets go of Julia's legs and says, "What did you get for my birf-day?" He has trouble with certain consonants, something the teachers are working on with him. They've told Julia not to worry, it's normal. They can probably tell she's a nervous mom, and she's fairly sure there's a big red X near her name in some secret book they keep.

"It's your birthday? You should have told me."

He doesn't laugh at that. Instead, he gives Julia a stern look and says, "You know it."

Julia smiles. "I'll show you after dinner, when Grandma and Grandpa are here. Aunt Leanette might come, too."

At this news, Marcus makes a sound like a monkey he saw once at the zoo, which is his sign that he's excited, or possibly that he wants a banana. Marcus loves Leanette, who always gets on the floor and plays trucks with him. Once, when he was particularly pissed off, he said he wished Leanette was his mom. Julia told him she'd get the papers ready and would just need his signature.

Julia puts out some cookies and juice on the table for Marcus, and she sits with him, cutting vegetables for the dinner while he eats his snack. She watches him. Her son is the most beautiful person she knows. She thinks it every time she sees him, at the same time as she wonders how someone so beautiful could have come from a mother as screwed-up as she is. He has dark red hair, which looks brown unless he's in direct sunlight. His cheeks are freckled, and he has a coin-sized birthmark on his neck, the kind that looks like a wine stain.

She can see Sam in him. It's something that disturbed Julia when Marcus was a baby, the way he reminded her of what had happened. But she'd made the decision that she couldn't go through with the abortion—she felt too guilty about all the harm she'd caused to prevent another life from moving forward—and so she'd had to tell herself she was going to love this boy completely, without hesitation, for the rest of her life. There was, and is, no other option.

And this works; it's allowed her to push any doubts from her mind. Sam had something in him, a sickness, a failure, that couldn't be changed, but Julia chooses to believe he wasn't born with it. If you're going to raise a child, you have to think people can change, that character is something you can help form, and that with all your flaws and obsessions and petty hang-ups, you have some small role to play in the human story. You have to believe that your life matters a little.

That night at the cabin, when Sam finally pushed out of the van doors, Marcus—the Marcus Julia went to college with—leaped on him, wrestling him for the knife, and Sam ended up stabbing him eleven times. Marcus never had any intention of running into the woods, of meeting Julia by the road. His leg was injured too badly, Julia knows it now.

After Julia ran over Sam, she waited for five minutes on the road for Marcus, and when he didn't come, she turned off the car and ran into the woods, not caring if Sam was alive, if he would come for her. She found Marcus herself. He was bleeding in the snow in front of the cabin, alive but incoherent, hardly conscious, and she dragged him to the cabin and locked them inside. With his cell phone, she dialed 9-1-1. By the time she'd finished the call, he was dead.

Julia has put it together in her mind again and again, the fact that Marcus sacrificed himself for her. It was why he'd told her to drive away, even if he wasn't there. She knows it, as certainly as if he were telling it to her himself, as certainly as she knows she shouldn't have let him do it. She should have seen he was lying to her, and she should have given herself over to Sam. She should have been the one to die.

The only part of it she doesn't understand is why Marcus did it. She tried asking his parents once. She went to visit them in the country, and when she knocked on the door, his dad answered. He looked so much like Marcus—tall and hunched, with that slightly distant manner—that Julia nearly fainted. Behind him, a TV was playing, and on the floor she noticed a dinner plate scattered with crumbs.

When Julia told him who she was, he said, "And you thought we'd enjoy a visit?" He was smiling widely, but the remark was made with such acid that Julia took a quick step back, as if burned. She told him she guessed not, and she was sorry for bothering him, and she left.

All she has now is her son. Julia feels that she's been given this person, this child, not as a gift, but as a way to make amends for the harm she's caused, damage that can never be undone. She can't bring back the dead. She can't apologize to Marcus, or to her brother. She can't trade her life for theirs. She can only raise her son, a small and insufficient gesture, but the best the living can offer the dead.

Sometimes, though, after Marcus is asleep and she's by herself in the middle of the night, she wonders if she is wrong about this. Time isn't such a rigid thing. She feels like these people are with her, like there's a world ahead where they all live, where she can touch them, where her voice can reach their ears. How could a world like this not exist somewhere, in the boundless wealth of creation? How could death be so final? How could you want something with all your heart, and yet know that it would never be? The universe should crack under the force of all our wanting.

"Mom?" Marcus says now, and he has a look on his face that Julia knows. It's the face he makes—the crease between his eyebrows, that small frown—when he's going to ask an important question. He's an inquisitive child, always has been.

"Yeah?"

And a strange thing happens. Her son says, "Can you tell me about my dad?" almost as if he's been reading her thoughts.

Julia knew she would get this question one day, that there were pieces she'd have to put in place, though she never expected it so soon. He must have heard kids in his class talking about their dads, and wondered about his own. It's okay. She has her answer ready.

"His name was Marcus, too," she says.

Acknowledgments

I would like to express my deep gratitude to the following people for their help with and support of this novel: Ayesha Pande, Claiborne Hancock, Maia Larson, Jessica Case, Michael Fusco, W. W. Norton & Co., Adam Gidwitz, Michelle Falkoff, Rebecca Schinsky, Vinnie Wilhelm, Terry Lucas, and Lynn Trieu.

READING GROUP GUIDE FOR
THE PRESERVATIONIST

1) Why do you think Julia is initially attracted to Sam? What does this say about her personality? Do her reasons change over the course of the book?

2) The second chapter of the novel introduces us to Sam. The first paragraph of this chapter ends with the sentence, "Who didn't want to keep a good thing going as long as he could?" Why is Sam so interested in preserving things? What does this say about his motivations in the novel? What makes him act the way he does?

3) There is an epigraph to the novel from Banana Yoshimoto that reads, "Death isn't sad. What hurts is being drowned by these emotions." How do you feel this quote relates to the book? Each of the three main characters has experienced a major loss. How are their attitudes toward death and loss different and how are they the same? How do the themes of death and loss play out over the course of the novel?

4) When we're introduced to Marcus in chapter 13, we discover that Julia's similarity to a girl from his past causes him to experience a great deal of emotional turmoil. Do you think that Marcus's character was shaped by what happened with Tree? Or do you think he would have been the same person regardless?

5) We get glimpses into the family lives and childhoods of all three major characters. How would you characterize the different families we see? Would you say that the novel takes a certain view about family or its importance in people's adult lives?

6) Why do you think the author chooses to explore the thoughts of all three major characters? How would the book be different if it were told only from Julia's point of view? Or only Sam's? Or Marcus's?

7) Would you say that the novel offers an overall view of love? Or would you say that there isn't one singular view expressed?

8) What other thrillers and suspense novels or movies would you compare this book to? How is it similar to or different from other novels you've read in this genre?